WITHDRAWN

IN CASE OF EMERGENCY

COURTNEY MORENO

McSWEENEY'S

SAN FRANCISCO

McSWEENEY'S
SAN FRANCISCO

ISBN: 978-1-940450-26-1

www.mcsweeneys.net

For Christina Black

When conducting the triage of a multi-casualty incident, start by taking charge. Consider the textbook example, based on the events of July 16, 2002, in Santa Monica, California. On a Wednesday afternoon, against the sparkling backdrop of summer sky and swaying palm trees, an eighty-six-year-old man drove his burgundy 1992 Buick LeSabre down three blocks of Arizona Avenue's crowded farmers' market. He was going about sixty miles per hour. He killed eight people and injured forty, and by the time his vehicle came to a stop there was a body pinned under the engine, a body resting on the hood, and an empty pair of shoes on the roof.

It will take some time before you show up to a scene like that and feel comfortable. It will take even longer before your only thought is *here we go* as you snap on gloves and get to work. But if you happened to be there, standing on Arizona Avenue between the rows of produce, the bag of kale your girlfriend asked you to pick up still dangling from your wrist as the Buick shuddered to a stop, you wouldn't have time to think. Just remember the golden rule of emergency medicine: air goes in and out, blood goes round and round, any variation on this is bad.

While you don't want to call yourself the incident commander, not out loud, anyway, that's what you are. As the only person with some medical training in the face of this disaster, you are the acting incident commander until a higher medical authority relieves you.

Which means you're going to have to improvise.

It's your day off. You have a community college class in sign language later that evening, so the backpack on your shoulders holds, in addition to the slim course textbook that binds together hundreds of photographs of hands, a few pens and highlighters. You can work with this. Stand in a space where most of the victims can hear you and shout as loudly as you can: "Everyone who can walk, please make your way over to the fruit stand." The people who can do so, the "walking wounded," are considered the lowest priority. They are represented by the color green. With broken bones or minor soft tissue damage, they might have been grazed by the Buick or trampled by people trying to get out of the way; they might be sent home or told to sit quietly, or even asked to help with the care of more critical patients.

Next, quickly determine the status of the victims who remain. Decide who is dead and who isn't. Intermittent gasping that sounds like air escaping from the lungs—the "death rattle"—means they are already dead, even if they still have a pulse. In fact, don't check pulses. Dig a black pen out of your backpack and put a dot on their forehead; other rescuers will know not to treat them.

Any victims breathing at a rate of over thirty breaths a minute are immediate, or critical, patients. If they are breathing less than thirty breaths a minute, but have a weak pulse or can't follow commands, they are also immediate. Mark these victims with a red pen. Finally, use a highlighter to label the yellow group: people who are breathing fairly well, have a radial pulse, and can follow simple commands. They might have serious injuries, but they will receive treatment and transport only after the critical patients have been handled.

Remember your triage methods, simple to use even in the face of a catastrophic incident, such as eight dead, forty wounded, hundreds traumatized, and an eighty-six-year-old man who can't comprehend what he's done. Do your best to stick to protocol. Take no more than thirty seconds to assess each patient. Do not treat; only label. Check breathing, circulation, and ability to follow commands. Assign colors.

Green, green, red. Black, yellow, red, yellow. Red, yellow, yellow, black—
And so on.

PART ONE

1

"What do you do? This guy is circling the drain! Think!"

I'm kneeling in front of a mannequin that represents an unresponsive patient with slow breathing, warm skin, and dumping vitals. The long-sleeved collared shirt I chose to wear feels ridiculous. The man conducting the interview, Vincent, leans over me, yelling. We're both sweating in the Los Angeles summer heat, and I push the hair out of my eyes using the inside of my elbow. In EMT school I learned to avoid using my hands for anything but handling the patient: it's best to think of my gloves, and therefore my hands, as covered in germs at all times. The plastic dummy's eyes have no pupils and look oblong instead of spherical. I don't have a clue as to what's going on with this patient. He needs advanced life support—firefighter paramedics or a hospital emergency room. Emergency medical technicians can give oxygen, help administer some drugs, and do CPR. He's going to need more than that.

"What are you going to do, Piper?" Vincent asks me again. "If this was your boyfriend, your mother or sister or best friend, what would you be doing?"

I know he's just trying to agitate me, but I consider it. "I'd probably be crying."

He leans in closer, his face inches from mine, and roars, "Pull your *shit* together, this is EMS!"

"Yes, sir."

The thin carpet of Vincent's office chafes my aching knees. What's going on with this patient? I can't afford to lose momentum now—I spent the last of my savings on the four-week EMT program, and I refuse to slink out of this office anything but employed. Warm skin, lowered pulse rate, slow, deep breathing, and loss of consciousness. Could the slow, deep breathing be Kussmaul respirations?

"Oh!" I say with relief. "He has DKA."

Vincent tilts his head slightly. He's impressed but tries to hide it. "And what is that?"

I tell him what he already knows: diabetic ketoacidosis occurs when someone's blood sugar skyrockets without the presence of insulin and is unable to enter the cells. All the cells in the patient's body are starving. If this goes on for too long, he may slip into a coma or even die.

I'm hired. Vincent gives me a tour of headquarters, the offices, the supply room with its stacked oxygen tanks. We walk outside so I can admire the fleet of ambulances and the mechanics' shop before circling back to the hallway outside his office. And Vincent tells me what I already know: A & O Ambulance is the best company in the Los Angeles area, with widespread coverage, the most 911 exposure, and a killer reputation. My field training officer will be Ruth McCarthy, who is also, I see, employee of the year. Her ferocious grin on the placard hanging in the hallway looks more like she's gritting her teeth than smiling. I know she must have proved herself many times over to earn that plaque, but mostly I'm just relieved I don't find her attractive. Field training will be hard enough already.

Vincent points at a large map, big enough to cover the side of a bus, as he explains the company's basic operations. A & O has twenty stations throughout the Los Angeles area. They cover east to west LA, as well as Long Beach and as far north as Pasadena. I find the YOU ARE HERE sticker, which represents the Gardena headquarters we're standing in. I've lived in LA my whole life and haven't spent an hour in Gardena before today.

"We need someone in the busiest area, so I hope you're ready for this." He points at a yellow circle representing Station 710, at the intersection of Normandie Avenue and 65th Place. "South Central, 24-hour shifts. You'll do your training there, too."

On my way out of the office I run into a kid, maybe ten years younger than me, who even as he's washing down an ambulance gives the sense that he's seen everything. He probably wouldn't get nervous if his own mother was flopping like a fish in front of him. Maybe his tattoos remind me of my ex, or maybe it's the way he works over the wad of tobacco in his mouth before letting loose a stream that lands near my shoe, but I take an instant dislike. After the obligatory cool appraisal, he asks where I'm going to be working and nods when I tell him. "Get ready to grab your ankles," he says.

2

Home is a two-story apartment in Echo Park, with a view of downtown even from street level and the constant white noise of the 101. "Guess who got her dream job!" I shout to my roommate. Marla turns off the TV and waddles into the kitchen to join me. She's wrapped in so many blankets that if it weren't for the familiar soft face jutting out of the multicolored cocoon, she would be unrecognizable. I blame her new layering habit on her recent breakup—freshly hurt hearts run cold.

Grabbing her leftovers off the stove, I slop them into a bowl as she rummages through the bag of my recent purchases. She sniffs a cookie before biting into it, retrieves the bottle of rum, and starts mixing us drinks. I show her my new Thomas Guide and the A & O Ambulance handouts that cover what to bring to my first 12-hour shift, the pages obviously photocopied over and over.

Marla helped me get through the EMT program so I know she's almost as excited as I am. For months I made flashcards with signs and symptoms of different medical or traumatic injuries; she'd choose one and follow its prompts while I tried to figure out what was wrong and how to treat her. When we practiced the emergency childbirth scenario, she grabbed a cantaloupe from the fruit bowl and put it under her shirt, shrieking so convincingly a neighbor knocked on the door, phone in hand, ready to call the police.

But instead of asking me about the job, she asks about last night's date with her friend Nathan. She's made me promise to go on at least five dates with him because, according to her, I never give anyone a chance. I've secretly nicknamed him NutraSweet. To me, he's only a sugar substitute.

I don't tell her that last night, our third date, NutraSweet took me to an expensive Italian restaurant that had tiny lights embedded in the ceiling and a whole lot of fake foliage. Or that he tried to hold my hand and asked for advice about an old wrist injury—because now that I'm an EMT, I must know about things like wrist injuries. For four weeks, all I did was listen to lectures on life-or-death situations and study from a textbook thick with pictures so gruesome I wanted to think they were fake. At no point did we discuss carpal tunnel. Grabbing our glasses, I get up to make us another round of drinks. I tell her if she was really my friend, she would have set me up with the girl at the grocery store, the one I've had a crush on for months.

"Yes, that would have gone well. 'Hello, grocery store girl, will you please go out with my roommate? Perhaps you've seen her here, skulking about?'"

"I do not skulk."

"You're filling our apartment with fennel toothpaste and organic tampons."

I wrestle with the ice tray. "Don't be a hypocrite. You went berserk over the heirloom tomatoes."

Marla takes the drink I hand her, looking up at me from her cocoon. Together we flip through the pages of the Thomas Guide. I tell her that I have to learn how to map the driver when we're responding to a call. "We're required to give correct directions in less than sixty seconds," I say with awe.

She scoffs. Marla is a mechanical engineer. "That's easy." She jabs at Hollywood. "Map me to the wax museum from Elysian Park."

It turns into a drinking game: map your partner from point A to point B in a minute. You can't use freeways. If it takes you longer than a minute to figure out the best route, you drink. If you map your partner in a circle or into a dead end, you drink. We quickly figure out which parts of Los Angeles do not run in a simple grid, and we quickly get drunk.

Toward the middle of the night, traffic dies down on the freeway and everything gets quiet. The DKA scenario has been replaying in my head all day. When a real person and not a mannequin lies in front of me, I'm going to have to be much faster. As if she knows what I'm thinking, Marla looks at me, resting her chin on a drunken fist. "Are you scared?"

Terrified. "Scared of what?"

"Scared of the kinds of things you're going to see. Scared of what you're going to be asked to do."

The objects in the room seem to narrow into focus, and their edges sharpen. Marla's blankets mushroom up around her face. How long have I been absentmindedly twirling a shot glass in my fingertips?

"I'm pretty sure I have this in me."

Marla pokes me.

"I was a total idiot today," I say. "I'd think the right thing but couldn't say or do it. It was like my hands were working at a different speed than my brain. I actually told the interviewer I'd be crying if the mannequin were a real person."

"You *what*?"

"Well, not exactly." I tell Marla that I refuse to work in a bar again, or as an extra, that I don't want to eat cheese while a bitchy actress complains about her lighting. "But what if I kill someone, or, worse, what if I get shown up by some crusty little know-it-all ten years younger than me?" I'm thinking about the tattooed kid outside Vincent's office, how he reeked of capability. The one thing I haven't felt for a long time is capable.

Marla hiccups. "Did you just say it would be better to kill someone than be bad at your job?"

I think for a moment. "You know what I mean," I say.

3

Ruth McCarthy gives me a tour of Station 710. My new headquarters is a small, beige, one-story house that looks out of place sitting in a large concrete parking lot with no plants or yard. The interior has been converted to mimic a fire station, and all the windows have thick iron bars. Ruth tells me Station 710 operates with two crews of three rotating shifts: A, B, and C. "We're the A shift," she says. Her copper hair is pulled back impossibly tight; she wears no makeup and stands erect with big-boned shoulders. "Carl and I are partners on the one-car. J-Rock and Pep are the two-car. They're on a call but you'll meet them later."

She points out a workout room with lockers and a shower and marches me through the sleeping quarters, where four twin beds are pushed against the walls. At the station's entrance, the communal area includes a pseudo-kitchen, as well as a dining table with mismatched chairs and four brown recliners circling a giant television. She reminds me that every room has a phone. "If it rings with a call for 7102, do *not* go sprinting for the parking lot. Just yell it out so the other crew knows they have a call. We're 7101. As in the *one-car*. Get it?"

I nod, trying to look determined and thoughtful. Perhaps if I look determined and thoughtful she will stop talking to me like I'm a golden retriever.

"That's my partner, Carl Hagan, by the way."

From the dining room table, Carl blinks at me before returning his attention to a surfing magazine. He's younger than her, about twenty years old, and has an impish face: ears that stick out, close-cropped hair, and eyes set a little too close together. I can tell that these two finish each other's sentences, though Carl has said nothing to me while Ruth, every inch the training officer, has been instructing me in a clipped tone from the moment I walked through the door.

"This is your first job in EMS, right?"

"Not exactly—I used to be a lifeguard."

"Oh, over at County?"

"No, in high school."

From the dining room table, Carl makes a noise but doesn't look up. Ruth pinches her lower lip before letting out a sigh.

"Okay. Here's how it works. Each call takes about an hour. Average of five to eight minutes to get on scene, ten to twenty minutes to run the call, then drive to the hospital either Code 2 or Code 3. Obviously, you're not *done* until you've transferred care, which means giving a report at the hospital and getting your patient a bed. Okay so far?"

"Sounds fine."

"I'm going to run your ass off, and I don't want to hear any complaining. The best way to learn how to be efficient in the field is to run as many calls as possible. This is a busy station, so that won't be hard to do."

My first task is to fill out the daily ambulance checkout. I sit in the back of the rig with my new clipboard and the checklist, going through compartments one by one. Triangular bandages, Kerlix, blood-stoppers, emergency childbirth kits, biohazard bags, isolation kits, gloves, tape, dressings, splints, trauma shears, suction catheters, airway adjuncts, oxygen masks, emesis basins, linen, backboards, portable oxygen tanks, soft restraints, cold packs… Ruth may assume I'm an idiot, but I was top of my EMT class. I got the highest score on the final my teacher had ever seen. And while I don't picture myself running out of a collapsing building with a baby under each arm—at least not on my first day—I do know what compassion looks like. Even when I've been working in the field as long as Ruth has, I bet I'll be able to spare a few words about the importance of helping people. Everything with her seems to be about paperwork, supplies, and protocols.

About halfway through the checkout we get our first call. I look at the vibrating pager. It's gibberish, a tangle of acronyms and numbers. I start to panic. They didn't teach us about this in EMT school. As I climb into the passenger seat, Ruth shoves my map book at me. She's sitting behind the wheel, the engine is running, and she's already spoken to Dispatch over the radio. She is waiting, not so patiently.

Carl sits behind and between us in the captain's seat, his chin resting on his fists, his face a becalmed smirk. He obviously knows exactly how to get where we're going. All I've been able to gather is that our call is somewhere on 82nd Street, which zigzags east to west across Los Angeles. I scramble with the map book, flip pages, look desperately at my pager for some clue. Someone called 911 and I'm no help whatsoever.

"Time!" Ruth says, indicating my sixty seconds are up. She throws the rig into drive, flips the lights and sirens on without so much as a glance at the different switches on the panel, and takes off. "We'll talk later," she adds over the scream of the sirens.

* * *

Later is relative. At the twelfth hour Ruth sits me down at the station's dining room table. A single hair has come loose from her ponytail, and it sticks straight up. As I sink into the chair across from her, I notice for the first time she is so pale she's almost translucent, and despite being five years younger than me, the dark rings under her eyes appear to be permanent. Then again, as she stares at me, I'm suddenly aware of what I must look like. My hair is a frizzy mess and my uniform disheveled. Because I kept breaking out in a sweat on scene, because I burned through my deodorant hours ago, I smell bad and my undershirt is sticking to me. She looks exactly like she did twelve hours ago except for the one errant hair. She didn't break a sweat once.

Ruth can do anything. Ruth hates me right now.

My hands were shaking when I tried to get a blood pressure on the first call; I forgot to get the appropriate signatures on my paperwork three times; I put a tiny pediatric oxygen mask on a 250-pound man, snapping its elastic and almost giving myself an eye injury; and only on the last call did I map Ruth in somewhat the right direction. I didn't handle the gurney properly and mistook a distraught woman experiencing anxiety for a person dying of a heart attack.

Nothing has been what I thought it would be. Vaguely I remember a pale patient with shallow breathing who had a thin sheen of unnatural sweat over his face and neck, and whose fingertips looked kind of blue. There was a drunk guy, too, with yellow eyes that Ruth whispered were a sign of jaundice. He grinned blearily at me, and smelled like a mixture of dumpster rot, sewage, and formaldehyde. For the rest of the day I kept catching whiffs of him like he was standing right next to me.

"Do you have any questions?" Ruth asks.

What causes jaundice? How do you tell anxiety from a cardiac problem? How had Ruth known the man's entire medical history just from his lung sounds? How good will I have to be before people stop looking at me like I'm an idiot?

Somewhere in my shift was also a car accident: a two-vehicle incident on the busy nearby freeway. While we were on our way with lights and sirens, wearing helmets and reflective brush jackets, I was especially jittery. I pictured carnage and broken glass, a car fire and the Jaws of Life. But the vehicles had minor damage, the people seemed virtually unharmed, and the trickiest part of handling the call wasn't the medical assessment, or the spinal precaution gear, or the transportation of the two patients to the hospital—it was pulling the victims apart. They'd been screaming and clawing at each other in the middle of the freeway.

"How can I do better?" I say finally.

"Mapping," she says. "Do the mapping homework I gave you. Try to multitask on scene. Be able to distinguish critical patients from stable ones; that will come with time. And paperwork, paperwork, *paperwork*. If you don't fill out the forms right, it's as if the events never happened. Don't forget, there are legal consequences for the decisions you make."

Ruth oozes calm capability, but earlier I saw signs of frustration. She would try to let me make mistakes, but due to the extent of my ineptitude, she kept taking things out of my hands in order to do them correctly and in half the time. And then there's the fact that while Ruth isn't compassionate toward her patients, there is something generous about her efficiency. All day I watched people respond to the knowledge that they were being taken care of. Now, aching and exhausted, I wonder if it's too late to go back to working as an extra or something equally useless. There's nothing so painful as desire: wanting something only reminds you of your shortcomings.

As I gather my stuff, Carl makes it clear he will be making fun of me the moment I leave. He has already started to imitate my high-pitched stress-voice, and halfway through the shift he started referring to me as "Ricky Rescue," making even the stoic Ruth snort. Before I pull the door shut behind me, Carl calls out, "Just remember, not everyone gets the color red."

* * *

When I was sixteen years old, I witnessed a hit-and-run. Car versus pedestrian. Today I heard an EMT joke about that type of call: the car usually wins. I still remember exactly how everything looked—downtown Los Angeles, the skyscrapers leaning in on me with their boxy silhouettes, mirrored contours directing the setting sun's light in a hundred directions at once. I'd been on my way to a bus stop. When I heard the sound of impact I turned around in time to see a body flying through the air.

The event was so out of sync with my daily life I almost laughed. For just a second, I was sure it was some kind of joke. The airborne object looked so lightweight, its flight so effortless, that it seemed to be an inflatable doll, not a human being. A black jeep tore out of the intersection and whizzed past me. I heard a small group of people crowded around the object, calling for help. "Does anyone know CPR?" someone yelled.

I did. High school lifeguarding had taught me that. I walked over in a daze and observed a woman in her early thirties; it looked like the car had hit her squarely in the chest. Her eyes were open and unseeing and she was covered in blood. Someone was already trying to breathe for her, so I did compressions, badly. As soon as I placed my linked hands over her sternum I forgot everything: the appropriate rate, the ratio of breaths to compressions, the depth I was supposed to be pushing. I don't know if it mattered. We never could get her chest to inflate; probably the impact had popped her lungs. Certainly she had broken ribs. Giving compressions felt like snapping toothpicks suspended in Jell-O.

The fire and police departments appeared within minutes and took over. Only then did I notice the force of her trajectory had knocked the woman out of both of her shoes and one of her socks. I saw her stupefied husband, eyes also unseeing but very much alive and uninjured, being helped into the passenger seat of the ambulance. Later, on the news,

I learned she was a mom of two kids, visiting LA from South Dakota. They said she died in the hospital due to sustained injuries. I knew she died on the corner of 5th Street and Figueroa.

As I drive home, I lose my adrenaline rush. Traffic isn't bad, but everything moves like it's sedated, even the cars. I circle Echo Park Lake, watching the ducks through the window. The dirt-filled pickup truck behind me honks. I notice I'm gripping the steering wheel, and loosen my fingers. How strange that I went through four weeks of EMT training, talking about trauma, blood, injury, and death, and didn't think of that woman once. But then again, that class was all about how to help people, and I didn't do anything except be witness to her last few moments.

What I remember most clearly was how after the ambulance took the woman away, I kept trying to find a bathroom. I wanted to wash my blood-encrusted hands. I tried gas stations, restaurants, and cafés but everything was out of order or off-limits. Finally I boarded a bus, fumbled with the money I handed the bus driver, and expected him to notice. But he didn't. Her blood was all over me—my hands were the most obvious—but he didn't notice a thing and no one on the bus did either.

My little Corolla seems to park itself. Retrieving my phone from the glove compartment, I see that NutraSweet called twice, leaving messages both times, and sent me a handful of texts throughout the day.

I remember how soft his lips are, how guileless his smile.

When he answers the phone, I don't tell him about my day or ask how he is. I tell him I don't want to see him anymore. No, I'm sorry, but that's how I feel. Yes, I should've told you in person and not over the phone. No, I'm not dating anyone else. The truth is, I'm just not interested. Then I hang up and go inside, suddenly starving.

On my first day of the four-week EMT program, we were given a diagram that was meant to encompass everything we would learn throughout the course. It showed an ever-branching algorithm: the top pinnacle started with the scene of a call; the middle, a patient-assessment flow chart, branched out like a Choose Your Own Adventure book; and at the bottom, every arrow pointed to the box that said your patient arrives safely at the hospital. My whole life had been spent waiting for such an algorithm.

4

Your eyes absorb light in cone-shaped fields of vision, the center point sharpest, the concentric edges increasingly indistinct, like a photograph in which a single seagull is perfectly captured and the rest of the flock blurs into the sky.

Vision is one of those rare senses that, while involuntary, you have some control over. As soon as you open your eyes, you take in light. You take in light and therefore shapes, movement, trajectories, the passing of time. Your eyes constantly move about, sampling your surroundings, your fields of vision roving like the rings of a target. You don't take in dimension so much as fluctuation. Proportions are implied. After all, everything would look two-dimensional if nothing moved.

Six oculomotor muscles attach to each of your eyeballs and rotate your sight up, down, side to side, and diagonally. These muscles also act as anchors, keeping your eyes from bouncing around in their sockets while your body hurtles through space.

When you're given a specific task, the difference between amateur and expert is obvious even in how you direct your gaze. Sight can distract and overwhelm. Driving around a curve in a narrow road, an amateur constantly judges the distance to parked cars, whereas an expert keeps the gaze fixed ahead, scanning for oncoming traffic. The eyes of an expert athlete don't follow the ball but instead anticipate its movement.

Light enters by way of the pupil and gets cast, upside down, upon the retina, which translates the image into signals your brain can understand. No photoreceptor cells fill the space on the retina where the optic nerve attaches, so there's a blind spot. Your codependent eyes fill in each other's holes, cover for the other's mistake. This snag in your vision always occurs in your periphery: the blurred object in the corner of your eye, the one you're not looking at, is the object that disappears.

Except you don't see out of the corners of your eyes. There are no corners. Your eyes are globes, sitting in orbitals, and sight occurs in circles, concentric cones of vision, and even the crystalline lens, just under the round hole of your pupil, is dimple-shaped as it refracts and projects light onto the rounded wall of your retina. There are no corners, and yet every form of visual representation—from photographs to paintings to movies to magazines—is constrained to squares and rectangles, as if to better imitate the action of your eyelids closing. As if to suggest that the narrowing of sight is more important than the act of seeing.

5

"We're going to be late," Ryan says.

"I just need a few snacks. I forgot to eat dinner."

My brother gives me a suspicious look. He peers down each aisle, carrying an empty basket, and I trail after him, scanning the store and trying not to be obvious about it.

"Fine, but then we won't have time to get a drink."

"We have to get a drink."

"Is Tin Lizzie even open on Sundays?"

"Of course it's open, it's a bar."

"But it's Orange County."

"*And* it's tradition."

"Some tradition. Dad will have alcohol."

"I need alcohol before Dad."

"It will take too long."

"It's hump day, Ryan. Live a little."

"It's *Sun*day, you asshole. I work at 6 a.m. tomorrow." He picks up a package of roasted almonds with sea salt. "What do you want, anyway?" He puts the almonds in the basket without waiting for an answer. "I have to get up early, Pipes." When I still don't respond, he says, "Fine. But if Tin Lizzie's is closed, we're going straight to Dad's."

"Fine."

We're at Sustainable Living, the organic food market on Sunset Boulevard. The food is delicious but the checkers are snobs. The produce is always perfectly ripe and colorful—not that I come here for the produce.

Ryan starts drifting down Aisle 7. Despite his supposed hurry to drive down to Dad's place in Costa Mesa tonight, the only time Ryan ever moves quickly is when he's working. The rest of the time he's got one speed, and it's a kind of dreamy, slow meandering.

He stops in front of the baking supplies. "I swear, this time if you don't ask her out, I will."

"I have no idea what you're talking about."

Ryan picks up carob powder, then some kind of cake-making kit that comes with icing bags and little jars of color. "It's a shame she's the reason you come here. There's beautiful food in this store."

"Keep your voice down." I poke my head out of the aisle, looking around the store one more time. Since there's no sign of her I finally give Ryan my full attention, which means telling him about my new job. I decide to leave out how incompetent I was and instead stick to describing basic operations.

When we get to the produce section he can't hide his excitement, so I wait by the scale while he carefully selects peaches, kiwis, a bag of cherries.

You would never know Ryan's gay. He came out when he was twenty-four years old, and no one had any idea. I was in my first same-sex relationship when I was only seventeen, but Ryan says it's a shame I lost my curiosity at the halfway point. We like to joke that Ryan went fully atheist while I took the more benign, agnostic route, by keeping my options open and insisting there was no need to make up my mind.

Before Ryan came out, he had a bird obsession. All through college and after, he dated a lot—girls were always chasing him—but all he ever wanted to talk about were the canaries and macaw he owned, dirty animals who never stayed in their cages and left bird shit all over his apartment. You'd go over there to find his blinds closed, streaks of white on the stove and banister and refrigerator, feathers and crumbs of their food pellets in the bathroom sink and crushed into the carpet. The macaw was loud and aggressive; the canaries never went to sleep when they were supposed to; the neighbors started to complain. Ryan always talked about them like they were friends, and then one day he donated them to a pet store and announced he liked men.

He comes up to me looking blissful, the basket nearly full. Then he gets serious. "Hey, remember, next month would have been Mom and Dad's thirtieth anniversary, so he might be in a bit of a mood. Maybe you could go easy on him if he starts—" He stops when he recognizes the disinterested expression on my face. "You're so good at that."

"What?"

"Not talking about things you don't want to talk about." He places his hand flat on the metal pan of the scale and pushes down until he gets the red needle to read one pound exactly. "Malcolm wants me to go to couples therapy."

I'm indignant on his behalf, but he shrugs and asks how things have been going with Nathan. Instead of answering I pluck a kiwi from the basket and wave it around. "Is it true you can eat the skin? Hair and all?"

He throws his head back and laughs. I love when he does that; the sound is full and good-natured and seems to percolate up from his navel. "Marla's going to kill you."

"She's distracted," I huff. "She's got a date with some guy from work tonight."

"Already? She's worse than a gay boy."

But I'm not listening to him, because a new employee has emerged from the back stockroom. She stops to take inventory of the citrus about twenty feet from me and I can't stop staring. I envy the crate of oranges wedged between her hip and the fruit display. Her presence makes me feel hot and magnetic. A little shorter than me, with strong, round shoulders, she has an athletic body that moves with an androgynous sway, and feminine hands with long fingers. The pensive tuck of her chin causes her short dark hair to tumble into her face. As she refills the mountain of fruit, she looks powerful and elegant, despite the fluorescent lighting, despite her earth-toned apron, despite the sweaty bald man who bumps into her left shoulder and almost yells his apology.

"Pipes," Ryan says softly. "Go talk to her. Do it already."

But I just stand there.

Ryan is the keeper of our visits to Dad. About once a month he'll call me up and tell me it's time. That's how he always says it: "Pipes. It's time." I resist as long as I can. It's not that I don't love our father, but all he ever wants to talk about is our mother, and I don't see why we should talk about someone who ran off when Ryan and I were kids. To make matters worse, she died two years ago. Since then, Dad's nostalgia has felt especially unbearable. I barely remember her, there's nothing to reminisce about, and even if there were, what would be the point?

We arrive at Dad's place, and as usual he pretends not to know who we are. "I'm not interested," he says, one blue eye peering out from the cracked-open door. "Go bother the neighbors."

"Already did."

Ryan spreads his empty hands. "We sold everything."

The door opens wider. The strong hand wrapped around the edge of the door looks older than the rest of him, the knuckles gnarled and veiny. "Well, what was it this time?"

"Porn," I say before I can stop myself.

"Kittens," Ryan says.

He lets us in. "Porn and kittens! Your pockets must be heavy with wealth." He waves for us to follow him to the living room. "Come in, come in."

We file down the hallway. Even from the back, Ryan and Dad look nothing alike, but they move alike, chins lifted, broad shoulders swinging lightly. My father is stocky and barrel chested; Ryan is tall and graceful, no freckles but the same blue eyes, the same unwieldy light brown hair as I have, only Ryan's is cut short and somehow made stylish, framing his open face. I'm long and wiry, only slightly curvier than I was in my adolescence, and my late twenties have stripped the last traces of baby fat from my narrow features.

"Well?" Dad asks, sinking into the dimpled black leather of his favorite chair. Crossing his meaty forearms over his chest, he looks at me, then at Ryan. "How's work, you two?" Hooded light blue eyes turn to mine. "Piper?"

"Work's fine. I got that ambulance operator position. It's all kind of new still."

Dad makes a humming noise. He's trying to remember if I told him about this new career path. I did. The last time I was here, I told him about my upcoming interview at A & O. He was sitting in the same chair.

"I'm surprised," he says, "that you thought to take up a job like that. But you never know, do you? In fact, your mother—"

I want to say to him, "Mom *left*, Dad. She left. Stop talking about her already. And especially stop talking about her affectionately, like she was a good person or something." But I don't.

"…which is why you've always reminded me of her," Dad finishes, patting my shoulder with a thick paw.

Ryan clears his throat. "Dad, the restaurant job is going really well." He tells us about working as a line cook at a family-run Mediterranean restaurant, how he hopes to work his way to head chef. But after a brief congratulatory exchange, Dad turns back to me.

"Are you making money doing this ambulance work?"

I try to laugh. "Not at all. It pays minimum wage." Fearing he'll launch into a lecture on his second favorite topic, money, I'm quick to add, "I mean, with the overtime and 24-hour shifts, it works out to—"

"What's the point?" he barks. "How's this job going to help you in the long run? One of these days you're going to have to pick a career and really stick with it, Piper. You can't just keep—"

"I'm thinking about becoming a nurse," I say. "Or a firefighter. I don't *know* yet. I need to be at the job longer than a day before planning the rest of my life."

"You want to be a fireman?" My dad makes his humming sound again. "You're not strong enough for that."

"How do you mean?" I have the brief hope that he is talking about emotional strength. Maybe what follows will be a sermon on how to take the severity of the job in stride, and keep going.

He leans forward and squeezes my relaxed biceps, like he's testing a pear for ripeness. "Have you been working out? You're going to have to lift weights if you want to be a fireman."

Ryan smirks at me from the couch, his relaxed, interlocked fingers resting in his lap. My brother figured out long ago how to let these visits be exactly what they are, and I envy him that.

I decide to back down. Playfully, I poke Dad in the shoulder and chest and down the length of his arm. "What about you? Huh? Have *you* been working out lately?"

He makes a few bodybuilder poses. "Finally made it back to Wild Card last week."

The only thing really Irish about my dad is his love of boxing. His gym, Wild Card, is the dive bar version of a fitness center. Two boxing rings frame the footwork and bare torsos of shadowboxers and spar mates, and the stereo system gets drowned out by the pounding of heavy body bags and the drumming taunt of the speed bags.

"That's funny, you don't look any different."

He pretends to have a heart attack, grabbing his chest and heaving. "How dare you," he gasps.

"She's just jealous," Ryan says. "Don't mind her."

Dad shifts in his chair. "My trainer told me a funny story when I saw him. His elbow is all bandaged up, like it should be in a sling—and this is not the kind of guy to fool with first aid. He's missing teeth and covered in tattoos of big-breasted women. So I say to him, 'What'd you do to your elbow?' And he gets all embarrassed. Turns out he was riding his nephew's Razor scooter—you know those skinny metal things?—and fell right off. Hard to picture a guy like that on one of those. He's gotten a real hard time about it."

Ryan picks up one of the beer steins from Dad's collection on the coffee table. The steins make a circle around a large silver platter that looks so untouched I wouldn't be surprised if time had glued it to the table. Ryan turns the stein over in his hands, tracing the Celtic knot on the side.

"Those old things." Dad sighs. "One of these days I'm going to get a smaller place, and then I'm going to get rid of all this crap. Too much stuff."

"Sure," says Ryan, though we all know he'll never move. Even though not a trace of her is visible, her absence is on every wall, in every room, a void so present it's like a roommate.

"Tell you what." My father's eyes light up. He slams his hand on the armrest and leans toward me. "I challenge you to an arm-wrestling match."

Not for the first time, I wonder if it ever bothers Ryan that I'm the one Dad treats more like a son, but he jumps up with a grin on his face and before I know it, the three of us are dragging Dad's chair down the hallway and into his dining-room-turned-office.

The dining room table is covered with stacks of paper, computer wires, a laptop, and two dusty candles that have never been lit. Dad works as a software engineer for some big company; he often brings his work home with him. I have no idea what being a software engineer means.

Dad drops his elbow onto the table and holds out his hand. "Shall we, my dear?" Placing my elbow on the table with a soft sigh, I pretend for a moment to be more feminine than I feel, as if that will throw him off somehow. He might be stronger, but I have more endurance. If I can just hold him in place, I should be able to force his hand down once he's gotten tired.

My thin fingers disappear as we wrap hands. His palm feels dry and feverish. I keep my arm loose and relaxed, with just enough tension to maintain the place-hold. My dad flexes his biceps and puffs up his chest. When we're settled and ready, we swivel our heads to look at Ryan, standing to the side and between us.

"Go," he says.

It lasts only a few seconds. I slam Dad's hand down, barely sensing his resistance, almost disappointed by how easy it is. His face registers disbelief and then warps into an unrecognizable expression. Leaning forward, almost panting, I feel the exertion only now that the match is over. My eyes widen with a daughter's guilt; my ears are pricked and nervous. Was that the sound of his robust Irish male ego shattering? But no. He looks bewildered and—can it be?—proud.

"Good!" he says. "Very good."

6

The clock says 0238.

After I got hired, I took Vincent's advice and got a watch that could be set to military time. I switched the digital clock in my room to the 24-hour setting. It's been strange these last few days, to see times like "1330" or "1645." So it's oddly comforting to look at a clock in the middle of the night and know exactly what time it is.

0238. No math required.

I lie in bed, still, staring at a dark ceiling I can't see but know is there. It feels like I'm waiting for something. I'm not hungry or sick or anxious; I don't have to pee; I didn't have a bad dream. I'm just awake.

Across the room, in the back of my closet, behind sliding doors thick with too many coats of white paint, a small cardboard box rests on the highest shelf. Each time I move I don't bother to unpack it; the label just says STUFF in faded black marker. Somewhere in the stratified contents lives a postcard that arrived in the mail when I was twelve years old, Ryan fourteen.

She's wearing a Santa hat and khaki shorts, my mother. She has water shoes on. Behind her, looming, the black and red crests of Westwater Canyon, the expansive Colorado sky.

The postcard arrived two years after she left. Back then, everything was separated into before and after, and Ryan and I still talk in this way sometimes.

I memorized it a long time ago. Every detail. A matte-finish photograph, sort of a Christmas card, the postcard serves as an advertisement for the river rafting company my mother and her boyfriend, Sergio, operated for over a decade. They probably sent out a hundred of those things; I don't know why I kept it. The gold cursive along the bottom edge reads: SEASON'S GREETINGS FROM WESTWATER'S DISCOVERY TRIPS! My mother with her Santa hat, one arm wrapped around the waist of the gangly youth standing next to her, the other hand holding an oar with a wreath hung on it. She offers it up to the camera like it's a fish she's proud to have caught. Sergio is fifteen years her junior and he looks it, standing by her side flashing a peace sign. I hate those fingers, their skyward-facing twin points. That one detail I have fixated on for years.

At 0402, I decide to go swimming. I dig through drawers until I find my dark blue T-backed swimsuit. Not wanting to wake Marla in the next room, I'm conscious of every amplified sound. Stripping down, I pull over my reluctant body (sluggish legs first, uncoordinated arms next) what feels like a rubber band. But when it snaps into place it feels like home.

Before Mom left, the thing I wanted most in life was to grow up to be her; I thought she was the most beautiful woman in the world. My mother's wavy brown hair hung all the way down to her waist; she had a singsong laugh and always drank out of a bowl-shaped blue mug, whether it was coffee or tea or water or beer. She wore bright, flowing clothing, and I would play dress-up in her hand-me-downs, in skirts and blouses that didn't move the way my clothes moved, that barely seemed to exist between my fingertips and settled gently on my skin. We read together almost every night, *The Phantom Tollbooth*, *The Happy Prince*, but there were also the stories she made up, like the one about the underwater castle a few miles west of Manhattan Beach, so perfectly camouflaged along the Pacific Ocean floor that sailors and scientists had never spotted it. I discovered later that some of the stuff she told me was true—how an octopus grows a new arm if it loses one, how an earthworm has five hearts.

After she left, Dad could barely look at me and Ryan. He lost himself in long work hours, turned on the television as soon as he got home. Mom called us about every two weeks, then once a month, then once every several months. Her inability to know what to say was obvious in her too-cheerful tone and its shifting lightness. Like a tightrope walker who knew it would be suicide to look down.

I shut the front door softly, click the deadbolt into place, and leave the key underneath a potted plant. I set off down the hall, passing the other apartments. Marla and I have lived here about eight months. She never uses the heated pool, but I go at least twice a week, either early mornings or late nights. Never this early.

After Mom left, swimming was instinctual, a survival mechanism. Ten years old and I thought of my gear, that flower-print suit complete with cap and goggles, as a superhero's outfit. I practiced stances in the mirror. The save-the-world stance was obvious enough: feet spread apart, hands on hips, a determined gaze looking up and past one shoulder. The save-the-world-and-look-sexy-at-the-same-time stance, at least according to my prepubescent brain, was to lower the gaze, bring the feet together, bend one knee, and rest one hand on the propped-up hip.

Ruth says there are four steps to effective mapping.

Step one: know where you are. Find your exact location on the map page and point to it with one finger.

The pool is an unremarkable cement rectangle, and its deep end is a mere eight feet. But the light shining through the clear, still water is a luminescent invitation. I pad barefoot to the edge, toss my towel over a lounge chair, and set the goggles over my eyes, feeling the suction as they seal onto my face.

I close my eyes when I first pierce the water. There's a familiar rush as my body registers the cold against my skin. The initial contact overwhelms my senses, but then I open my eyes and start to kick. It's too damn small, this pool. I flip-turn at the shallow end and I'm more than halfway across before my first stroke.

Step two: know where you're going. Make sure you are looking at the correct map page and grid, and find not just the street of the address but the cross streets as well. When you've got the exact block of the destination, place a second finger there.

Already I'm working too hard, wasting motion, forgetful of my limbs' ability to be efficient. When I get into the water I always want to go as fast as I possibly can. Switching to the breaststroke, I remember how one of my coaches used to remind me that speed isn't everything. If you get shipwrecked you'll want to conserve energy—it might be days before you see land.

Step three: figure out your route. Work backward from the second finger to the first, like when you solved mazes as a kid, working from the heart of the labyrinth to the entrance instead of the other way around.

I cut to the surface with a gasp when I realize I don't remember the fourth step. A two-vehicle incident. A Santa hat. Dad turning on the television, Ryan in his room, working on some project or another. He was always the creative one—the musician, the mechanic, the tinkerer. The car usually wins. And then there was me—I did *nothing* for that dying woman. I would have forgotten all about her if being so useless on my first day hadn't reminded me. Grabbing the cement lip at the deep end's edge, I hold on with one hand and look out at the rippling water, dangerously close to crying.

Step one: know where you are.

Step two: know where you're going.

My legs sway in the current I created. What have I done with my life since graduation? My postcollege years led to ambiguous goals. And to learning things that had nothing to do with what I learned in school. And to Jared. My ex-boyfriend: a lovely, attractive human being right up until he wasn't. We met at a glassblowing workshop he taught, and he didn't act like I wouldn't know how to use tools because I was a girl. I thought he was exotic and artistic, with eyes like flat black stones and a sly smile. He had unusual arm sleeves tattooed in heavy black ink, the lines, curves, and circles molded perfectly to the shape of his muscles and joints. I used to trace the lines after we had sex—but only then, because otherwise he found it ticklish.

We dated for four years, lived together for about two; one night we threw a party at our apartment and I walked in on my friend Elizabeth giving him head in our bathroom. I'd never made a speech before but I made one that night; I turned down the music and clinked a fork against a beer bottle and announced to about thirty of our friends that Elizabeth was a filthy whore; she was giving my boyfriend a blow job in the next room; maybe it was a good time for everyone to leave and thanks so much for coming. I moved out in hysterics that same night, leaving my CDs and potted fern behind, staying with Ryan and Malcolm at their place in Culver City for a while. Ryan tried to take care of me; when I started losing weight he force-fed me fatty foods, ramen and pizza. Later I learned Jared and Elizabeth had been sleeping together for months.

In the EMS world, you could call that particular kind of trauma a double penetrating injury, the mechanism being two knives in the back. The field remedy would be to seal the exit and entrance wounds with occlusive dressings and treat for shock.

I push off for a few more laps.

Soon after Jared and I broke up, I got the news that Mom died. Even after her skiing accident, and after the funeral, I would see the photograph she sent when I was twelve years old, as clear in my head as if it were in my hand, and I would think: *she's not dead*. There she is, promoting river rafting in Colorado, her mousy brown hair streaked with golden highlights, her bleached teeth beaming.

Step two: there's your career, your home life, and your social life. Pick one. Or at least that's what Mom used to say. I guess you could say she chose social life. Dad chose career. Ryan and I were the home life nobody picked.

I get out and towel off, dripping into a puddle at my feet, no save-the-world stance. Which one have I picked? Life experience?

That's not on the list.

As I make my way back, edges of pink in the sky behind me, I remember.

Step four: after determining the clearest route, choosing main streets and as few turns as possible, give your driver all directions up front. But also give updates. Keep an eye on your location at all times, call out when the next turn is coming up, and estimate how many miles will be spent on each street. Be ready to map a new path in case of traffic, detours, accidents, or roadblocks.

Step four: be vigilant with the task at hand.

I take a shower but don't go back to bed. I do the mapping exercises Ruth gave me until it's time to go to work.

7

Ruth says I need to see South Central. She throws Carl and me in the rig and drives around 710's district. "We're first up for all calls," she says. "And we're not going back until you're better at mapping."

She and Carl point out landmarks. The pale pink church at the corner of Van Ness and Arbor Vitae, where you sometimes respond to congregation members who've fainted. The crack house at 92nd and Dalton, a dark green shoebox whose color contrasts sharply with the straw-colored weeds. It has a BEWARE OF DOG sign but no dog, the empty leash drooping from a wrought-iron fence. Carl tells me everyone wants to run a call on that place, to see what the inside looks like, but no one has.

I learn about the dive bars, the convalescent homes, the elementary schools. Which restaurants get people sick. Which intersection has the highest homicide rate. Carl points out two small parks within a mile radius of each other, explaining that the men who ride their bicycles in circles, ringing the little metal bells on their handlebars, are actually drug dealers, the ringing sound an advertisement. We pass another landmark, the abandoned warehouse on the corner of 112th Street and Normandie Avenue with its tilted rusty sign and mural of gang tags, the remaining shards of glass hanging in the frames like an ever-shrinking jigsaw puzzle. The deserted Buick on Central Avenue could almost serve as a landmark, too, covered in parking tickets like feathers, at least until they tow it away. I wonder if Ruth and Carl are as familiar with their own neighborhoods as they are with these streets. Their attitude toward South Central falls somewhere between resident and tourist.

Looping through the neighborhood, Ruth explains which avenues and boulevards are the easiest to oppose traffic on, and Carl warns against a convenience store that's had three robberies in the last month. I look at the piles of trash on the sidewalk, the crumpled shapes and decay-coated buildings, the way the early morning light casts quiet over everything. There's something here I hadn't expected, a deeply rooted sense of community in this wrecked and broken place; it's apparent in the way everyone yells their hellos and seems to know each other.

Ruth and Carl wave their own hellos at a trio of transients standing in an alley. "I'll bet you lunch we pick up Sadie before eleven," Carl says.

"By nine," says Ruth.

Our first call comes in at 0816. I'm beginning to recognize my pager's language: "57/ M ALOC" means a fifty-seven-year-old man has an altered level of consciousness. Ruth pronounces every acronym as if she were reading off the letters of an eye exam, but Carl refers to this one as "A-lock."

Ruth hits the gas as she flips on the lights and sirens. "Map me to my call!" she yells. "If I make it before you've mapped me there, you're going to polish our boots."

I open my Thomas Guide and quickly reel off directions to 134 Kansas Avenue, but Ruth shows no sign of approval. She switches to quizzing me as she swerves around cars, her aggression clearly habitual. "What are possible reasons a person might be altered?"

It's shocking to witness how many drivers refuse to pull over to the right.

"They could be hypo- or hyperglycemic, or it could be a drug overdose or a stroke. They could be in shock, maybe from trauma. Like a blunt force injury to the head?"

"Normal range for blood sugar?"

"Between 70 and 140."

"What's hypoxia?"

"Hypoxia. Hypoxia. That's when brain cells are deprived of oxygen…" My brain is being rattled for loose change. "Oh, right! If a person has a seizure, there's the post-ictal phase afterward, when they're disoriented."

"How do you treat a seizure?"

"Turn them onto their side so they can't choke on their tongue, give them oxygen, do a rapid trauma assessment for injuries."

"Stroke?"

"Check eyes, motor, verbal, try to get onset and duration from witnesses." Carl adds playfully, "I'm usually ALOC on my days off. Due to EtOH."

"What is that?" Ruth uses even Carl's sense of humor as a means to quiz me. "We talked about this."

Other drivers' faces are a blur as they ignore the emergency vehicle's howl and flash. People talk on the phone and sing along to music. One guy is picking his nose and looks up, caught, as we fly past. I remember the jaundiced patient the other day, the way he had reeked of booze and his eyes had lolled.

"Alcohol? You say that if someone has been drinking?"

"Correct. EtOH is the chemical abbreviation for ethanol. It's a way of saying your patient is drunk without them knowing what you're talking about."

She slows and parks, aligning the rig with 134 Kansas Avenue. Leaving the emergency lights on, she uses the radio to tell Dispatch we're on scene. In front of the leaning one-story, a rusted Chevy sits on blocks in the oil-stained driveway, and a couple of stray cats clean themselves amid the tall weeds of the front yard.

Carl puts on a pair of gloves with a loud snap. "Let's go say hello to Teddy boy."

We fall in line with the firefighters, who arrived moments before us, moving up the driveway, the gurney bouncing along in concert with the gaping cracks in the pavement. One of the firefighters, who looks as though he is never not in uniform, thrusts his chin in my direction.

"Who's the boot?"

"Piper."

"They treating you okay, Piper?"

"Yes, sir."

"Don't call me 'sir,' it makes me feel old. I'm Vick."

"Hi, Vick." I smile at him and turn my head just in time to see Ruth glowering at me.

The front door is ajar and leaning off its hinges; we lift the gurney inside. Vick is in charge. He calls out and there's no answer. We walk into the next dimly lit room and see a shape sprawled on the couch. One of the firefighters searches for a light switch with his flashlight. I can just make out his reflective yellow pants moving around the room, the glow of the flashlight's halo swiveling above.

When weak light spills from an overhead lamp, I see Vick already kneeling by the couch, briskly rubbing the man's chest with his knuckles. The whole place smells dank, stale.

"Theodore? Come on, Teddy, talk to us."

The man doesn't respond. Seizure? Drug use? EtOH?

Ruth nudges me. "Go."

I stare blankly at her and then spring into action. I don't yet have the confidence they do, that unique assumption that I can just stroll into a stranger's home and start touching and talking to him. But I rush to get a blood pressure and a D-stick with my shaking hands; Carl hooks him up to the EKG monitor and the pulse oximeter.

"His sugar's 33!" I call out as the glucometer accepts the drop of blood and a number flashes on the small screen. I am at war with a Band-Aid: I am losing. One of the adhesive ends clings to my gloves. If he's in this kind of shape, who called 911?

But then she appears, an unconcerned woman holding a cup of coffee and a pack of cigarettes, her belly pushing out against her tank top and pajama bottoms. She tells us that he hasn't eaten since yesterday, but she gave him his insulin as usual this morning.

As if that's his cue, Teddy turns into a monster. A swinging, grunting, drool-slinging brute who would've clocked me in the face if I hadn't leaned back just in time—and yet even after this transformation, his expression remains oddly relaxed, childlike.

This is what it looks like when someone's brain is dying.

I'm rooted to the spot while three firefighters and Carl pin down Teddy's violent appendages. Ruth helps Vick get an IV line ready. The firefighter wearing moon pants holds up his flashlight so Vick can get a better view of a promising vein.

My options are: (1) ask to hold the firefighter's flashlight so at least it looks like I'm doing something, (2) try to administer oxygen to a person who's behaving like a crazed gorilla, or (3) bum one of the woman's cigarettes so I can smoke while I watch everybody work.

With the IV line established, Vick pushes fifty millileters of dextrose through one of the ports and flushes it with saline. He's able to achieve this only because four grown men are practically sitting on top of his patient.

Teddy's eyes open and focus on the room around him. "Oh, hey guys," he says.

"Teddy!" Carl says. He and the others climb off. On my last shift, Carl told me combative patients are his favorite type of workout.

Our patient sits up, blinking. He looks at his arm, the crisscross of skewed tape holding the IV catheter in place. "Did my sugar get low again?" He manages a weak smile as he rubs his leg in the spot where Carl's knee had pressed him.

I wait for someone to explain to him his close call with death, or advise him to monitor his sugar more often. No one does. If anything, the vibe as we leave is casual. *See you next time.*

"Piper, you have to jump in more," Ruth says as we climb back into the ambulance. "I give everyone a pass on their first day of training, but this is your second. Which means starting now, every single moment of every single call you should be figuring out what you can do to help."

But she's not talking about helping the patient, she's talking about helping the firefighters. "Does that guy know he almost died back there?" I ask.

"Teddy isn't the brightest star in the galaxy."

"Maybe because he's gone into severe hypoglycemia too many times."

The ambulance slows from Ruth's usually leaden foot. "Maybe it is," she says. "I don't think you should be changing the subject right now. We're talking about you, and how you can be a better EMT. Not Ted and how he can be a better diabetic."

"I only meant—"

"No, you listen. Don't make excuses. Don't change the subject. If I tell you that you need to get better at the job, it means you need to get better at the job."

"You're right," I manage to say.

Carl and I wash the ambulance in the parking lot of Station 710, which faces Normandie Avenue and borders a nightclub. The club's unlit neon sign, hanging over the entrance, reads DYNASTY, but everyone at A & O Ambulance calls the joint "Dy-*nasty.*" Ruth is inside the station, having her monthly meeting with the district supervisor, and as we soap up the rig walls I think about the girl at Sustainable Living, imagining the day when she will choke on a piece of gum or a speared slice of honey crisp apple, and I will rush to save her—I will do perfectly executed abdominal thrusts—and she will collapse into my arms and stare soulfully into my eyes.

"Ruth and I have a bet going about you," Carl says, interrupting my reverie. "About whether you're going to be a badge bunny." He cocks his head and studies me. "Personally, I don't think so. Not sure what it is about you, but I just don't see it."

"What does Ruth think?" I'm careful to keep my voice casual, as if the answer won't matter to me.

"Ruth hates other girl EMTs. Most of them are husband-hunting or looking for uniforms to hook up with."

I wiggle my toes, feeling the hard plate in my steel-toed boots, and try to fight off my disappointment. Here I've had so much respect for her, and she's making bets with her partner about how many firefighters I'll sleep with.

Carl gazes at the suds-filled bucket. "I can't wait to be FD. I'm going to collect badge bunnies like baseball cards."

As I hose down the rig, Carl lectures me on how to endear myself to my training officer. When he tells me to steer clear of lady killer Vick, I grunt in frustration, but then he tells me that the real way to kiss ass is to start calling Ruth "ma'am."

"That's ridiculous. I'm older than her!"

"Not in EMS you're not."

"I'm not calling her ma'am."

"Fine, don't take my advice. But keep talking back like you have been, and you're going to get yourself spanked."

We hang the wet towels on the low brick wall to dry them in the sun. I pour out the soapy water and we watch it spread, coating the parking lot, seeping into its cracks and potholes, pooling around the weeds.

"Want to see something?" Carl asks. I wonder if he ever doesn't have that smirk on his face, the lopsided one that makes his right ear and right eyebrow lift higher than the other side. It's impossible to hate him.

He pulls out his phone and shows me a picture from a call he had last year. On the little screen, a dead woman lies on her side on a couch. At first glance it looks like she just slumped over and never sat back up, but then I notice that half of her face is gone. So much skin and muscle have been removed that one eye looks normal while the other stares out from the orbital of her skull. Perched above her, sitting on the couch's backrest, is a small, fluffy white dog whose black eyes and pink tongue turn up toward the person taking the picture. But the cute face thrusts forward guiltily; the flat-eared expression belongs to an animal expecting punishment.

I look up with a growing feeling of horror. "Did the dog…?"

He nods, gleeful. "Her neighbors hadn't seen her for a week, so someone called 911. We broke apart the door with an ax and went in there. She'd been down a while. Little Fluffy must have gotten hungry at some point."

I look back down at the phone. The woman looks withered and crumpled, a small pile of bones folded into a flower-patterned dress. Carl shouldn't have this on his phone. Health care professionals aren't supposed to share any information about patients, much less take pictures of them. "That's a HIPAA violation," I say. "You're not allowed to do that."

Carl nods, his face mocking. "See, I knew I'd win that bet. You're a pretty big nerd, Piper Gallagher."

The man reaches for me, lets his arm collapse back onto the gurney. I look around for Ruth; she's near the front of the ambulance, craning her head to talk to Carl as he drives.

"Baby girl," my patient says. "Baby girl, I'm not okay." He can barely keep his eyes open but he's trying; his eyebrows are pulled up like ship sails trying to catch a breeze.

When we pulled him out of the bushes near the neon signs of Hollywood Park Casino, he was alone, with no wallet or ID, utterly incapable of answering any questions. A comical, towering six-foot-five that spilled over both ends of the gurney. Now, on the way to the hospital, the largest rag doll I've ever seen is coming to life.

I awkwardly pat his shoulder. It seems the thing to do. "What happened, sir?"

He shudders and grows still, his eyebrows relaxing, eyelids drifting shut. "I lost all my money," he says. "I gambled it away."

I nod even though he can't see me. "What did you take?"

He tries to remember. Definitely he drank, maybe even for twelve hours straight, and then he recalls taking about seven pills given to him throughout the night. One or two of the pills was Ecstasy, but other than that he can't remember a thing. Which, it sounds like, was the point.

"Baby girl," he says again. His low tone is intimate, and there's something about those two words and the way he keeps saying them that's getting to me. He fumbles for my hand, and as he grasps it I blush, amused and caught off guard by my own vulnerability. Ruth's attention is still on Carl, but I hate to think how she would react if she turned and saw this. His warm, drug-addled hand wraps around mine with the tenderness of a lover.

My patient rolls his head to look at me; it's a fluid, slippery motion only drunks are capable of, and for a moment it looks like his head will keep rolling right off the gurney. With supreme effort he keeps his eyes open and peers at me, solemn as a priest.

"Baby girl, I'm sorry."

At the end of my shift, Ruth lets out a groan when she sees my paperwork. Slamming one of my forms down on the table, she points out mistakes.

"How old is she? How do you spell diaphoretic? Why is there a number *missing* from her zip code?"

I'd been doing so well. I'd jumped to holding C-spine for a patient who slipped in the bathroom, recognized sepsis in a frequent flyer, restocked the ambulance in between calls without any reminders, and gave a report to a triage nurse for the first time. But our last patient was a middle-aged car thief who was covered in Taser barbs from her escape attempt from the cops. She cussed loudly and creatively the entire way to the hospital ("mama-pissing-pig-bitch-butt-wrench"), and seemed to be under the firm impression that her own mother was the one who had outed her to the police. The way she struggled against the restraints shifted the silver-cylindered barbs, and as I watched the folds of her jowls turn raw and pink from the points of puncture, and as she proceeded to call me every name she could think of, I had felt, strangely, a swell of excitement, a sudden self-assurance that I would be able to handle the job, and this assurance echoed old choices—my previous escapes from the ordinary—and an almost-forgotten version of myself, which is to say that I got so overwhelmed with a rush of simultaneous emotions that all I accomplished in the back of the ambulance was staring at her.

Ruth presses her palm to her face, and I watch as her fingertips drum against her forehead. Finally she says, "Listen, Piper, you have four days off before we see you again. I suggest you make the most of them."

"I'll get better," I tell her. "I absolutely will."

8

By now you're starting to realize the simplicity with which it's all possible. If you want to memorize something, turn it into a mnemonic device. Rhymes help, as do melodies; throw in visualization and associations for good measure. To memorize that the normal range for an adult pulse rate is 60 to 100 beats per minute, picture a snake curled up next to a bucket in one room, a skinny man blowing smoke rings in another.

The ability of your neurons to remap themselves, to change their strength and connection, is thought to be the reason you can form and retrieve memories or learn new behaviors. You're constantly creating pathways that can get triggered, recalling information voluntarily or at random.

For example.

For paperwork purposes, you memorize hospital, treatment, and medication codes. You learn the fire station numbers and addresses for five battalions, as well as all the freeways, major streets, and zip codes in your district. You memorize your rig, assignment, and employee number.

"Okay, ma'am," you say.

Height, age, weight, date of birth, phone number, social security number, address, zip code, medical insurance number, phone number of an emergency contact. What your patient rattles off by rote is just the beginning of our memory vaults. These digits are nestled in with those of bank accounts, passwords, pin numbers, and credit cards. This little computer chip sits alongside old addresses and phone numbers, security questions and answers, email addresses, and mothers' maiden names.

"Please sign here."

Roughly translated, the average patient looks like this: (323) 467-8792, 555-66-9827, 5'7", 42 y/o, 145 lbs, 01/13/1968, 34689 103rd Ave, 90044, 555-66-9827A, (818) 227-6900.

When you're giving the report at the hospital, your partner wanders over in the middle of it. He's been standing next to your gurney-riding patient in the ER hallway, using the portable vitals monitor to collect "a fresh set of numbers."

"Ready for her?" he asks, and you nod, pen ready. "She's 156/90 on the blood pressure, 102 beats per minute, about 18 breaths per minute, a temp of 98.6, pain scale is 7 out of 10, and 99 percent oxygen saturation on room air. Hospital medical record number is M110462890."

Consider a neuron, its cell body a spiderweb suspended in brain matter, its axon sending signals to one or several of one hundred billion other nerve cells. A conduit for the electricity running through your body, the translator for how to make electrical signals meaningful, a neuron's physical structure fortifies with each memory stored. One pluck of the spiderweb's string and all the neurons involved in a single memory light up. They reconstruct the visual—the shape of the numbers on a page, or on the card in your wallet—and they reconstruct the action. With kinesthetic sensibility, your tongue gallops across the roof of your mouth for "twenty-two"; your lower lip sweeps against your upper teeth for each "forty-five."

You watch the memory traces come alive in another human being and you want to believe it's enough, these numbers; you want to believe there's something meaningful, even altruistic, behind the reduction. You look at your patient, rolling the pen between your callused fingers. She looks blankly back at you.

323-467-8792 555-66-9827 5'7" 42 145 01-13-1968 34689 103 90044 555-66-9827A 818-227-6900 156/90 102 18 98.6 7/10 99 M110462890...

You suddenly want to tell her: "Ma'am," you'll say. "You are an abacus. A license plate. A chi square. You are an exponential equation, a rosary, an irrational number, a fundamental theorem. You are singular simply because you represent a combination of numbers not represented by anybody else."

You are unique only because the possibilities are endless.

9

As soon as the glass double doors slide shut between me and the night air, I spot her: she's in the bulk section, refilling plastic numbered vaults with grain and flour. To do this, she hefts large barrels onto her shoulder from a skinny metal cart and pours from them into the propped openings. She makes it look easy but it isn't. The sound of heavy barrels slamming against the metal cart attests to their weight.

It's not too late to run away. The closer I get, the more I catalog her features. Olive skin, strong jaw, pursed lips, perfect ears, a small birthmark on her straining neck, and beautiful, moody green eyes that stare back at me. How long has she been looking at me? I'm standing here like a slack-jawed stalker. This is awkward.

"Hello," I say.

She nods at me. "Hey." She's completely still, waiting. "Can I help you with something?" Her voice is pure sex. It's low and husky and growling without even trying.

I manage, "What's your name?"

She wipes her hands on her apron. "Ayla."

"Ayla. Hi. I'm Piper. Can you tell me where the tea section is?"

She points to her left. "Middle of Aisle 7."

My "thanks" is a whisper. I move past her, careful to hold my head high, careful not to sag into my breastbone. These days the people I'm surrounded by guzzle coffee, soda, energy drinks; even if I brought tea to station, no one would drink it. Ayla isn't fooled. She can't be. She must know I came here just to talk to her, she probably thinks I'm crazy, and she might even joke around with other employees later. *Did you see that weird girl?*

By the time I reach Aisle 7, my entire body feels shamed and electric, angry and alive. It's not my fault I'm awkward; it's been years since I liked anybody. Smoothing down my frizzy hair and T-shirt, I try to remember how it felt to be in a racing swimsuit and goggles in Las Vegas right before we won a meet, or the time I climbed up movie-set scaffolding to watch a take from above, unnoticed by the cast and crew except for Christopher Lloyd, who winked. People are either attracted to me or they're not. The ones who are tend to say things like, "There's something about you." Still, I don't want to imagine what I look like right now.

I stare at the shelves, pretending to search for something. Maybe a powdered juice mix. Maybe an aromatic chai spice. I want to hear Ayla's voice again and find out what she smells like and ask about her day and run my tongue down the side of her neck.

I try to think of it like a flow chart. If I get up the nerve to ask Ayla out, that will be a reward in and of itself, because it will mean I've reached some kind of turning point. Even if she says no, at least I will have an answer; if she says no, I can stop pining after a stranger. No one has ever actually died of embarrassment, and perhaps Ayla will be one of those people who realizes there *is* something about me, despite my frizzy hair and crumpled T-shirt.

Forget it.

I snatch a plastic-wrapped box of organic jasmine green tea with lemon and licorice root and walk back the way I came. Ayla gives me a sly sideways glance as I pass the bulk section. My stubborn chin lifts up; I'm suddenly filled with a sense of injustice. After making it five steps past her, I whirl around and march back. She shifts suddenly in a reflexive effort to get away from me.

"Look," I hear myself say. "Look, I'm not good at this, and I know that, but I came here because, well, I thought you might be here. I know that probably sounds weird. I swear I'm not a stalker or anything—I won't ever bother you again, I won't even *come* here, if it feels like I'm bothering you. But I wanted to know if you want to get lunch. Sometime. On one of your breaks or something."

Ayla relaxes and doesn't lean back quite so much. She looks at my flushed face and raises her eyebrows. "Lunch?"

"Lunch."

Her short dark hair is unkempt chaos, boasting accidental style rather than prim deliberation. Strands stick out in every direction, hang over her face, collect behind her ears, curl up sweetly at the nape of her neck. She's one of those people who can look out at the world through bangs and not seem to mind. At any given moment, with even the smallest shift from her or from the light, she appears now more masculine, now more feminine. The lower part of her face juts out, boxlike and fierce, but the grace of how she moves is obvious in the curve of her neck. There's a toughness to her, sure, but there's also a softness in her frame, and her eyes—flashing intelligence bordered by dark lashes, partially covered by her habit of hiding behind her hair—are easily the most stunning thing about her.

"Why not?" she says. "Piper, is it? Meet me here on Friday, Piper. Out back at one o'clock." She leans over the cart; her tumbling hair can't mask her grin.

10

After several days of not seeing my roommate, I sit with Marla at our kitchen table on Thursday night and watch her new love interest, Tom, cook us dinner. I try to see him as she does. Tom is an obvious introvert. His enormous build is an apologetic demand for attention. He smells faintly of clove cigarettes, and as he moves around our kitchen, his hair pulled back into a ponytail, he makes origami of his large frame in order to chop up ingredients. Green onions, celery, peppers. Blood-red beef strips for a stir-fry. Everything he touches gets mangled in his clumsy hands. I don't get it.

"Tell me everything," Marla says to me.

I start with work, and once I start talking I can't stop. I describe patients' homes and people's faces, Ruth and Carl and their badge bunny bet. I can't shake the image of that woman's face and her little dog, but I'm not ready to tell anyone about Carl's photograph yet. When I get to the story about the convulsing hypoglycemic, Marla's eyes stretch wide in concern. "That poor guy," she says. "You must have felt so bad for him."

"There's no time! Everything happens so fast. If I get overwhelmed there's no way for me to do my job. That's what's so weird. Probably the best way to help someone is to treat an emergency like it's the most normal thing in the world." I think about Ruth and her efficiency, how she can seem cold, uncaring.

Once the food is ready, I force myself to stop talking about work. There's an unnatural silence. What follows stories of life and death?

Marla asks about Nathan and it takes me a moment to remember who he is. I tell her I ended things, and that I finally had the courage to talk to the girl at Sustainable Living.

It's as if she didn't hear me. She nods and returns to her food.

The sound of metal scraping ceramic.

Sometimes the best way to show someone's being an asshole is to ooze politeness. I turn to Tom. "So tell me—how did you and Marla meet?"

He looks up from his hunched-over seat. "We work together."

"At Birchwood & Brown?" I've been there only once. A fifteen-story engineering geekdom located squarely downtown.

"I told you that." Marla laughs, a little shrill, and smiles at Tom. "Piper's so busy, she must have forgotten."

Now she's really starting to annoy me. It can be hard to keep track of her rebounds, and Tom is clearly not a keeper. In a couple months her affection will dry up—she'll admit she's not over Alexander, her ex, then swear she's going to take a year off dating—only to do it all over again and break the next rebound boy's heart. In the meantime, though, if she's happy with Tom then I'm happy for her, and maybe she could do me the same favor. I pile green onion shrapnel on one side of my plate and avoid her eyes.

"Actually, I noticed Marla months ago," Tom says. "One day we were on the elevator and started talking, and I rode up twelve extra flights, pretending I needed something from HR. But apparently I didn't make much of an impression."

"That's not true!"

I suddenly remember Marla talking about "some ponytail guy" at work. *That* Tom?

"How great," I gush. "You mean you had a crush on her for months and then you were finally able to ask her out?"

"Exactly!" Tom says. "It wasn't until I sent" —he lowers his voice— "well, I used our internal mail service to invite her to a Ben Harper show, because I remembered we'd talked about his music in the elevator. But she didn't remember me, so I—"

Marla touches his arm. "He thought I'd report him for sexual harassment! But then I ran into him and he apologized. It was so cute."

A spattering of small talk occurs as we eat. I try to remember who Ben Harper is. Marla refuses to make eye contact with me. Tom has a strange way of looking up at the ceiling after he takes a bite, as if the answer to how flavorful the food is will be written on the ceiling.

Marla's ex, Alexander, wasn't nearly as statuesque as Tom, but he was much more charismatic—we used to joke that he was sex on a stick—and he was a lot stronger than he looked. When he and Marla would fight, sometimes he'd pick her up, turn her upside down, and shake her a little. And she would scream at him to stop, she'd complain that he drove her absolutely crazy, but by the time she found her feet again, she would have forgotten how to be mad at him. During the three years they dated, whenever Alexander had anything to drink, the drinking would spin him toward old habits, habits he managed to hide from Marla for a long time, like borrowing money, calling up old contacts, finding pills to pop, and, eventually, and more noticeably, heroin to smoke. Marla never talks about how much she misses him, but I know she does.

When Tom gathers our streaked plates I thank him for dinner. As soon as he heads outside to smoke, the screen door whining to a close behind him, Marla wants to talk about Nathan again. She says I've been in hiding for two years and that I should have given him a chance. Her voice sounds pleading. "All I'm saying is you need to let yourself have some fun. Break the cycle by going on more than a few dates."

When Marla and I were in college we had a conversation that I still think of as the moment when something shifted, the beginning of our transition from being acquaintances to close friends. Bisexuals are treated like unicorns: tell someone you're bi, get treated like you don't exist. But when I told Marla, her acceptance came easily. The world is lonely enough without following useless rules, she said.

Right now the last thing I want to talk about is Ayla—all my euphoria feels flattened—but I force myself.

"If all you want is to see me back out there," I say, "then you should be happy for me. When have you known me to ask someone out? This is big."

She looks worried. "No, it's great, and I'm happy for you—"

"But what?"

She doesn't answer. She goes to the sink to do the dishes, filling one side with hot water, squirting in a liberal amount of soap. At first I help her, stacking dirty pots and pans on the counter, but after a few moments the silence gets to me. I turn the faucet off and square her shoulders to mine.

"It's really nothing," she says, finally. "It's just, one day I was at Sustainable Living and I saw—what's her name?"

"Ayla."

"Ayla. Okay. She just strikes me as volatile, I guess. That day I was there it seemed like something was really wrong with her. Her face was red, her hands were all balled up, and it looked like she was going to punch something. I didn't like it."

"When was this?"

"Maybe two or three weeks ago."

"Was she arguing with someone?"

"I don't know, I only saw her for a minute. It didn't look like she was with anyone. She just looked really upset."

"What had just happened?"

"I don't know."

"Well, what'd she do then?"

"For the love of god, Piper, *I don't know*. I just noticed her, it made me feel kind of scared, I guess, so I walked the other way."

I sit back down at the kitchen table and carefully link my fingers in front of me, the way I imagine a diplomat would. "You seem upset."

Marla leans heavily against the counter's edge. "You're impossible."

"No, it's true, you look upset. Maybe even mad? I'm not sure."

She flattens a cloud of suds sitting on top of the water. "Why do you like her so much?"

"I don't know yet."

"It would really kill me to see you... how you were before. That was so hard to watch. I want you to date someone *good*. You know? A good person."

I don't know what to say back to her. That I just know, somehow, that Ayla won't hurt me? That I won't let anyone do that to me again? By the time Tom comes back inside, Marla and I are silent. She plays with her bracelet. I use the condensation rings from the bottom of my water glass to create the symbol for the Olympics on our beat-up table. Tom stands in the middle of our kitchen, shifting his weight from one foot to the other, pretending to take an interest in our refrigerator magnets. Blending in with the appliances. It's heartbreaking in a way. Marla wants me to go with Nathan because he's good and kind and safe, but look where that's gotten her.

She goes to Tom, stretching up on her tiptoes like a seal angling for bait, and he bends his bulk toward her upturned lips. Then he looks at me, his expression friendly, playful. "You know what you guys look like right now?" he says. "Houdini, after he got sucker punched. Every hear that story?

Greatest escape artist in the world, and he died because someone socked him in the gut before he had the chance to flex his stomach muscles."

11

It's Friday morning. I have a date in two hours. Maybe I'm supposed to be excited, but instead I keep thinking about my conversation with Marla. Restless and irritable, annoyed that no one is around to witness my restless irritability, I decide to take a long shower.

After I step into the tile cell and slide the frosted door shut, I turn the water full blast and stand there, teeth and eyes clenched, arms crossed over my nipples, while I wait for it to heat up.

When was the exact moment when something switched between Jared and Elizabeth? I still want to know how it happened. It was after I'd already moved out that I realized: when he and I were making plans to vacation in Hawaii, they were already fucking; when he and I were discussing whether to become pet owners, they were already fucking; when he and I were rear-ranging the living room furniture, and got into a stupid argument about a lamp I didn't even like, which led to us yelling at each other, and then to having sex on the floor (even though the couch was five feet away), they were already fucking.

The last vision I have of either of them is my boyfriend standing, head tilted, jaw tight, one hand resting on the pumping hair of Elizabeth's thick ponytail. This took place in the bathroom, *our* bathroom, the bathroom with awful peach tile and the photograph of Rodin's *The Thinker* scuplture over the toilet, which we bought for two dollars at a garage sale. We took soaking salt baths in that bathroom, while Jared displayed his latest glass sculptures along the edge of the tub, the swirling colors he'd created mixing with amber light.

When I get to my room, my hair dripping down my back, instead of getting dressed I reach for the phone. When my brother answers, I tell him I don't want to date anyone ever again, to which Ryan says what he always says when I'm being resistant to something he thinks is good for me: "Pipes, it's time."

The back of Sustainable Living is less attractive than the front. No mural of colorful vegetables dances over the loading dock. Instead there's a large blue dumpster and some kind of compost bin. Ayla sits on the edge of the concrete bay, her green apron removed to reveal dark blue jeans and a black T-shirt. Her Vans-covered feet swing, hitting the side of the low wall. She hops down when she sees me.

"Let's just walk to Luna Café," she says as a greeting. "It's close, the food's good—they have sandwiches, soup, that kind of thing—does that work? You're not going to find any parking over there."

"That's fine," I say. The roots of my hair are tingling. Ayla's friendly expression disappears; she shoves her hands into her pockets and keeps her gaze just ahead of her, occasionally darting her eyes to the cars and pedestrians. If I weren't queer already, she would turn me. Even moving slow with her hands in her pockets, her energy is palpable, coiled up, humming just beneath the surface. I picture us in some dark hallway, her pinning me against a wall, sliding her hands under my shirt.

She leads the way up Silver Lake Boulevard, its four lanes taken up with honking drivers all trying to get somewhere on their lunch break. We pass a small bakery. I breathe in the fresh-bread smell.

"I've got an hour," Ayla says.

"Okay." I have to think of something to ask her. Not about her job, not how long she's lived in Los Angeles or what neighborhood she lives in. Something else. My hands are shoved into my pockets. I chose my best pair of jeans and a form-fitting orange tank top, and topped off the outfit with white flip-flops, earrings in the shape of two thin spirals, and lip gloss. My straightened hair is pulled back.

We arrive at Luna Café. The flooding sunlight gives its oak floors and tables a warm glow while the fans and open windows fend off the eighty-degree heat. I feel a strange satisfaction when the hostess says "Two?" before reaching for a couple of menus. She seats us near a window in the main space and I focus intently on my meal decision. I've said only three words so far.

"You know, you don't look gay," Ayla says after a few minutes have gone by. She folds her menu, tosses it onto the table, and interlaces her fingers in front of her, a wry expression on her face. "But I could tell you were."

I must have been holding my breath, because when I try to respond there's no air to move words. Lifting one knee at a time, I release the trapped hands I've been sitting on and decide not to correct her. "How could you tell?"

"You hook your keys on your belt loop with a carabiner," Ayla says. "That's pretty gay. I could hear you coming over to me from the tea aisle."

"You didn't think I was a rock climber?"

"It might as well have been a pink triangle."

"Did you know I was going to ask you out?"

"Oh, is this a date?" She peers out at me from under her tousled hair. "How did you know *I* was gay?" I suck on my teeth while I contemplate this; she grins. "Only kidding—everyone knows. It's flipping obvious."

The waitress arrives. I pick the chicken sandwich with a cup of tomato soup and Ayla asks for a hummus wrap. As she looks up to order I see her jugular vein running along the right side of her neck, from her jawline to the jut of the collarbone poking out above her black T-shirt. It is a thing of beauty, this vein. A blue tendril like a tree root.

"Where'd you go?" Ayla asks, turning back to me.

I dive into my water glass and try to recover. "How long have you been working at Sustainable Living?"

She nods, as if expecting this. "About a year. But I've worked a lot of jobs. Long story."

She seems embarrassed, and there's an uncomfortable pause. "I like long stories," I offer. I can't help thinking there is no context more ill-suited for getting to know a stranger than a first date.

"What about you, Piper, what do you do?"

"Ambulance. I mean, I'm an EMT on an ambulance. Emergency—"

"Medical technician, sure. How do you like doing that?"

"I love it." I find myself for once not wanting to pretend I'm tougher than I am, so I add, "I kind of suck at it, though."

"You suck at it?" She's amused. "If I suck at my job, things don't get arranged right. If you suck at *your* job—"

"Well, I'm new. Only a couple shifts in."

"Ah." She rubs her palm against her sternum, her fingers tapping her collarbone. "I moved to California a little over two years ago," she says, "and work was hard to find. I took random jobs for a while, I mean every kind of crap job, and pretty much left them as soon as I found them. Distributed posters, worked as a security guard, got trained in home lice removal— don't get me started on that, I quit after one day—and answered an egg donation ad."

"I've heard that's really painful."

"It is—don't ever do it. I'll spare you the details since we're about to eat, but I got fifteen thousand for it."

"Where did you move from?"

"Wisconsin. You know, cows. They play any pranks on you yet?"

"No, but they don't really have to."

She cocks her head to one side, interested. So I tell her about snapping the elastic of the pediatric oxygen mask I heroically managed to place on the 250-pound man, putting gloves on backward *and* in the wrong size, filling out my birth date instead of the patient's on paperwork, and staring blankly at a cursing car thief. The reward for my self-deprecation is the way her mercurial eyes lock on my face as I spin one story after another. She laughs in all the right places.

"Sounds about right," she says when I stop to catch my breath. "You're lucky. In the military, you would have earned some awful nickname by now."

The waitress arrives, and we lean back as our plates are placed in front of us.

"The military?"

Her fingers hover over an enormous hummus wrap, as if deciding how best to capture it. "I was in the army, did two tours in Iraq." She saws the wrap in half, ignores her fork, and takes a bite out of one triangulated edge. Swallowing, she says, "One guy I knew was obsessed with adding hillbilly armor to the piece-of-shit Humvees we had. I'm talking plywood, chunks of two-by-fours, sandbags, scrap metal, anything he could find. Sometimes he'd just sit and tack welds onto it, as if the extra cauterization would help." She snorts. "He would have pulled into a scrap yard in the middle of a mission if we'd let him."

Taken aback by this new information, I ask the first question that comes to mind. "What was his nickname?"

"We called him 'A-Team.' For the time he did something incredibly stupid, but fortunately it worked out really well." She pauses. "Funny, I can't remember what it was."

I run my tongue over my teeth to sweep for bits of arugula, and she continues, telling me between swallows that she got an honorable discharge for injury. "It was bad when I first got back," she says. "I had nightmares all the time." She picks up the second half of her wrap, stares into the face of it, sets it back down.

"And now?"

She shrugs. "I got discharged in 2006. So, what? Almost six years." Picking up her paper napkin, she folds and refolds it until she's holding a thick white square. "It's not gone, never will be, but at least it's better. These days the only thing I have nightmares about is the giant teddy bear that likes to chase me down the street, but I've had those since I was a kid."

I'm drawn to how frank she is, but this time I don't buy it. "What—"

"TBI. Traumatic brain injury." She starts to shrug but falters. Her expression has shifted—what was warm is now wary—and her eyes are flat. Her voice is so emotionless she could be talking about anything. I remember how I used to casually tell people that my ex had been fucking my friend behind my back, as if I could make it a small and unimportant thing that way. There's also something in her voice I can't quite place: a challenge. Like she's saying, *If you think you're interested in me, you need to know these things, and then maybe think again.*

We stare at each other for what feels likes several minutes—that weird close-up that happens when you're looking into someone's eyes and some part of your brain hits the zoom button. Her eyes are green-gold streaks flecked with amber, a mix of wistfulness and resolve, and I can see her respond to the empathy that is swelling in me, see her soften and even look a little frightened, until she breaks the eye contact and shifts in her seat.

The table suddenly seems wider between us. Finally, I say, "I'm glad you're here and not there, Ayla."

She laughs, looks out the window, laughs again, and shakes her head. "Me too."

12

When I pull into the lot I notice both of the rigs are gone, which means yesterday's 24-hour crews are out running late calls instead of sleeping. Technically the oncoming crews don't relieve the outgoing crews until 0700, but I wanted to get here by 0630 to restock the rig supplies. I park my

Corolla next to Ruth's hatchback, because of course she is already present and accounted for. The stiff uniform collar is a cold edge against my neck as I grab my bag from the car.

It feels like a first day again, and not just because of the four days off. I've been daydreaming since saying goodbye to Ayla yesterday. I can already tell we will have great sex, and I will struggle to understand her three years in the army, and part of me will continue to scream that I should run the other way. I can already tell she's worth it.

I go inside and say hi to Ruth, who looks up at me from above a bowl of oatmeal. Throwing my duffel bag onto the floor of the workout room, I button and tuck in my uniform shirt, finish lacing my boots. None of the other oncoming crew members have arrived.

The wall of lockers. Two stories of metal rectangles; only Ruth's is bare. J-Rock's has a black-and-white picture of a mob of zombies, but most are plastered with firefighter logos. One locker, belonging to someone named Phil, is covered in muscles. Faceless, headless close-ups of taut and shiny biceps, bulging lats, a waterfall of abs, a medley of quads, calves, and even feet.

Because Ruth wants to ensure I run as many calls as possible, I haven't seen much of the two-car crew. I have yet to learn J-Rock's real name or have a conversation with him. He's a quiet guy, a little older than Carl and Pep but probably younger than Ruth, always hunched over either eating sunflower seeds or chewing tobacco, and a small plastic cup of soppy, dark material is a virtual extension of his uniform. The company-issued baseball cap J-Rock wears has the A & O logo on the front, but he must have paid extra to get his nickname stitched across the back. He wears the hat backward—the blue cursive stitching arcing between his thick eyebrows—and flips the bill forward when he climbs into the rig for a call.

His partner is gorgeous and knows it. Pep's dark skin is flawless, and he has dimples and thick eyelashes. Even though he's much prettier than I am, he gave me a look when we first met that seemed to suggest if I ever found myself experiencing a lonely evening, I shouldn't hesitate to ask for his company.

If I clear training, there is a spot already waiting for me, on B shift with a guy named William Leone. I've been trying not to think about what Carl told me, that William is a cocky son of a bitch and no one likes working with him.

First call of the day comes in at 0732, and delivers us a chest pain from the glass office buildings at 88th and Vermont. As we wheel the man into the back of the ambulance, Ruth whispers to me that it doesn't get any more "standard" than this. Our patient is fifty-nine years old, has a history of hypertension, and is experiencing an episode of sudden onset crushing chest pain that radiates to his left arm. His suit is rumpled, his tie loosened, and sweat has soaked from his undershirt to the tips of his white collar. He nods at us anxiously, hands fluttering along the side rails of the gurney, and he keeps lifting the oxygen mask off his face in order to talk to us, insisting he feels better after the nitroglycerin and aspirin. Ruth firmly reminds him to leave the mask on. I've taken his blood pressure three times, and it has finally lowered from a frenzied 212/108. I don't know what that feels like, but it can't be comfortable.

Carl begins the ten-minute drive to Crossroads Hospital. In the back, Ruth and I are accompanied by the lead medic, who's giving our patient another dose of nitro. If a patient's fairly stable, just the two-person EMT crew handles the transport, one driving and one in the back, but when a patient needs advanced life support we're required to be accompanied by the fire department paramedic, the person who acts as the lead medical authority for the entirety of the call.

Ruth hands me the stethoscope. "You need to get better at lung sounds. He has rales in the bases."

As I put on fresh gloves, place the earpieces in, and warm the bell with my palm, I'm acutely aware of the rig's every bounce, the shrill wail of sirens, the conversation the medic is having with the patient, and the hissing of oxygen through the thin green tubing. I look wearily to the lead medic for approval.

He checks the man's rhythm on the monitor before giving me the go-ahead. Leaning toward our patient, he says loudly to him, "Sir, my partner here is going to get another set of lung sounds."

Encouraged by this small sign of respect from the lead medic, I peel up the man's sticky undershirt and tell him to breathe in and out as deeply as he can. I hear nothing. I place the bell above, to the side, and below the fleshy part of his chest, ask him to lean forward, and press into several places on his back. I find myself pushing the bell's diaphragm harder into his skin as well as raising the top of my shoulder to meet the side of the earpiece, in order to shove it farther toward my eardrum. At the very least I should hear air moving in and out as he sits here, sucking on high-flow oxygen with exaggerated effort.

"Anything?" Ruth asks. I shake my head, knowing better than to lie to her. "Keep trying," she demands, giving a significant look to the medic, who smirks in response.

Yesterday, at the end of our date, when Ayla and I stood blinking in the sunlight next to the loading dock of Sustainable Living, she wished me luck on today's training. "Just focus on doing right by the patients," she said. "The rest will come." I liked her shy smile, the way she didn't quite seem to know how to say goodbye, and I especially liked her advice, the openness of it. But now I feel a selfish stirring, a resentment that has nothing to do with the man in front of me. I want to feel smart for a change. It's really too bad my hands are prone to shaking, my instincts so easily overwhelmed, my sense of hearing so unsophisticated, because my book smart brain is much more intelligent than this job makes it appear to be.

The prongs dig into my ears, deafening the noise around me but somehow still not enhancing the sounds inside my patient's body. I watch his slick chest rise and fall, his intercostal muscles tugging doggedly at his ribs. This is the first time I've seen any nakedness in a patient, and it only adds to the feeling that I'm unqualified. I'm playing doctor while a man with a busted heart tries his damnedest to accommodate me.

Crossroads Hospital is located on Hoover Street near Florence Avenue, not far from where the Rodney King riots began. I heard of it long before I ever rode there in the back of an ambulance. Most people call the hospital "CRH" and the city where it's located "South Central," even though Crossroads redid its sign under new management about four years ago, in an attempt to get rid of unfavorable associations. Likewise, at some point the city was officially renamed "South Los Angeles." But they're still CRH and South Central.

The hospital resembles a pile of cinder blocks, three bluish-gray boxes, each bigger than the last, stacked in ascending order along Hoover Street. Patients who get a window can look out at the dollar store, Ed's Liquor, and the taco truck that crouches every day on Florence Avenue. The backside of the smallest cinder block houses CRH's emergency room. It's early still; when we pull in to the ambulance lot, we're the only ones here. I put the stethoscope away and transfer the oxygen tubing from the rig's house oxygen tank to the gurney's portable one.

We roll our patient up the ramp; he seems calmer but he's still trembling. Steering the foot end of the gurney, I push open the double doors to the ER and look around, unsure where to go. The emergency room wing of CRH is shaped like a horseshoe, with the outer perimeter feeding off to twelve ER rooms with three beds each. The inner perimeter contains the triage station and work areas for nurses and doctors. An arched hallway free of machinery separates the two areas, and is usually filled with loaded gurneys, ambulance crews, police officers, and ER patients who got unceremoniously yanked out of their rooms to create space for higher-priority newcomers. I know there's a system on how to stack patients in the hallway, but I don't know what it is.

My confusion must be apparent. "We're not going to park him," Carl says. "We'll get a room right away."

While Ruth and the lead medic give a report at the triage station, I get the man's squiggly signature and check some more boxes. Carl leans on the headrest of the gurney, seeming not to notice that his folded arms are inches from the back of the man's head.

"You heard about this place?" he asks.

Our patient thinks Carl is talking to him, and his face clouds over. "Terrible," he says, his voice muffled through the oxygen mask. "Just terrible."

Most of the infamy surrounding Crossroads has to do with how shitty the ER care used to be, even though its reputation has improved greatly in the last four years. It was known for being overloaded, for long lines of gurneys out the door and down the ramp, and even for people dying before they ever got triaged. People sometimes waited twenty-four hours or more before being admitted. But the real scandal happened a few years ago, when the hospital was almost forced to shut down because a woman with a perforated bowel died on the waiting-room floor—after vomiting blood for forty-five minutes. People became so alarmed they started calling 911. The infamous picture someone took of her, sprawled and lifeless on the blood-and-excrement-covered floor, made the front page of the papers. And people had plenty of time to take pictures, because the body didn't get cleaned up or removed for another forty-five minutes.

The medic gives his report, and the triage nurse calls out to us: Room 1, Bed A. Moments after Carl and I transfer him to his bed, our pagers start vibrating. Carl rushes to tuck the corners of a new bedsheet over the gurney's mattress while I read out the call details on the flickering green screen. Female behavioral at Florence Park, just five blocks away. Ruth appears at the doorway, barking orders, and we file after her, through the double doors and down the ramp. Carl looks thrilled.

"Are you hoping she'll get combative?" I ask him as we race toward the rig.

The woman sits on a park bench, humming. About thirty-six years old, with a bombshell body and a very pretty face, she looks out, over, and past us as we stand a safe distance away, talking to her boyfriend, Frank. He explains that just a moment ago she'd been screaming and beating her fists against a nearby tree. It must be true; her fingernails are ripped to pieces and her hands are caked with dirt and blood. But they're also folded serenely in her lap. The sounds coming from her throat remind me of cooing pigeons.

Ruth is trying to explain to the gangly Frank that we have to wait for the police before approaching her, and he's frantically arguing that the police aren't necessary, he doesn't want her to go to jail.

"I'm sorry," Ruth says. "Our protocol is that in any potentially dangerous situation, we have to wait for the police before approaching our patient."

"Betty isn't dangerous! She's all right, I swear she's all right, she just gets like this sometimes."

"Well, we'll be happy to take her to the hospital and get her checked out," Ruth says. "But we're not allowed to—"

Betty stands up dramatically. The humming sounds she's been making take on a new frequency: a sudden diva quality radiates from her whole body. She looks down the small hill we're standing on toward a cluster of maple trees on the other side of the playground and begins to run, shrieking terribly, pulling off her clothes in frenetic abandon. She's still running, almost tripping, when her shirt ends up around her head, her arms pinned up by her ears and bound inside her shirt.

"We're not allowed to chase after our patients," Ruth finishes absentmindedly.

Carl would very much like to chase after and tackle our patient, judging by the grin on his face.

When her bra comes off near the base of the hill, my cheeks grow hot with embarrassment; her breasts are enormous, heaving and surging in a waterfall of flesh as Betty sprints barefoot, a trail of clothing on the grass behind her. Then, just as suddenly, she flings herself onto the ground. She appears to be making snow angels in the dirt.

"Faster than you can say 'fifty-one-fifty,'" Carl says, and Ruth shoots him a warning look.

When the police arrive, four officers surround her. By then Frank has vanished. Betty lifts her head, looking at them with an unconcerned expression. One cop approaches Betty carefully, his voice friendly, his body rigid, his hand resting on the back of his utility belt. He coaxes her up off the ground, but when she realizes we mean for her to get onto the gurney she starts flailing and screaming again. It takes all four officers to pin her down. I hold myself together for once, determined not to get distracted by the sound of her screams. I rip open the thin plastic packaging of the soft restraints and hand the contents to Ruth and Carl; they attach a cloth handcuff to each wrist and use the long adjustable straps to tie one hand high above her head and the other down by her hip. She lies there panting, not a mark on her, glaring at us all. Ruth and I hurry to cover her up, first with a sheet, tucked under her armpits, and then with a blanket, pulled all the way up to her chin.

At 0938 we arrive back at CRH with Betty and a police escort, to find that it's now a busy day. I hear catcalls and moans coming from the beds as ER nurses pass by with files and carts, rolling their eyes at each other. There are five patients in the hallway with their accompanying ambulance crews, and the triage station is deserted. I recognize J-Rock and Pep in the corner; they wave sullenly.

"How long have you been waiting for a bed?" Ruth asks.

"About twenty."

We find a spot in the lineup and Carl wheels over the portable monitor to get a fresh set of vitals. I ignore everyone and focus on paperwork. I discover that there are no fewer than five places on the patient care report in which I am to document the use of restraints, as well as fill out a separate form indicating she had good circulation and sensory and motor function both before and after applying them. Which means…

I look up from my clipboard and take a step forward. As I lean over the gurney, Betty's large brown eyes focus on me and she has a wide, helpful smile on her face.

"Betty?" I ask. "Are you able to wiggle your fingers?"

She makes a sound from deep in her throat and I bolt out of the way when I realize she means to spit on me. Carl lets out an appreciative chuckle. He's standing behind her, and Ruth several feet away. They both have a perfect view of her, but are well out of spitting distance.

"You might just make it in this business after all," Carl says, and then a wistful look crosses his face. "He's lucky." It takes me a moment to realize he's talking about J-Rock, who's over in the corner leaning against the wall with his hat pulled low over his eyes. "He's learned to sleep standing up."

Pep, however, is wide awake. He stands in the hallway, arms crossed, casting wolfish looks at any woman passing by, whether she's a doctor, nurse, ER tech, or patient. But when a beautiful nurse wearing bright pink scrubs charges past him, shiny blond curls spilling down to her waist, he doesn't even glance in her direction.

I look at Carl. "Let me guess. Pep already seduced that one?" He beams at me like a proud parent.

* * *

The triage nurse today is Shilpa, a plump Indian woman who exudes stern but matronly warmth and takes extreme measures in matching her accessories to her scrubs. She adores Ruth. After we have been waiting for forty minutes, she appears at the triage station, pulls a novelty pen out of her front pocket, and raps it against the counter. Attached to the end of the pen are colored springs, and they bounce brightly.

"Who else?" she says in her accent, looking around. Her socks, fingernails, earrings, and eye shadow are all the exact same shade of teal. "Has everyone given a report?"

An EMT I don't recognize slouches forward, his shirt partially untucked, one lone glove hanging out of his back pocket. He speaks in low tones but Shilpa's indignant voice interrupts him.

"*No*," she says. "Look at him. You *look* at him."

His head swivels toward his patient, as does the head of every other person in the hallway. The man sitting on the gurney is in a classic tripod position, leaning forward with his elbows on his knees, an inhaler in his lap, his breathing rushed and haggard.

In a quiet, dangerous voice that carries the full length of the ER, Shilpa asks, "Does he look like he's 18 breaths a minute to you?" She slams her pen down. "Come back and give me a report when you've got a real set of vitals." Spotting Ruth, she says, "Hi, Mama, what have you got?"

Ruth walks over and wraps an arm over Shilpa's shoulders in a sideways hug. "It can wait its turn," she says, "but I do have a favor to ask." As Ruth speaks softly to her, Shilpa looks over at me and makes a clucking sound. I feel acidic. The triage nurse disappears and comes back with a stethoscope.

Not again.

Ruth takes it and thanks her. She gestures for me to follow and I do, into Room 1, Bed A, where our previous chest pain patient is sitting upright on the hospital bed. His clothes have been exchanged for a gown and the oxygen mask replaced with nasal cannula. His hair is no longer dewy with sweat. Recent vitals on the overhead screen show that his blood pressure is down to a mellow 162/90. Other than the occasional beep from the monitor, the room is very quiet. My chances are much better in here than in the back of the ambulance, but I wonder what happens if I still can't hear anything. Will Ruth fail me? Will A & O Ambulance fire me? I only have one more training shift after today.

Ruth hands me the stethoscope without a word. It's much fancier than the one we use on the rig, probably costs close to two hundred dollars.

I clear my throat even though I don't need to. "Hello, sir. I'm Piper. I met you earlier?"

"You're new."

"This is my third day." Clutching the stethoscope with both hands, I hold it out to him, like it's some kind of peace offering. "May I?"

"Go ahead, little lady."

I listen to the tops of his lungs, just below his clavicle, and for the first time, I hear air moving. Moving the bell to the sides of his rib cage, I hear it again—air in, air out, what a relief—and then travel to the bases of his lungs, a few inches below his nipples. There's a slight bubbling there, like air moving through water.

"Rales! I can hear it!"

Ruth nods. "And what are rales?"

I'm so glad she asked. They're caused by trapped fluid, I tell her. It can happen from a near-drowning or because the heart isn't working properly, and signifies that backup from the circulatory system has entered the lungs. Specifically, I say, the *left* ventricle must not be working properly, because when the *right* ventricle doesn't work, blood gets backed up in the body, causing swollen feet and ankles, known as pedal edema. I smile at him, pleased with myself, but he looks bored. Ruth and I walk back to the hallway. It's just as chaotic as before. The halls are packed with gurneys, a patient is screaming at a nurse, and Betty chooses this particular moment to start singing opera.

She's good. She's really good. I have no idea what she's singing, or in what language, but I am aware that the whole ER stops, momentarily, to listen.

13

If they were removed from your body, your lungs would look like two inconsequential pink-gray sacks, hinged together only by their mutual attachment to the bony rings of your windpipe. If all the tissue were removed, your lungs would reveal an extensive series of narrowing tunnels that descend and branch off from the main bronchi. Each lung has what looks like an inverted and hollow oak tree hidden underneath its pink flesh folds.

There are very few involuntary bodily functions you have control over. Eyesight is one. Breathing is another. You can't tell your body to wait until 5 p.m. to digest the cereal you ate for breakfast, but you can hyperventilate until you pass out. You can hold your breath, cough, or deepen your respirations, forcing yourself to become dizzy, irritated, or calm. By shifting the focus of your breathing, you can make your back expand more than your chest, or your right side expand more than your left, or fill up your belly with so much air it pushes out the walls of your abdomen.

The structure works like a bellows, the ribs, intercostal muscles, and diaphragm expanding and contracting, the pulmonary tissue quick to inflate on the inhale and elastic in its recoil. The inner surface of your lungs is honeycombed with three hundred million air sacs that specialize in gas exchange. When trapped fluid, airway blockages, or damage to these air sacs occurs, your lungs start to sing. Depending on the source of injury, a listener will hear coarse crackling, high-pitched wheezing, bubbling, or coughing.

This effect isn't singular. Anything that moves creates vibrations; where there is motion, there is sound, whether or not the human ear or technology can hear it. Musical instruments live inside you: wind, percussion, and stringed. Your tongue clicks against your palate every time you swallow; air pushes against your tightly strung vocal cords, giving pitch to your breath. Flooding happens in all of your various cavities, cascades of saliva, intestinal juices, bile, blood, and mucus. Gaseous by-products bubble and gurgle their way out of your organs in as many directions as they can. Eating is a cacophony from start to finish, carried out by an uncooperative orchestra.

And subtler music-makers are also at work. If only it were possible to listen closely enough, you would hear the sweeping sound of cilia rhythmically moving particles toward your throat. You'd hear the tap of your eyelids closing, the plunk of your cells separating as they reproduce, the lapping of cerebrospinal fluid bathing your brain, the rubbing of muscles sliding over each other as you move, and the creak of bones swiveling in their joints.

There are silences, too, tucked away in hushed pockets amid the tricklings and murmurs and thumps. Most distinct is the deafening pause right before the clamor, such as occurs before the *ga-gush* of blood ejecting from your heart. Or when the rib muscles and diaphragm contract—pulling the chest cavity outward in all directions, followed quickly by the lungs—and the smallest suction of soundlessness occurs before a great rush of air.

14

About once a month I have Sunday brunch with Ryan and Malcolm at the house they bought together in Culver City. Malcolm is an accomplished legal advocate (although he likes the word *ombudsman* better) and there's something very meticulous about him, with his tweezed eyebrows and straight, square teeth. Ryan deals really well with any kind of upheaval—he's a bit of a fixer. He got practice at an early age, of course, holding the family together after Mom left, and even now, if your car breaks down or your house gets broken into or your girlfriend dumps you and you need a shot of whiskey stat, Ryan's the person you want to call. But Malcolm—prim, cheerful, smart, pushy, needy Malcolm—always wants to psychoanalyze every last thing, and Ryan is not that kind of fixer. Even when they are on an upswing after their most recent bout of fighting, smiling lovingly at each other, it's hard for me to understand how they've lasted six years.

On my way to their house, I stop in Hollywood to pick up a loaf of za'atar bread from our favorite Armenian bakery. Sometimes Ryan will devise omelets that complement the za'atar spices, the thyme, sumac, and sesame; other times he doesn't and we eat it anyway. I drive down De Longpre Avenue, east of the 101 freeway, past the apartment Jared and I lived in for two years, and then past the restaurant I used to love so much, an old-fashioned deli that serves a tower of large dill pickles on a small white plate as an appetizer. This isn't the well-known part of Hollywood. There are no pink terrazzo stars embedded in sparkling sidewalks, no elaborately made-up celebrity look-alikes doing their routines for tourist tips. For a long time I avoided this area because I worried about running into him, then I started coming here whenever I was depressed, inexplicably half-hopeful about running into him.

The last time I heard from Jared was an email he sent about six months after we broke up. I remember sitting at my computer, staring at the screen, acutely aware of all that had taken place since I'd last seen him—how I rushed out of our apartment in a daze, refused to answer any phone calls, only dealt with the logistical aftermath of our breakup and resisted any emotional processing; how I showed up late many times to Mad Dog Bar & Grill, where I used to bartend, got drunk off snuck shots of whiskey on an empty stomach because I'd forgotten to eat again, and the owner was forced to fire me (and I cried like a baby when he did); how Ryan called me not too long after and told me in an unfamiliar voice, a voice that sounded somehow shattered, that our mother was dead, and I stood in a gas station with a bag of Skittles and a water bottle in one hand, the phone pressed to my uncomprehending ear in the other, and didn't cry at all—and after all this, I got an email from Jared saying he would like to be friends.

He told me that he and Elizabeth had stopped seeing each other, and apologized in what appeared to be a heartfelt and genuine way that was simply not enough. This tiny bit of bait almost prompted me to pick up the phone and arrange a meeting, to hash out all the painful things, to yell at him in person, as Ryan so often advised me to do, rather than punish him with a wall of silence. But Jared also included a postscript saying that he'd heard about my mom, and to let him know if I needed anything. The extent of my rage upon reading those last lines actually stopped me, my feelings too complicated to sort out. It wasn't my desire to punish Jared that made me ignore him. I was scared of how ugly I would be if I saw him, how angry and vicious; I was scared of all the questions I would ask that I didn't want answers to. After he sent that email I retreated so far into myself that Marla and Ryan—the only two people I saw with any regularity anymore—really started to worry. Jared's betrayal was hard enough, and my mother's death confusing enough, but the combination of the two laid me flat for longer than I like to admit.

I park on Keystone Avenue. Ryan and Malcolm live in a light green, shapely one-level house that has a backyard and a mailbox. It's the smallest structure on the block; they're surrounded by multilevel apartment buildings, awkward and boxy, fitted on four sides with balconies too small to be useful. Still, when we were kids I never pictured this kind of domesticity for my brother.

Malcolm answers the door, looking pristine even in pajamas. "Piper!" He says it with surprise, like he hasn't been expecting me. "Come on in." Stiff blue cotton frames his long body like a nice suit; black hair hugs his scalp in even rows. It's as if he spent hours in front of the mirror this morning, ironing the pajama set, wetting and combing the shiny strands just so.

Ryan is hard at work, a dishtowel slung over one shoulder, a crackling bed of country-style potatoes in front of him. He sprinkles paprika over the mixture. Sitting on a cooling rack on the counter is a muffin tray, its pockets filled with red pepper goat cheese frittatas. The whole kitchen smells like browned butter.

"You amaze me," I tell him. He smiles.

We sit in the living room, the boys on the couch, me on the floor, and talk loudly over each other as we eat. Once my belly is bursting, I push my plate away and lean my elbows on the coffee table.

"Have you rescued any cats from trees?" Malcolm asks, chasing what's left on his plate with a pinch of bread.

"Not in my job description."

"Is it true you should always wear good underwear in case you get in an accident?"

"Yes, it's the first thing I check."

"Tell me you have a crush on this Ruth person," Malcolm presses.

"Actually, I went on a date with someone much cuter the other day."

"What? I haven't heard about this! Guy or girl?"

"Pipes, we got a new kind." Ryan leans his cheek on the kitchen doorway. "You want regular or Lime-zest Jima?"

I make a face. "I'd rather drink cowboy coffee than that citrus crap."

Ryan holds his hands up and backs slowly out of view.

"What's cowboy coffee?" Malcolm asks.

"You pour hot water directly on the grounds, no filter."

"That's disgusting. So who are you dating?"

In my halting, awkward way, I tell Malcolm about Ayla, wishing I could capture how it felt to talk to her, trying to render her wry sense of humor and shy smile. In return I get a monologue about why certain coffees taste nutty versus fruity, how the ones with citrus overtones have been grown in mountainous regions and wet-processed, because once Malcolm has smelled out an argument of any kind he can't ever let it go. We're busy bickering when Ryan comes back with a French press and some half-and-half.

"I don't care how gourmet it is, coffee should not taste sour. That stuff always makes me think the milk has curdled."

"Coffee is *fruit*," Malcolm says. "The beans are actually coffee cherries."

"I never know which one of you is more stubborn," says Ryan. He sits down, kisses Malcolm's shoulder, and places his palm over the plunger. "Or why I always surround myself with stubborn people."

"What about you," I say to Malcolm, "any exciting cases?"

"I've got a new workman's comp case, really interesting. Poor guy ended up with a doozy of a TBI. Stands for—"

"Traumatic brain injury."

"Exactly. Apparently my client is a completely different person now than before. Crazy mood swings, and I mean crazy. Never seen anything like it. And he has memory problems, but that's really common."

"Who doesn't have mood swings?" Ryan says. "And I'm the king of losing things." He turns to me, his voice purposefully light. "We had to change the locks to the house last week. I think it's the fourth time."

"I mean *mood swings*. This guy never started a fight in his life and now he's gone completely—here, wait, I'll show you the reports."

"Malky—" Ryan warns.

"What? She's a medical professional now, this kind of information might come in handy." He disappears into the bedroom.

Ryan fills my mug, the one I always choose, that has the words NONE SHALL PASS on the side in thick calligraphy, and he mixes in the cream until it's the exact shade of tan that I take my coffee. He passes it to me, but won't let go until I look up at him. "You finally met someone who might have half a chance," he says. "Don't you start spinning now."

"I'm fine," I tell him.

Malcolm comes back with an armful of papers. "Here." They land on the coffee table with a thump. "Take a look at these."

I sift through articles and research papers describing blast injuries and the coup-contrecoup phenomenon. I learned about the latter in EMT school, but it feels different to think about Ayla's brain, floating behind her face, colliding with the thick and bumpy interior of her skull, getting battered into a whole new shape.

"It was an explosion that caused it?" I ask, hoping to change the subject at least slightly.

"Blast-related TBI," he says. "Causes more severe injury. My client worked for a sewage treatment plant, and a water tank blew." Leaning over the table, Malcolm taps his middle finger on a graph filled with data points and a swirl of connecting lines. He talks about the relationship between the extent of injury and proximity to the blast. His depth of knowledge is impressive; I'm interested despite myself. First there's an explosion, he explains—a huge increase in air pressure—which compresses the surrounding air, creating winds more forceful than the blunt impact of a car accident. If that weren't enough, between the blast waves and the winds, internal organs get crushed and bruised. "And then there's the force of the body hitting the ground afterward. All of this happens in seconds."

Ryan shrugs. "I have no idea what you just said."

"Which part?"

"All of it."

"Okay, fine. Consider an orange lying on a table. An explosion creates a vacuum. Like a tsunami. The shoreline draws back, revealing miles of ocean floor, before a wall of water crashes down. In an explosion, there's the same vacuum effect, and then there are blast waves. A wall of air. When the blast waves hit, the orange gets lifted off the table and up into the air. But there's also enough force to send shock waves *through* the orange, imploding the pulp, denting the skin, rupturing pockets of air. Make sense?"

"Did you know the fish soup we make at our restaurant has orange juice in it? A whole cup's worth."

"Here we go again." Malcolm looks at me. "Your brother has a one-track mind."

"All things food."

"Exactly."

They continue but I lose the thread of the conversation. On the wall behind the two of them hangs a print of a Salvador Dalí painting: two elephants walk on toothpick legs across a blood-red landscape. Even if Ayla were a specimen of perfect health and sanity, there would be risk. Malcolm and Ryan discuss which fish are bottom-feeders and whether it is bad to eat a bottom-feeder. Their voices fill the room and I sip my coffee and the elephants walk toward each other, bulk balanced on gossamer.

15

"I think I'm over-caffeinated," I tell Ayla.

"You'll fit right in," she says.

We walk on the strand at Venice Beach, amid the heavy crowds of street performers, bodybuilders, tourists, and merchants. There's grass on one side, storefronts on the other, and palm trees in the shape of fireworks dance overhead. We pass a woman dressed as a mermaid who does tarot readings; the Rollerblade Guy skates by playing electric guitar. When we've had enough we buy a giant Elvis beach towel and climb our way onto the sand, the noise fading behind us, a few bobbing surfers in front of us. It's windy today, making the waves choppy. The sand scuttles and tumbles toward the ocean, and the fray from Ayla's torn jeans flutters. We claim a patch of beach, marking our territory with four evenly stretched corners of Elvis's face, and as we lie down and get settled, I am hyperaware of how close we are. The pad of her left big toe hovers an inch from my ankle.

I tell Ayla about Ryan and Malcolm, how when they started dating neither of them expected it to work out, because they were both just out of relationships and planned to use the other as a rebound. She tells me about the worst date she's ever been on, how they met for breakfast and the first thing the woman did was order a vodka drink, and the second thing she did was to try to read Ayla's palm.

"Did she know how?"

"Clearly no idea. Just made stuff up, and talked so loud people turned to look. She went on about my childhood for a while, then at some point realized I wasn't left-handed and switched to reading my right. I remember it was kind of demeaning. Like she was telling a joke, but one that was funny only to her. She had a shit-eating grin on her face the whole time."

"What did she say?"

"Oh, you know. I'd experienced a great loss by the time I was seven that had left me bitter, I would date a woman whose pubic hair would terrify me—"

"She said what?"

"You heard me. I'd have three major loves in my life, would have to overcome enormous obstacles, and unless I took up scuba diving by the age of thirty-five, I'd be fated to die young."

Ayla tells stories with the practiced face of a storyteller, of someone who may or may not be bluffing. I don't care either way. I'm glad for the excuse to look at her.

"Do you scuba?"

"No."

"Then what happened?"

"Her vodka arrived. She got even more belligerent, which was when I realized she'd been drinking before we met up. I caught a cab home with the money I would've spent on breakfast."

"And have you had three major loves?"

"Two and a half. Must be why I'm sitting on this towel."

"So this is a date."

She rolls over onto her side, which moves all of her body parts about six inches away from all of mine. "You bet your ass it is."

She peers at me as I lie on my stomach, propped on my elbows, looking down at her. Her lips parted, eyes like a doll's—glassy, iridescent. It would take very little effort to lean down and kiss her.

"I've never understood that expression."

"Which?"

"Shit-eating grin. Why would eating shit be a good thing?"

I stack my fists on top of each other and rest my chin on the hollow created by my fingers. "Do you miss the army?"

She doesn't respond at first. I watch a family of four struggle over the sand with a mountain of belongings, feeling her eyes on me.

"I guess I miss the wacky sense of structure. You always know where you're supposed to be, even if your orders don't make sense. You know when mealtimes are even when you don't know if you'll get to go on leave."

"And now—"

"Now I have to make my own choices all the damn time." Her fingers try to twist the flattened plush of the beach towel, but she can't get a grasp.

The family stakes ground about fifty yards from us, and as they unload, their wiggling, energetic Jack Russell runs circles around them, kicking up sand, looking at each of them for approval. Again the image of Carl's photograph flashes across my consciousness. "I don't ever want to own an animal," I blurt out, and before I can stop myself I'm telling Ayla the horrible story.

"That's awful," she says when I'm done. "And I thought I already hated little dogs."

I laugh, more out of relief than anything. "Do you have any pets?"

"Now, don't do that. Don't change the subject." She's serious even though her tone is light. "Have you been thinking about that photo a lot?"

"It's more like the woman pops into my head sometimes. Which is weird since I didn't even go on that call."

"She just kind of stayed with you."

"Yes."

"Ever heard of 'intrusive images'?"

I shake my head.

"It's therapy-speak for being a crazy person." She rushes to correct herself. "I mean, temporarily crazy. A lot of vets have intrusive images when they get back. It's exactly what you're describing."

"You're saying I'm a crazy person?"

"Maybe a little." She grins. "I guess I'm saying it's kind of normal, but I don't know if that makes you feel any better."

I smile back. "It does, actually."

She nods.

"What did you have nightmares about?"

"When?"

"When you got back from Iraq—you said you had nightmares?"

"Oh. I don't remember too well, honestly. But they must have been bad because I used to choke my partner. Sometimes she'd tell me what'd happened the next day, other times I'd wake up to her yelling my name over and over. My arm would be around her throat like we were fighting."

I picture her finding out in the morning the things she had done to her lover during the night and fight the urge to change the subject. "Is there a name for that, too?"

"Night terrors." She rolls onto her back and looks up at the sky.

"Shit-eating grins, human-eating dogs, and night terrors... honey, we're so romantic." At the last second her tone loses its sarcasm and hits a more genuine note. And something in me flinches. The feeling is not uncomfortable; it's as if she's reached in, discovered a long cord running from the base of my skull to my tailbone, and plucked it.

I pinch sand into my palm and tip it out to meet the ground again. On the boardwalk, a man in head-to-toe gold sequins is about to do his routine for the third time.

"You know, I noticed you in the store a lot," she says. "When did that start, about three months ago?"

I gape at her. "So you knew? That whole time?"

"Knew what?" Her storytelling face is gone, replaced by the beginnings of a smile.

"Oh, you're an asshole."

"Now wait, I didn't *know* anything. I just thought maybe—oh, you're blushing. Hey, I'm sorry. Didn't mean to embarrass you." I watch as her fingers make their way over to my forearm and rest on the inside of my wrist. When I lift my gaze to meet hers I find myself unable to move. We stay like that for a few moments, her barely-there fingertips drawing small circles on my thumping pulse.

"I was going to ask you out," she says, the breeze nudging her thick hair. "You were always there with that friend of yours. I thought of trying to make conversation but everything I thought of was just so cheesy. You beat me to it is all." The late afternoon sun makes everything appear more supple, buoyed, three-dimensional, and the glow of her skin and green eyes leaps off her face as she stares at me. "Listen, this isn't the best way to put it, but..."

"What?"

"Should we just get it over with?"

* * *

Time stretches itself long and quiet. We move slowly. We are skin to skin. Already, this is more than I can handle. I wrap my arms around her waist and feel her body swell as she breathes in. She rolls over on top of me, cupping my jaw with her fingers as she presses her mouth to mine. My thin sheets settle around our new shape.

I keep reminding myself that I've done this before.

"You're trembling," Ayla says, breaking off our kiss to study me.

"No, I'm not."

She removes my right hand from her naked, warm waist and holds the fluttering traitor up between us. "No?"

I silently demand my hand stop quivering. It does. We watch the five-pronged silhouette hanging in the air between us, now motionless. I take hold of her hips and tug, feeling the pressure of her hip bones against my palms, and bury my face in her neck. Ayla's hands tighten and release, trail to a new spot, tighten and release, and when her fingers reach my left leg, just underneath her, she pauses. "Now your leg is shaking."

Yes, it is. I tell it to stop but it won't—the agitated limb responds to the attention by trembling more. I shut my eyes tight and try to disappear.

What she does with my vulnerability only makes me feel more exposed. She puts her mouth on my ear, tracing my earlobe with her tongue. She takes her time before murmuring, "You're beautiful, Piper."

Propping up on my elbow, my weight sinking into the pillow, I study Ayla's profile, motionless except for the slight tremble of eyelashes. Her oversize trap muscles don't fully relax even when she's resting.

"Worried I'm going to kill you in my sleep?" Ayla asks without opening her eyes.

I snort and dig my finger into her ear. Laughing, she bats my hand away and pulls me into her. Collapsing my head onto the pillow next to hers, I throw an arm over her, and we lie like that for a moment, still and breathing, listening to the silence of my dark apartment.

"What's your last name?"

"Gallagher."

"Piper Gallagher. You Irish?"

"Half."

"Any family banshees?"

"Not that I know of."

"My mom used to tell me a spook story, about the banshee who'd come for me if I was bad."

I trace her arm until I get to the crook of her elbow and pause there. Her skin is soft and hot, like she's still sitting in the sun. "Are you Irish, too?"

"Mostly Russian and German. My mom loves to tell stories is all—the one about the banshee was her favorite."

She tells me about her mom, a schoolteacher, who she describes as the kind of person a whole family revolves around, and then she says, "After I got discharged—well, let's just say I'd be in a loony bin or dead if it weren't for her."

I open my mouth to ask *what happened*, but I'm acutely aware that within my arms, Ayla's whole body has gone rigid. Her right hand twitches from its position underneath my back. Listening to the silence between us, I realize we are both holding our breath.

Picture an orange on a table. Picture a shoreline drawing back, revealing miles of ocean floor.

"I'll tell you all about it sometime. But not tonight, if that's okay."

"Okay." I trace her arm again, trying to soften her brooding body, but she seems held in place, almost lifted off the mattress.

"What about your mom, Piper?"

I find myself hesitating. Here it is, the moment when I have to decide which version of the story to tell. I start with Mom's river rafting trip, how she went to Colorado with some college friends and ended up falling in love with the guide. How she decided to leave us, barely taking anything with her when she did. How the phone calls tapered off, things slowly filled in around her absence, and how Ryan and I eventually got used to it, probably because kids can get used to anything. I rush through the whole sordid story with a hint of apology in my voice, and then wait for Ayla to tell me how sorry she is, how horrible. For a while she doesn't say anything.

"What do you remember about her?"

"Not a lot."

"Hard to trust people."

"Yes."

"Did your dad ever remarry?"

"He tried dating here and there. He never got over her." I burrow in closer. "Do I get to hear about the banshee?"

"What, you a fan of ghost stories?"

"Maybe. Will you hold me if I get scared?"

"Maybe." Her weight relaxes and she squeezes my arm. "Let me think. You know, I've never tried to tell this story."

"There's no backing out now."

Her cheek moves against my scalp: she's smiling. "She haunted an Irish family by the name of MacNeal for hundreds of years. The MacNeals had stories and songs about her, passed down generation after generation; the children were warned to watch out for her and grown men would wake from their sleep thinking they had heard her." If you hear the banshee's wail of mourning, she tells me, it means that exactly three days later, you or a member of your family will die.

Her voice becomes uncharacteristically wistful. "A hundred years go by. All that's left of the MacNeals is a ruined castle."

One night, she continues, a young American tourist traveling the countryside in search of his heritage sees a speck of white floating in the hills.

As he gets closer, he sees a woman, pale, with long black hair, wearing a tattered white dress. Then he sees her feet don't touch the ground. But it's too late. She rushes toward him, shrieking, her face full of despair, and he falls backward down the hillside, getting hurt so badly he can't move his arms or legs. He calls for help; he can still hear her floating above him, moaning softly.

"When he dies three days later, the last of the MacNeal line is lost. The banshee's never seen or heard again."

We're both quiet. Ayla's fingers dig into my hair and massage my scalp, then come loose and wrap around my shoulders. As my hair settles back down, the smallest of the strands give the sensory impression they're standing erect.

"What does she sound like?"

Ayla leans into me until her nose presses against my cheekbone. Her voice low in my ear, at once musical and gravelly, she moans an oddly terrifying "*aiee.*"

16

Centuries after he died, you can hold the skull of Phineas Gage in your hand and admire the large triangular hole, like a misshapen third eye, just above the crest of what must have been his hairline. You can contemplate how, in the 1800s, Phineas Gage lived to the bright age of thirty-six despite the fact that when he was twenty-five, an almost-four-foot-long solid steel tamping iron blasted through his left cheekbone and out the top of his head. You can turn the skull toward the light and see evidence of his rudimentary surgery. The physician at the time, a Doctor Harlow, managed the wound as if it were a jigsaw puzzle, placing large bits of skull fragments where they seemed to fit, discarding smaller fragments as useless, and even inserting the full length of his index finger into the tunnels of Phineas's enormous entrance and exit wounds in order to check for any remaining pieces of bone.

Your brain weighs three pounds and is most recognizable for its fissures and folds, the coiled tissue sitting atop the brain stem like a bouquet of miniature sausage links. Its resilience and adaptability have long been recognized but remain mostly inexplicable. You can talk about neuroplasticity and cortical remapping; you can point out the different case studies, the miraculous recoveries, or how startling it is that when a blind person learns to read Braille, it isn't just the tactile part of the brain that gets activated but the visual cortex, dormant for so long. Your brain knows how to rewire itself in order to recover function.

Or, rather than ponder the fate of Phineas Gage, these days you can consider Li Fu, a Chinese man from Yunnan Province, who for four years complained of migraines and a bad taste in his mouth, until X-rays revealed a ten-centimeter knife blade lodged in the middle of his brain. You can consider Kate Dendrinos, who, in 2002, endured a motorcycle crash without a helmet. Because of massive amounts of swelling, doctors were forced to remove the left frontal and temporal lobes of her brain completely. She wasn't expected ever to recover cognitive function.

But what do we have except hope? And what is hope except the persistent belief in the unlikely, if not the impossible? As in: you won't get hurt, you won't fall, you'll survive, you'll recover, you can beat this, you are loved, you're going to live, you're not alone.

These incidents weren't without consequence. Phineas Gage became unrecognizable to his loved ones after the accident, prone to violence and bouts of rage. When he was refused his old position as a crew foreman, he appeared in live shows, always holding the tamping iron that hadn't bested him. Kate Dendrinos experienced profound relapses over the years, but made a full recovery. She now teaches the disabled how to ride horses. And

Li Fu, the mild-mannered family man who once had a slowly rusting knife blade lodged in his brain? Li Fu's headaches are gone.

17

"Man, I hate slow days."

"Yeah."

"Yeah."

Silence. They listen. The phone does not ring.

"You know we're not sleeping. We're going to be up all night."

Carl, the most forlorn I've seen him, looks at his watch. "I'll make a pot of coffee later. Maybe at 2100. Get us through the night."

The five of us have been sitting around the table at station for about three hours. It is something of an honor to be sitting with the two regular crews like this, and I'm guessing this means Ruth feels more confident about my skills. We haven't had a single call. We ran a couple of station drills, using the infant-size mannequin and the unfortunate "Jenna" doll, whose gender is debatable and whose fake-blood-splattered rubber skin sorely needs a washing. After lunch I vacuumed the carpet in sleeping quarters, while the boys played video games and Ruth graded my mapping exercises. The lack of calls makes everyone nervous, especially Pep. Everyone expects some kind of retaliation later for all the free time they've had so far.

"I should take a nap now," Pep says.

J-Rock spits tobacco into a red plastic cup. "Man, all you ever do is sleep. You need your beauty rest? I'd do you. Put a wig on that dome and you'd look like a girl."

"I can't help it that I'm prettier than your girlfriend, Rock."

"You're not nearly as pretty as your mom. She says hello, by the way."

Carl told me on my second day that if I wanted to impress other EMTs, and Ruth in particular, I shouldn't laugh, join in, or speak until spoken to—not until I earn my badge. Today this is not a problem. Today I have a goofy smile stretched across my face and I float above the conversation, thinking of Ayla's hands on me, Ayla's voice in my ear, Ayla's kisses and moans and warm, soft skin.

The boys continue.

"Fuck you."

"Go suck a horse."

"Don't want sloppy seconds where your mouth has been."

Ruth places her hands flat on the table's surface and pushes her chair back a couple of inches. She does this so efficiently, not a single copper hair in her perfect ponytail stirs. The effect is a loud scraping sound of wood against linoleum, and the conversation ends. J-Rock and Pep look like children expecting a reprimand, and Carl looks upward appreciatively as if he's thanking God for the hilarity.

But soon they're arguing about zombies. Conversations at Station 710 often circle back to this, to the upcoming, and inevitable, Zombie Apocalypse. How to train for, defend, and survive an invasion of the living dead. J-Rock appears to be particularly obsessed with this topic. J-Rock is a bit more of a geek than Carl or Pep, with his backward hat and hunched posture, his lack of affect. He has the enviable skill of looking completely serious even when he's saying something hysterical.

Although Ruth hasn't said a word on the subject, I think my Zombie Apocalypse Plan would be to hide behind her. J-Rock's newest plan is to gather weapons, food, and animals, and head to Catalina Island.

"That's the dumbest thing I ever heard," Pep says.

"It's the perfect defense," J-Rock replies. "You've got a 360-degree lookout. Plus, zombies can't swim."

"Yeah, but there's nothing to do there," Carl says. "Better to load up a cruise ship and travel around the world than be stuck on a boring island."

"The Centers for Disease Control actually cover this," I say. "Their website has a page on zombies; it talks about virus transmission and government containment and there's a recommended list of supplies…" I trail off, remembering I'm not supposed to speak unless spoken to. By the looks on their faces, everyone at the table, with the exception of Ruth, just fell in love with me.

To distract myself, I slink down in my chair and try to count how many times today the boys have broken the rather long-winded sexual harassment policy of A & O Ambulance. So far: twenty-seven times. They continue their stream of chatter about their regular patients, nurses at CRH, someone who got fired last week for forgetting the height clearance at a Carl's Jr. drive-through. The mechanics at A & O's headquarters in Gardena are still doing repairs on the roof of the rig.

"Lucy finally got let go, too," J-Rock says with a satisfied nod.

"The queen of the badge bunnies!" Carl laughs. "Didn't she have sex with someone at CRH?"

J-Rock wraps his hands around his reversed hat and leans back. "You're getting her mixed up with our favorite neighborhood transient, Sadie." He looks at me with that stoic expression of his. "Sadie has the highest frequent flyer points out of everybody."

He tells me that video cameras in the Crossroads Hospital waiting room caught the full action of a very intoxicated Sadie copulating with another transient in front of patients and their families. She has since been banned from admittance to the hospital, and rumor has it she temporarily relocated to the streets of Hollywood.

Pep begins the discussion of whether it was the illegal Code 3 or the blow job given to a firefighter in Station 3980's parking lot that got Lucy fired. Ruth's voice is startling when she interrupts. "I have a trainee! For fuck's sake."

Silence again. The three boys straighten and stare down at their laps. They seem to be earnestly considering what topics won't become inappropriate. Finally they settle on their bucket lists.

"Amputation. Oh, definitely."

"Cardiac tamponade. But what are the chances?"

"Yeah, good luck, they usually get stabbed in the gut. Speaking of which, I'm going with an evisceration. Piper, what about you?"

"Um, well, I guess I'm curious about a sucking chest wound."

The four of them stare at me. "A sucking chest wound?" Pep says. "That's like saying you want to run a call on a drunk. People get shot so much around here, you're bound to get one of those."

"Or two or three." J-Rock spits dark liquid into his cup. "Pick another one."

They give me a moment to think about it.

"I want to deliver a baby."

The boys shudder. "I can think of a *lot* of things I'd rather do," Carl says.

"Don't listen to them," Ruth says. "It's fun."

When we finally get a call, Ruth, Carl, and I arrive closely behind the fire department paramedics, and soon all of us have infiltrated a crowded birthday party, where we begin our search for a sixteen-year-old seizure in a sea of ten-year-olds. The small one-story house has been squeezed to capacity. The front room looks like a dining room as well as a children's bedroom, judging by the four tiny mattresses pushed up against the walls. The decorations are standard fare: a giant white cake, a couple of drifting balloons, and some cardboard cutouts held to the walls with Scotch tape. Through the postage stamp of a kitchen window I see there is a backyard, too, with presents piled on a small plastic table. There isn't a game in sight, but I can make out the unicorn piñata dangling from a tree.

It's unusual to be at any birthday party and see the adults crying. Eager and nervous as always, practically hugging the green oxygen tank

I unhitched from the gurney, I look around, trying to locate our patient. We get ushered into a corner room with much dramatics. One woman has dark mascara trails outlining her nose, tears waterfalling off her face. Lying on the couch is a teenager with a fragile build and long, thick hair. Her body looks held in place; she doesn't seem relaxed enough to be sleeping. She's pale and her eyelids flutter. This must be our seizure patient. I start to rush in but get stopped by the paramedic. He's surly-looking, his face riddled with gray stubble. His arm bars me as I try to enter the room.

"Let's just load her up," he says, dropping his arm, still not looking at me. He turns to the girl's mother. "Did you guys get in an argument?'

"No!" she wails. "She was fine and then she just started shaking."

They continue to talk as Carl and I negotiate a two-person lift of our patient and Ruth supervises. The girl isn't heavy but the space is narrow, and as I shuffle backward and Carl forward, the way the girl hangs limply between us causes the woman to go into fresh hysterics.

In the back of the rig, the lead medic tells Carl to shut the doors but not to drive away yet. After the slam of double doors there's silence. He leans forward, cracking his knuckles one by one in a steady rhythm. "Hey," he says, "stop faking it already."

Our patient doesn't move and I look at Ruth, bewildered.

He leans in closer. "I said, stop faking it."

The girl doesn't move. He picks up her wrist and raises her arm so the drooping hand hangs directly over her face. I notice he's not wearing gloves. When he lets go, her arm takes a strange trajectory. Instead of falling flat on her face as gravity would dictate, it swoops and manages to land on the soft bed of the gurney just above her forehead.

His slow smile is unctuous. "Okay. Here's how it's going to work. Either you're going to cooperate and start talking to us, or I'm going to do tests and treatments that will be very uncomfortable. I will shove tubes down your nose and needles into your feet. I promise it will hurt. Is that what you want?"

She doesn't respond. He slides down to the end of the bench seat and flips up the thin hospital sheet we used to cover her.

"Do you want me to get vitals?" I ask.

"Don't do a thing," he says.

Her shoes are checkered black and white, with pink laces, and after he pulls them off he removes her white socks, dropping all of it onto the floor of the ambulance. His hands still ungloved, he runs a finger along the bony arch of her foot, poking for a vein. In the seat next to me, Ruth's posture is stiffer than usual.

The girl's eyes flutter open and she issues a soft sound. It breaks the tension somewhat. The medic seems to have expected this: he slides back up toward the head of the gurney and stares at her. "All better now?"

He questions her for a few minutes, but none of the questions seem medical. Did she get in a fight, is she stressed, is it that time of the month, did they forget to leave her a piece of cake? Instead of answering, she stares calmly out the back windows of the ambulance. She doesn't seem the least bit surprised to be dealing with his disrespect, and to see such youthful resignation is chilling.

"Why'd you pretend to have a seizure?" he asks finally. For a moment something dark, bleak, and lonely crosses her face but then it's gone. She doesn't answer; he shrugs and climbs out of the ambulance. "Take her to CRH," he says. "Go with whatever chief complaint you want." And he shuts the doors.

I sit on the rig's bumper in the parking lot at Crossroads, staring at paperwork. What used to take me sixty minutes now takes me twenty-five. The boxes are checked, the codes filled in, the narrative complete. Ruth comes around the corner of the ambulance and sits next to me on the perforated aluminum. I hand her my report, which she scans and hands back. "Any questions?"

"Who's the shithead?"

At first it looks as though I'm going to get a scolding for my language, but then she says, "Randall." After a pause, she adds, "That was the drop arm test."

"Is he always that rude?"

"Yes. And he would have done what he said, shoved an airway adjunct in her nose, probably without lube, and started an IV in her foot."

I grimace, shaking my head.

"What would you have done differently?"

"She's sixteen," I say. "She shouldn't have upset her family and brought 911 to her house, but maybe something really was wrong. A medical problem she didn't know how to talk about, or some kind of violence in her family. At the very least, I would have done a real assessment, not just threatened her."

Ruth doesn't say anything. There it is again, the reminder that perhaps I am too sensitive for this job. People don't say it so much as think it.

When I was sixteen, I saw someone get killed in a hit-and-run accident. Who knows what this girl has seen? She lives in a tiny house crammed with at least two families, and although I don't like being lied to, there was something genuinely wounded about her. It might have been just teenage angst; she could have been acting out for attention. But she also could have had a petit mal seizure, which would have resulted in more subdued symptoms, or some other kind of injury or illness that can't be recognized with something so primitive as the "drop arm test." Either way, I don't like Randall. I don't like the way he talked to her, and I don't understand why someone like that would be in this line of work.

Ruth surprises me by saying, "Hold on to that, Piper. See if you can." She kicks at a few small stones strewn over the parking lot asphalt, and watches as one dips and disappears into a hollow. "I can see that you give a shit about patients, that that's what you're here for. You'd be surprised how rare that really is. And—you're going to be good out there. Once you get a little more used to it."

I can tell there's something else on her mind.

"Carl told you about the bet we made?"

It's not really a question. A little shocked, I nod, my eyes still on the hollow where the stone disappeared.

"I'm sorry. I really am."

The double doors to the ER swing open and we both turn our heads as Carl charges down the ramp, riding one side of the gurney like a skateboard. He doesn't stop at the ambulance but flies past us, hollering.

When my laughter subsides, I say to Ruth, "He never was a rookie, was he? He was probably born into this job."

"Carl?" she says incredulously. "Carl was one of the worst. I trained him. He was all empathy and politeness. Southern manners and sympathy. Couldn't get his ass in gear to do anything. But once he figured things out, he was one of the best. Of course," she adds, shrugging, "*I* was never a rookie."

18

"Anything good?" J-Rock asks from under his cap as we file through the front door of Station 710. He's watching an action movie, one of the many Bourne installments, but the loud soundtrack doesn't stir his partner. Pep's limp frame sags in the seat next to him. Eyeing one of the empty recliners as I head toward the kitchen table, I lament the fact I can't kick up my feet until I'm done with training.

"Drop arm test," Carl replies with a shrug. He hangs the rig keys on a hook by the door and slumps into one of the recliners. Ruth pulls a frozen burrito from her stash and tosses it onto the counter near the microwave. It lands with a dull thump.

"Pass or fail?" J-Rock presses.

Ruth and Carl in unison: "Fail."

J-Rock nods, his eyes still on the screen. "Well, while you've been off saving the world, Pep and I have accomplished exactly nothing."

"It's going to be so busy tonight." Carl sighs.

"Yeah."

As my last, uneventful day of training comes to an end, a call comes in for 7101. When the phone rings, J-Rock jumps to answer and nods at Carl, Ruth, and me, sitting at the table. "You got something." He and Ruth say it the same way, "SOB," but I know Carl likes to say "son of a bitch." Either way, it means the patient has shortness of breath.

Ruth quickly pushes her chair back and stands, looking at the neat stack of my completed field training paperwork in front of her and noting the time on her watch: 1920. My shift officially ended twenty minutes ago. "Training's done," she says with finality. "You can come on this call, but you don't have to. Go home if you want."

But I've already grabbed my clipboard and brush jacket and am sprinting out the door, looking at my pager for details: #30026: 52 y/o M, SOB, 1 Byrd Ave, xs 2nd Ave/Van Ness, Apt 518.

I take the passenger seat and tell dispatch, "7101 is on air," as Carl and Ruth pile into the rig. The dispatcher's steady voice gives us the details. I recognize the address of the apartment as part of the tan-and-white complex on Byrd Avenue that takes up a whole city block.

There's an unusual pause in the radio transmission and then Dispatch continues. "7101, be advised. New update for incident number 30026. Call is now for a full arrest."

A fleeting image: my brain detaching from my spinal cord and floating away like a helium-filled balloon as I sit here, unable to absorb this information. I knew I would get a full arrest call at some point, but for the stakes to rise so high so suddenly makes me wonder if Ruth can retract her declaration that I've passed training. I hold the radio transmitter up to my mouth, and with trembling fingers press the side button. "Car 7101, copy that."

"Ice cream!" Carl yells happily from the back of the cab. The bewildered look on my face is so extreme even Ruth smiles a little.

"It's a firefighting tradition," she explains as she starts the rig and the heavy diesel motor turns over. "Any time you have a big first, like your first full arrest or you're on television, you buy everybody at station ice cream."

"Television?" I clutch the map book in my lap, but have yet to turn a page of it.

"News coverage," she says, throwing the rig into drive and flipping on the lights. "For big incidents, like multi-casualty car crashes or crime scenes. Plus we get a lot of stabbings and shootings, so sometimes you'll be on TV." She pulls the rig out to the edge of the parking lot so its nose dips down into Normandie Avenue.

My face feels numb.

"Piper, map me to my *call*."

"Yes ma'am." I snap my spine straight and shake my head once to clear it. Opening my Thomas Guide, I slam my right index finger down on the location of Station 710 and my left middle finger on the diagonal slope of Byrd Avenue. Briskly I tell her, "North on Normandie, west on Manchester, northwest on Byrd, and your trigger street is Van Ness."

The tires screech as Ruth takes off, and Carl says in a satisfied voice, "Get some."

His wife leads us to him; she was on the phone with the 911 operator when her husband went from gasping for breath to not breathing at all. She reports they are both in their fifties. In the hallway I pass a picture of the two of them from maybe twenty years ago, a curling yellow memory that hangs in a wooden frame so faded by the sun the wood looks almost pink. They stand erect and formal, holding hands, beaming warm smiles at the camera.

We find him sprawled on his back in the office, under an old Dell computer. The screen saver flashes a colorful montage, and I notice two things: the theme seems to be landscapes from around the world, and he doesn't look much like the picture hanging in the hallway. We—seven firefighters, Ruth, Carl, and I—descend on him like a swarm of insects. The captain hovers behind me, the only person still standing, and hurriedly documents the multiplicity of events on his clipboard. I jump on compressions as soon as a firefighter says the man is pulseless, and as soon as I do, I'm scared to look up. The flurry of activity around me is overwhelming, as is the man's stricken expression, and I can't afford to mess this up by becoming frozen and useless.

In CPR class we practiced on mannequins with blue foam torsos, pivoting plastic necks, and faceless heads that had fixed and modestly open mouths. If you gave breaths right, you could see the dummy's chest rise and fall. If you did compressions right, you would hear a little clicking noise. The EMT instructor played the disco song "Staying Alive," which sets an appropriate tempo for proper CPR. Some students sang along, laughing, and nodded their head to the beat as they pumped away at the foam.

This is nothing like that.

The sharp, rapid compressions I press into this man's sternum cause his gray chest hairs to quiver. Balanced on my knees, I focus my gaze on my arms descending straight down and crossing at the wrists, my interlocked and pumping hands, the ripples that shudder out through his fleshy chest. I watch his chest hairs tremble and I look at his blotchy skin, a mix of purple and pale—vitiligo, I think it's called—and I ignore my right eye, which is watering. A single strand of my hair clings to it, but I'm not allowed to pause until the thirtieth compression, and there is no way to wipe it away. Hoping to push the strand to the outer rim of my eyeball I blink rapidly, in time with the compressions, and the strobe light effect makes the act of doing CPR feel absurd.

8, 9, 10, 11…

"Lock your elbows!" Ruth hisses in my ear. "Look at the monitor, you're not pushing hard enough."

The monitor rests on the carpet next to him; she tells me I will know if my compressions are deep enough by how sharp the spikes are on the screen. "Really lean into him," she says. "And tell me when you get tired."

I follow her advice and shove harder; his torso shudders and wobbles underneath me, and the spike rockets up. Seeing the improvement, I feel a small thrill. These compressions are better than the ones I delivered to a blue foam mannequin, better than the ones I jokingly threatened Marla with when we practiced scenarios, and much, much better than the ones I gave when I was sixteen years old, to a hit-and-run victim whose life I couldn't save.

23, 24, 25…

The man belches from the caving pressure and the smell is sour bile mixed with decaying chicken noodle soup. Ruth peers at me; she sees the way I am blinking. My right eye stings from that stupid piece of hair. I've half-promised myself I will shave my head when I get home to avoid this problem in the future. She wipes my face using the side of her forearm, her gloved fingers bent awkwardly so as not to contaminate me, and clears away the offending strand.

30.

"Stop CPR," says the lead medic.

Finally bending my blood-filled arms, I lean my weight back on my heels. It feels weird to be touched by Ruth. Her gesture had been businesslike but tender. I feel the sweat at the roots of my hair and wonder how damp and flushed my face had felt on the thin skin of her forearm. "Thanks," I whisper. Her gaze fixed on the monitor screen, she doesn't appear to hear.

The dramatic spikes my compressions created plunge into a subdued quiver above and below where the man's asystole line would be. "V fib," a paramedic calls out to the captain. "Setting up a shock."

Squeezed shoulder to shoulder in the tiny office space, the large men work steadily around the patient's body, most crouching or on one knee. Three firefighters prepare IV lines and drugs, two unpack the intubation kit, and another, halfway in the act of cutting off the man's jeans with trauma shears, rocks to his feet and takes a step back. Carl, his fingers gripped around the man's jaw for leverage to open his throat, squeezes one more breath into the man's lungs with a bag valve mask.

Defibrillation is something I've never seen, and I feel another small thrill. In EMT class I learned what shocking actually does, and realized I'd been lied to by TV shows and movies my whole life. Sending 250 joules of electricity through a person's chest stops his heart completely. It's counterintuitive to think that to save a man's life you would first kill him, but two rhythms—ventricular fibrillation and ventricular tachycardia—create irregular electrical activity that doesn't actually pump blood, and are worth silencing. After defibrillation, a small chance exists that the barely quivering heart might suddenly restart itself and throw an organized rhythm, which would create pulses again. Unlike in the movies, no one would ever shock a person in flatline. Why stop a dead heart?

"Everyone *clear*?" the lead medic asks. He looks at the monitor and not at us; his finger hovers over a blinking button. A shock of 250 joules also stops the heart of anyone touching the patient, and there are horror stories of responders dying in the field because they weren't paying attention. Ruth narrows her eyes at me, and I hold my hands up and scoot my knees back in an exaggerated show of reliability.

"Shocking," he says, and presses the button.

The man's body jerks upward, forward, almost airborne, but his give-or-take 160 pounds is too much weight for flight. Our patient's arms land at different angles than before, and his face swings toward mine. Mouth open and covered in spittle, eyes fixed and dilated, he looks less like a dead person and more like someone who just received terrible news.

"Sinus brady!" yells the lead medic. The news ripples through all of us, pulling us together for a breathless, hovering instant. My eyes snap back to the monitor screen, and sure enough, there's sinus bradycardia, a too-slow but nevertheless functional rhythm. The number in the right-hand corner blinks at 48, then 50, then 47 beats a minute. The man has pulses again. We are lifesavers.

The moment over, I rest on my heels, dumbfounded and elated, amid the overlapping voices and resumed flurry of activity. Meanwhile, one fire-fighter finds a vein and plunges in an IV catheter as Carl hands him the line; the lead medic has cranked the man's jaw open with a laryngoscope blade and inserts the breathing tube; another firefighter removes the rest of the man's clothing. I've lost Ruth—apparently the excitement of getting pulses back caused her to forget about her role as field training officer. Of everyone's hands, hers move the fastest.

"Good flow on the line, keeping it TKO."

"Where's that epi?"

"No signs of trauma, no spontaneous breathing."

"Skin signs are warm and diaphoretic."

"Okay, tape it up. Can someone get me a D-stick and a blood pressure?"

"D-stick is 110, working on a BP now."

"Does he have any medical problems?"

"No! Wait, hypertension. Is he... that's good, right?"

In the midst of all this, I hear his wife speak and realize she's been standing behind me, looking on and talking to the captain in a trembling voice.

I had forgotten she was there. I lift my head a little, goose bumps erupting, wanting to turn and look at her, wanting to jump into the flurry and be useful, thinking, *I helped save a life*, and catch sight of something in my peripheral vision. The computer screen flashes the Eiffel Tower. We haven't even been here long enough for the computer to switch from its screen saver to sleep.

We lift him using a backboard and file down the hallway, but before we make it to the gurney, the lead medic halts the caravan and shocks him again. I get a look at his wife's face, the way her heart stops every time his does, and feel a tinge of horror.

In the back of the rig, Ruth explains the drugs being administered while I push oxygen into the man's lungs and feel the kickback of his diaphragm. My slippery latex-covered hands occasionally lose their grip, gloves glued to knuckles with sweat.

Ruth, Carl, and I shut ourselves up in the little break room dubbed the "Paramedic Lounge" in the northwest corner of the ER wing. As we get settled, Carl says, "Piper, you better quit now. You've got a perfect record—100 percent lifesaver. It's only downhill from here." He kicks his boots off and stretches himself out on the flower-print couch, resting the walkie-talkie on his chest.

Ruth digs through the fridge, grabbing a small carton of cranberry juice from the available stack of pink, red, and orange containers. She finds a plastic-wrapped ham and cheese sandwich amidst the pile of bologna and white bread and tosses an orange juice to Carl. "Want anything?" she asks me.

"No, thanks," I say. Spreading out a mound of paperwork on the gray plastic table, I stare forlornly at the work ahead of me.

Carl chuckles. "I'm so glad I'm not you right now."

I labor steadily, documenting over thirty treatments, looking up the corresponding treatment codes, writing a two-page narrative. Nowhere do

I mention what a nightmare it had been to remove our patient from the apartment complex, with its tiny elevator that barely fit the gurney. Four of us had squeezed him in diagonally while everyone else took the stairs. When we struggled to remove him from the elevator, I got a look at his bare feet poking out from the sheet we'd covered him with. I'd guess he hadn't cut his toenails in at least two months.

When I finally finish, Ruth and I look over at Carl, who is fast asleep. Ruth grabs the crumpled-up carton of cranberry juice and ball of plastic wrap from the table and stands next to the couch, looking down at her partner. With a heavy overhand throw, she pitches her trash into the metal wastebasket on the floor next to him, but the dull clanging sound doesn't wake him up. Undaunted, she plucks a pen from her front uniform pocket and tickles the inside of his ear. Carl slaps the pen out of her hand even before his eyelids fly open, and the pen clatters to the floor. Picking it up, Ruth marches to the sink to wash it off.

Carl looks at me sleepily, not bothering to cover his yawn. The mirth in his eyes is absent; he looks innocent and so, so young. Half-awake and solemn, he says, "I like mint-n-chip."

My training is officially over, and this is all the more evident by the fact that Carl kicks me to the captain's chair in the back of the cab and takes my place in the passenger seat. On the way back from the Baskin-Robbins on Ninetieth Street, he and Ruth talk excitedly about our last call. I listen, my ears perked forward like a puppy, every now and then interrupting to ask questions, already reciting the story in my head, practicing how I will describe it to everyone I know, imagining Ayla's face as she reacts.

"Did you see the way he landed—"

"The intubation tube? Solid on the first try. Stevens runs the *smoothest* full arrest."

"That was probably the best one I've ever seen, though. If it weren't for that—"

"Damn thing was puny. Should be against the law. No old people in apartment buildings unless the elevator can fit an elephant."

I'm jolted when I hear Carl call our patient old. I'm only twenty-eight but still the man had seemed young to me, too young to die of a heart attack. I wonder if Carl will still think fifty is "old" when he's nearing his thirtieth birthday.

Ruth pulls into the Crossroads lot and parks, and I ask in confusion, "I thought we were going back to station?"

Looking over her shoulder, Ruth coolly raises her eyebrows at me and says nothing. My excitement from the full arrest and the adrenaline still pumping in my veins give rise to quick heat in my cheeks. When will they stop ignoring me? How many tests must I pass not to be treated like a boot?

Carl hops out of the rig and uses the walkie-talkie to contact Dispatch: "Sir, 7101 requests permission to do a Code HLP." The scratchy transmission from the dispatcher reveals he is laughing; I remember that he and Carl are friends, so this must be some kind of inside joke. Carl's request gets approved, and I search his face—big smirk or little smirk?—for some clue as to what a Code HLP might be. He's unreadable.

Carl nods at Ruth, clipping the walkie-talkie to his belt. She tells me to bring the ice cream, then locks the doors and turns on her heel. She's headed toward the entrance to the emergency wing, and Carl follows after her, whistling.

I trudge after them up the ramp. We are doing a Code HLP at CRH after a SOB mutated into a full arrest and was delivered to the ER with pulses and a BP. A new acronym is not what I need right now. I rack my brain for all the jargon and slang I've learned recently, for A & O Ambulance's policies and paperwork codes, and wonder if Carl's slang has something to do with the hospital itself. If a "code" means there is some kind of action involved, like a Code Blue is a full arrest, and Code 3 means driving with lights and sirens, then "HLP" could mean... what? Nothing comes to mind, so I start to make things up. Hemorrhagic labor pain? High-level pressure? Heart liposuction?

Ruth pushes through the double doors but instead of walking into the belly of the ER department, she makes a left and goes through another set of double doors I hadn't noticed before. Close behind Carl, I listen as his whistling mixes with the rolling of carts, beeping of machinery, yelling of patients, chatter of doctors, laughter of nurses. When the second set of double doors swings shut behind us, his whistling stretches to fill the empty hallway, mixing only with the clipped percussion of our boots.

"Where are we going?"

Carl ignores me, as I knew he would. "You'll see," says Ruth.

We walk down a series of hallways, pass signs for RADIOLOGY, SURGICAL UNIT, URGENT CARE. We arrive at an elevator in another part of the hospital, and once we get inside I notice a small keypad underneath the usual panel of buttons. To choose the ninth floor, Ruth holds one finger on the button and uses her other hand to enter a four-digit code on the keypad.

When the elevator doors open we step out directly onto the roof. The early evening light soothes my pupils after the long trail of fluorescence. A strong wind has cleared away most of the haze, and from up here I can see the glittering downtown skyline to the northeast. I stretch up on my toes to look west, imagining I can see all the way to the Pacific.

Carl's white teeth flash in his grin. "This hasn't been used since 1993, but we keep hoping."

Ruth digs out the ice cream and bright pink spoons, and traps the plastic bag with the gallon container so it can't blow away. "For bonus points at the end of your training," she says, standing upright and throwing her shoulders wide, "what do you think HLP stands for?"

Looking around for clues, I notice the rooftop has a bright red circle with a thick gray cross painted on it. My hair whips my face as I smile. "Helicopter landing pad."

Carl raises his arms over his head and whoops loudly. I laugh, and add my own crowing to his sounds.

Ruth says, "Easy, children," but she is smiling, too.

We sit near the edge of the roof and carve pink spoons into melting neon green. We don't face west, toward the wide, tree-lined streets that lead to the ocean, or north, toward the serpentine concrete that converges downtown. We sit facing the south end of South Central, with its tiny houses and their tiny yards, its rundown churches and schools, its lack of freeways or greenery. From up here you can't tell how rusty the cars are, how filthy the streets, how tattered the sidewalks.

PART TWO

19

The beautiful, delicate object nestled at the end of your auditory canal has a complicated shape. On one end of your inner ear, the snail shell of the cochlea spirals down before rising upward into the concentric loops of the semicircular canals. Those fragile, overlapping archways make careful circles before feeding back into the nubs and nodes of vestibules, which descend into the trunk of the cochlea to start all over again. It's a self-contained system. You can trace it with your finger like an Escher drawing, unsure where it begins, unsure where it will end. You are moved to think like a sculptor: you would love to have been the first to design this elegant form, or even to re-create it.

The whole system becomes only more elegant when you learn how it works. Every last spiral, from the snail shell to the archways, is hollow and filled with fluid. If you were to slice apart this delicacy and look inside, you would see an even more intricate system held within, an underwater labyrinth of looping chambers.

Much like the perceptive areas of your tongue being divided into sweet, sour, spice, and salt, different receptor cells in the cochlea are oriented to specific pitches. Sound vibrations cause fluid to sway against receptor cells, producing nerve impulses that travel to the brain.

Perhaps your inner ear is a leftover piece of your evolution, a souvenir from the oceans that cast you on their shores 365 million years ago. A fish with four legs, sliding onto land, breathing air through the spiracles in its skull, was somehow unable to shake the object lodged in its head: a fluid-filled snail shell that maybe even now carries the scent of salt water.

This organ isn't responsible just for translating sounds into electrical messages. The archways of the semicircular canals sit at three different angles so your brain can distinguish up from down, left from right, and the tilt of diagonals. It can tell these three different types of motion apart because while the inner ear stays fixed in place, moving as you move, tilting as you tilt, the fluid filling its chambers always stays upright, like water trapped in a rolling cylinder.

Your inner ear tells you where your body is in space; it orients you even when your eyes are closed. But if small crystals float freely in these tunnels, you lose your horizon. These particles knock against these receptors, signaling that your head is moving no matter how motionless you are. Likewise, if the hair cells that serve as sound receptors get damaged, you'll be plagued with constant, albeit nonexistent, noises.

Hearing and balance sit so close to each other, and intertwine so carefully. It's not surprising that sounds themselves can change your sense of center.

20

My phone vibrates from its position on the passenger seat. My father is calling. I don't answer. I'm headed into my old neighborhood today, the grungy part of Hollywood, flat and residential. I drive past boutiques and kitsch-loaded storefronts until I see the corner strip malls that used to greet me daily, the ones that have store names so generic they seem to address only the most basic human needs. Chinese Food. Flowers. Barber Shop. Car Wash & Star Tours Maps.

Over the last few weeks I finished all my requirements for A & O Ambulance—the driver's training, the last of the physical testing and immunizations—and picked up a few shifts on 12-hour "day cars" out of headquarters while I waited for my permanent spot at Station 710 to open up. I've been told that before I start working my regular 24-hour shift I should get a navy blue zip-up jacket for the calls after midnight. Today I have a new basic need. Uniform Store. Although A & O doesn't issue these jackets, nothing else is company approved. Purchasing a work-related clothing item is especially painful right now. Depositing my first paycheck actually made me feel more broke than before.

Whenever Dad calls, we have the same conversation: "How's work?" "Work's fine." Even when I was unemployed he would ask, "How's work?" And I would answer, "Fine." But if Dad leaves a message, he always closes with one of his sayings, usually Irish, some joke or idiom, some blessing or toast or one-liner. Some of the sayings are funny, some are not, some I have heard a hundred times since birth. He'll attempt an accent now and then, his voice growing deliberate and robust, the syllables rolling and multiplying, and it always reminds me of being a kid sitting in his lap, how over the years I learned the timing, could recognize by the intonation and tug of his smile when I was supposed to laugh, at which line comprehension should be dawning on my face. By the time I grew old enough to understand, I no longer knew if these sayings were funny. They were already broken in, comfortable, a piece of my childhood; Dad's comic delivery was a measuring stick for my aging. It's my favorite thing my father does.

After picking up the jacket, I stop by Hollywood High to watch a cluster of skateboarding kids stare down the famous Twelve Steps. They sit or stand, leaning on their boards, simultaneously awkward and cocky, working up their will. I watch a teenager take flight—he has that glorious mid-air suspension—but then his body tips at the wrong angle and he's spilling and rolling by the time he meets the ground again. The board speeds away merrily. He stands up and walks it off. Never has it been so clear to me that this form of glory also involves convincing your brain concrete won't hurt.

The sun is setting by the time I get to Ayla's neighborhood in Silver Lake and park my car on one of the narrow, all-but-vertical streets.

Dad's voice rambles on about traffic on the freeway, an accident on the road that made him think of me—he hopes I'm being safe out there on the ambulance. "And Piper," says the recording. I'm waiting for it, already smiling, ready for the same buildup as always, the slowing of syllables, the deliberate pauses, the much-treasured coda, ready to form the words along with him and mimic the intonation, my father's particular brand of gruff-and-pleased delivery. "Remember, my dear, try to turn the hearts of your enemies. And if you cannot turn their hearts, at least turn their ankles, so you will see them coming by their limp."

It's with excitement and a slight sense of dread that I propel my body up the narrow, winding stairs that lead to Ayla's bungalow. As is my habit, I count as I climb. I admire the view—snaking freeways, the blurred red and white of speeding cars, all blooming under the kind of colors a smog-filled sky only enhances. This is what beauty looks like in Los Angeles.

Lately I've been watching a lot of nature shows, at work if it's slow, or late at night when I'm winding down. There are some species that don't just procreate, they mate for life. The albatross attends a breeding dance every year, observing its elders, imitating the steps, posturing, and vocalizations, and after years of practice, finally woos the mate of its choosing and settles down. Great hornbills sing duets to assure compatibility, seahorses link tails and flutter side by side, and elephants wander off from the herd in pairs to taste trunks and wrap tusks. But I relate more to the horror stories of insects who eat their mates during or immediately after copulation. Every time I walk up these stairs, I find myself thinking it's not too late to run away, and then I have to remind myself that if I never saw Ayla again, there are so many things I would miss. I have never found falling in love anything less than terrifying.

She answers the door and we have an awkward moment where we figure out how to greet each other. Whenever I see Ayla it's like we're meeting for the first time. She can be restless, distant, distracted. Vigilant even. But she softens eventually. Her focus settles, her voice finds its wry cadence. During our half-hug greeting, I kiss her on the cheek.

The setup of her studio is simple enough—the bedroom is the kitchen is the dining room—but the space feels large because of the hardwood floor, the windows, the minimal decorations in shades of orange and brown. A round table with two chairs occupies the middle of the room; a queen-size bed extends out from one corner. Along the wall that faces the hill, a two-burner stove and a refrigerator act as bookends for the kitchen sink; along the opposite wall sits the careworn centerpiece of Ayla's home, a bedraggled yet inviting coffee-colored leather couch, onto which Ayla and I now sink.

"I lost my job," she says.

She's seated but not comfortably—it looks as though at any moment she's going to spring from the couch and run laps around the room. I ask her what happened.

"There's this customer, comes in every single day, little angry man, always wears a khaki jacket. He's got this mustache—" She raises her hands as if to show me the shape of it but then continues. "He always goes to the coffee bar and orders the same thing. A cherry Danish, a quadruple latte. Every day except weekends."

I ask what kind of person needs that much caffeine.

"Right? Anyway, it's actually a double latte with two extra shots of espresso, and he calls it a 'red-eye,' all proud, as if it's something he invented. He gives explicit instructions, no matter who's working, no matter how many times they've made it for him. He wants a double latte in a *medium* cup, don't burn the milk, add two extra shots of espresso *after* the foam—"

I make a sound like a buzzer going off and she laughs.

"Yeah. My friend Lettie got me that job, and before he left the place, Lettie started a… tradition."

"What?"

She grins. "Decaf. The past year or so I've been working there, most of the time he gets a completely decaf red-eye. Four shots of non-caffeinated espresso."

I burst out laughing. "They fired you for that?"

"No. I don't even work the coffee bar. They fired me because I agreed to switch shifts with someone and then forgot to go."

"But I don't—"

"It's not the first time, Piper. I'm sure you've noticed by now I don't have the best memory." I follow Ayla's gaze to the quivering AC unit across the room from us, built into the wall by her bed. Small gray strands of dust splay out from the vents, rippling in the refrigerated air. "It's a dumb job," she says. "I didn't want to be there forever. But I'm going to miss that little angry man."

Ayla hasn't talked much about her memory problems, except to say she's been "off the notes" for about two years. She used to tape reminders on every surface—every wall, every cupboard, every door—to help her remember basic things, like to lock the door at night and take her keys with her in the morning, to set the alarm, to water the plants she kept killing off, and also to remind her of the order in which to do things, like put water in the oatmeal before putting the bowl in the microwave. Eventually she was able to switch to putting reminders in her planner, and most of the notes came down.

"Ayla, I've hardly even noticed your memory problems."

"Because I've been doing so well. That's what kills me. Katrina—my ex back in Wisconsin—we were together about a year before she couldn't take it anymore. I was so forgetful all the time, needed help with so many—" She jumps up, grabs her planner off the round table, waves it at me. "I've been doing so well with even the little things, like trash day and watering the cactus. Then Mark had to go and ask for a shift trade because it was his kid's birthday—she wants to be a veterinarian when she grows up and has a hard-on for some stupid monkey at the goddamn San Diego Zoo—and I was in a rush to catch a bus, and thought I'd remember to deal with it later, and I didn't"—she tosses the planner on the couch, it bounces and lands near my hip—"write it down, I didn't motherfucking *write it down.*"

On the open pages of the sprawled planner I read my own name. In the rectangle representing August 5: "Piper mom left ii you told banshee." August 6: "Piper heli full code cookies." August 9: "Piper 28 movie hand swim nerd."

"I'm in here?"

"Well, yeah."

"I'm a nerd?"

She looks caught. "That must have been something you told me, maybe something someone else…" She notices the heat in my face. Sitting down, she picks up the planner and looks at it. "Swim nerd," she says. "I think you were telling me about what's his name, your hero—"

"Michael Phelps? He's won twenty-two Olympic medals."

"Right, him." She flips through more pages, the vein on her neck standing out. "On our fourth date, you told me about your brother's birds, last week you said you've never been to Europe but you want to go to Spain, and—I can't read this. After your first full arrest, you ate cookies?"

"Ice cream."

"Well, there you go, I wrote it down wrong, another fucking—"

I grab her face with both hands and kiss her. "No, Ayla."

She tilts her head back. I rest the side of my face on her shoulder, my nose almost touching her neck. Eventually she says, "Someone told me once, you don't get better, you just figure out how to deal. I thought I'd figured it out."

I think of the teenager at Hollywood High, the way he kicked up the back edge of his skateboard while hanging midair above a flight of concrete stairs, how his arms stretched to either side of him for balance, the board pirouetting underneath high tucked legs. I could see it in his face, the moment he took off, he knew he'd never nail that landing, yet he took off anyway and almost did.

"Let's go on a road trip."

At first there's no response, then she lifts her head. "What?"

I don't tell her the truth, that although my regular shift doesn't start for a few more days, for me to leave town I'll have to give away the shifts I just picked up to make some extra cash.

"You don't fool me. I know how much EMTs make." She's considering it. "I'm not broke, you know. This is my uncle's place, I rent it for cheap. Plus I get disability."

I haven't ever thought of her as disabled. "Is that a 'yes'?"

She's watching me closely. "Listen, Piper—oh, *crap*."

"What?"

She places her forehead on her knees and wraps her fingers around the back of her neck.

"Ayla, what is it?"

"I don't drive," she says, her voice muffled.

I try to remember the dates we've been on, how she arrived and left from each of them, slowly coming to the conclusion that not once have

I ever walked her to her car as a way to say goodbye. "But everyone drives in Los Angeles. You mean you don't have a car?"

"I mean I don't *drive*."

"Ayla?" I want to touch her somehow but feel so awkward. I squeeze her shoulder. "Why not?"

"I get vertigo."

"Dizziness?"

"Well, yeah, but I get it in really bad episodes. If it happens while I'm…"

"I can barely hear you."

She lifts her head. "The last time I tried to drive, I got a massive panic attack. It was too much. People crossing the street, people parking, people *looking* for parking, the lights, the signs—so many signs—everywhere you look. I got the sweats. Couldn't breathe. Couldn't remember what I was supposed to do."

"How do you get around?"

"Bus."

"Doesn't that take forever?"

She makes an exasperated sound. "It takes ten minutes to get to work—or it used to. Thirty if I walked. People in Los Angeles are funny about their cars. Besides," she pulls at the hair hanging down over her face, "you'd be surprised what you can get used to."

I recognize how insensitive I'm being. "Sorry. Just took me by surprise, that's all. I thought—"

"Everyone drives in Los Angeles?"

"I guess I deserve that."

She bolts from the couch. Grabbing a roll of paper towels and a spray bottle of cleaner from under the kitchen sink, she squats in front of the AC unit and starts cleaning up the strands of dust. As I watch her wipe down each slat on the vent, I feel as though I'm no longer in the room. My tongue is swollen, immobile.

When I finally speak, my voice sounds like a petulant teenager's. I ask her if she still wants to go, and tell her I can do the driving.

She shakes her head, a guarded expression on her face. "Do you really want to do this?"

And suddenly I know she's not just talking about the road trip, and she's as terrified as I am. I go to her, remove the bottle and the towels from her hands, and make her follow me to bed. She doesn't resist. When she lies down, I climb on top of her, straddling her waist. I can feel her heat through my legs.

"Where should we go?"

She squeezes my hips, hooking her thumbs on my belt loops. "How many days off do you have?"

I slide her gray T-shirt up and kiss the soft place just above her belly button, then slide it higher and kiss the birthmark on her sternum. "Do you really write down what we talk about?"

"It helps me remember. I don't want to keep asking the same questions."

"That's so romantic."

"You better not be making fun of me." I can tell that she recognizes my sincerity but she's embarrassed anyway.

I press my lips against her eyelids and tug lightly on her hair. "I'm not," I keep saying. "I'm not kidding, Ayla."

The moment passes and it's like I never saw that vulnerability flash across her face. She finishes taking off her shirt and removes mine. I rest my bare stomach on hers and feel the quiver I always do when we're skin to skin, the reminder of how much my body wants this body. "My next shift is Wednesday," I tell her.

"How about somewhere on the coast?"

"I want to go to Monterey."

"Monterey it is," she says.

As she unhooks my bra and slides her hands across my back, I can feel the strain in her dropping away, the lifted shoulders melting down into their sockets. This is where we reverse: she slows down, gets patient. I fumble with her belt, trying to get her undressed before my excitement makes me even clumsier. There are plenty of times when she's distracted, her focus split in a hundred directions, but these are always the moments when I have her full attention.

When we're naked she rolls on top of me. She does this thing that kills me, every blessed time: she puts her fingers into my mouth, follows the crooked path of my teeth and the shape of my tongue, before putting her hand between my legs.

21

The I-5 is jammed in a few places, and my right toes itch for the depth of the gas pedal—nothing deflates the start of a road trip like traffic—yet I find it impossible to be anything but cheerful about my current situation. We listen to pop music and sing along loudly, laughing at ourselves; Ayla tries to get truck drivers to pull on their horns and they stare blankly at her. When we finally begin the grapevine climb, there is nothing to see, because everything is a sloped and treeless brown. The radio will play only static.

"Want to play a game?" Ayla asks. "You'd like it, it's a logic puzzle."

She gives me a scenario and tells me I can ask her all the questions I want in order to solve it, but only yes-or-no questions. Scientists have been working in Antarctica and find the perfectly frozen and preserved bodies of Adam and Eve. The question is, how do scientists know these bodies belong to Adam and Eve?

"Perfectly preserved as in, flesh and hair and everything?"

"Yes."

"Carbon dating?"

"No."

The traffic starts to loosen; the cars recover speed. I sit up straighter and move over to the fast lane. "Are they wearing clothing made of extinct plants?"

"No."

This continues all the way past Bakersfield, and Ayla tells me she knows a lot of these puzzles since they were popular with her unit while she was overseas. The puzzles helped distract on long convoys or after the card games got dull.

"I'm always afraid to ask you about Iraq," I tell her, "but I don't know if I should be."

She swings her feet onto the dash; her toenails are painted silver except for where the polish has chipped off. She leans forward, scratching at the polish. "You ever get that feeling, almost like you want to walk out of your own skin? When I'm with you, it's the opposite. You're steady. I like how steady you are. It makes me not want to bring up certain things."

"So I'm boring?" I tease. I place my fingers around her neck and rub my thumb down a tight cord of muscle. Then I ask her what she thought about the war when it started, what she thinks about it now. At first she doesn't say anything, then she sighs and says, "Here we go."

Her response is long and complicated, as I figured it might be. She starts out by telling me about the vegetable garden she and her mother used to take care of, how when she was stationed in Iraq—"in country," as she says—the few times she got to call home, her mother would give updates on how the carrots and fava beans were doing, and Ayla would sit inside the phone tent in 110-degree heat, her Kevlar helmet in her lap, and try to think of what to say.

When we finally turn off the 5 and take the 46 west toward the coast, stopping in Paso Robles to eat a late lunch, she's still not finished. I can feel the four hours of driving in my lower back and knuckles. We stop to get gas in King City and stretch our legs again, getting lost inside the gas station.

It's more like a mall inside, a sprawling mecca of gaudy key chains, mugs, magnets, hats, and T-shirts. The mechanics' section has air fresheners, sun visors, and license-plate holders that say RIDE IT LIKE YOU STOLE IT, and the food area has an entire wall dedicated to beef jerky.

"It's hard to explain," she says when we're back in the car. "I don't support the war, not knowing what I know now. I ran off to join the army for the same reason as everyone else—9/11—but I also wanted to get the fuck out of Wisconsin. I thought I was ready for something bigger than me, something I could believe in. And all of that got fucked. We got fucked, while a few politicians made money on our corpses, and there never seemed to be a reason for it. I'd like to think we did some good over there, but I'm not sure we did."

"That's exactly what I've been trying to say."

"Right. But the difference is, you don't know shit about it. When I came home, half the people around me didn't even realize there was still a war going on. Thousands of people dying and they thought the conflict was already over." She cranes her neck to look at a billboard we're passing. It says something about being a real Californian. "You know what I miss from home sometimes? Deep-fried cheese curds. That stuff is delicious."

I follow signs for G16 and turn onto a two-lane road by the name of Carmel Valley, which has walls of bright green vegetation on either side and winds through a series of hills. She's right, of course. My daily life changed very little in the last nine years, no matter what the headlines had to say.

"I got so reconfigured with the brain injury," she continues. "My friends kept saying I wasn't acting like myself. And certain things I remembered being good at, I wasn't good at anymore."

"Like what?"

"Like my perception is a little bit off, all the time. I used to know how to work with my hands; I could fix up my old car, work in the garden, build things. Now what used to be intuitive is skewed. Or things like logic puzzles. I couldn't solve one now if my life depended on it."

We drive for a few minutes in silence. Then I ask, "Did the scientists figure it out by using equipment?"

"No."

"Tools?"

Her face scrunches up. "Are you fucking with me right now? You asked that already."

"So they could tell just by *looking* that they were Adam and Eve?"

"For the last time, yes."

"What the hell kind of scientists were they?"

"Yes or no only. The funny thing is, deep down you think you're going to be fine—even in the middle of a war zone you think this—and then all of a sudden *you're* the story, you're the one people are talking about. 'My friend Ayla hit her head and now...' At first I wanted to stay close to people from before. Because they knew me. And then at some point that stopped feeling true."

"Is that why you came to California?"

"Go west, brain-damaged one."

I fake-punch her arm, trying not to laugh. "Stop it." But she's laughing, too.

"Did you get anything out of it? I mean, maybe a new appreciation, or a different way to look at things? You must have been so—"

"Pull over."

"What?"

"Now."

Ayla's eyes are squeezed shut, and she's pushing herself back into the seat, arms locked, hands gripped on her thighs, as if she were trying to stop the car with the force of her neck against the headrest.

I find a turnout. Before I come to a complete stop, Ayla throws open the car door, sticks out her head, and pukes. She does all this with her eyes closed, hands reaching for support as she leans out into unseen air. I hear the sound of liquid hitting dirt. Then she sits up and wipes her mouth.

On nausea/vomiting calls, we use the acronym OPQRST to guide our assessments. Onset, palliation, quality, radiation, severity, time. Her eyes are still closed; I touch her back gently, as if to let her know where I am, and ask, "Ayla? When did you start feeling sick?"

The shoulder blade moves slightly under my palm. She leans against the door frame, her head tilting at a wistful angle. You know you're in trouble when the person who just vomited looks beautiful to you. "The road's a little squirrelly," she says. "Must've set it off."

"Has the nausea been constant since it started? Or does it come and go?"

Ayla presses the pads of her fingertips into her temple, as if her head were a basketball that could be spun between her hands. "I'm trying not to let it get away from me. If I open my eyes right now the whole world is going to be completely flipped."

The only thing worse than watching her experience something intensely uncomfortable is knowing there isn't a thing I can do to help. I try to think of something funny to say. "Are you sure you're not faking it?"

She doesn't answer.

"Maybe you just don't want to talk about Iraq anymore."

"Big faker," she says.

"If I was really going to be an EMT right now, I'd ask— *Oh*." My hand jerks up from her shoulder as if touching something hot. "They didn't have belly buttons."

"No," she says. "They didn't."

It's dusk almost, the sun is low in the sky, and it's hard to see, because the landscape has a pinkish tinge and softened edges. My car's headlights come on automatically and I see a small shape crawling about ten feet in front of the car, its front four legs reaching tenuously for the asphalt from the dirt of the turnout. It's a tarantula. There's another one, a few feet from the first.

"Ayla?"

"Yeah."

I tell myself it's fine, just a couple of tarantulas, out for a friendly stroll. But then my eyes drift farther up the road, and I lose count after ten, twenty, there might even be close to a hundred, tarantulas spreading across the next half mile or so of road, all heading in the same direction.

"What is it?" Ayla asks.

"Are you afraid of spiders?"

"Depends. Are they tarantulas?"

"Yes." I'm scared to look out my side window, or down at my lap, for fear of seeing one up close, its many beady eyes fixed on me.

Ayla starts to nod then immediately winces. "They're early." She gives her eyelids one more squeeze before opening her eyes. When her softened gaze finally comes into focus, she looks out at the road and smiles. "They do it every year. All the males are looking for mates."

She gets out of the car slowly, pulling herself onto two feet, and convinces me to join her. We stand at the edge of the road facing Monterey. Ayla keeps laughing at the way I check the ground around my feet.

"Well, at least you're feeling better," I say sulkily. All the skin covering my body is suspicious of being crawled upon.

"They're not dangerous, you know. Very gentle creatures."

I wrap my arm around her waist, and she leans against me for support. In its own strange way, it's beautiful. The tarantulas are at once bestial and delicate, and the sheer number of them makes it look like an optical illusion, like the road is rippling away from us.

"See that?"

She points behind us, back toward the car, and at first I'm scared to turn my head for fear my little Corolla will be covered in a hairy suit of tarantulas. But she's pointing at a lone spider, still crouched in the turnout. He's smaller; instead of the lifted body and multi-limbed gait of the others, he's in the locked and low position of would-be camouflage, eight legs planted obstinately in the dirt.

"He's got two shadows," Ayla says. "The angle of the sun is giving him that long shadow, like the ones we have, and your headlights are giving him a second one. You see it? It's kind of a haze, right underneath him."

We both watch as the shadows of the trees dance around him while his two shadows stay fixed in place.

"It's exactly the kind of thing that took me forever to figure out," she says. "I'd see something like that, something that seemed off, and it's not like I could tell someone—I couldn't ask why a spider would have two shadows—because I couldn't even find the language to explain why something looked off. I just knew that it did.

"You asked if anything good came out of this injury. I hate that question more than anything. People want a bright side, a success story; they want to believe things happen for a reason, and meanwhile *they* have a brain they trust. You look out at the world, Piper, you take it at face value. Because you can. My whole life I wanted something extraordinary to happen to me, and what happened instead was I had to learn everything twice, even down to the simplest things. And the worst part is, that is extraordinary. I got what I asked for."

We watch our lone tarantula for a while but he doesn't move; he continues to pretend he doesn't exist. The sun is slipping away from us. Soon he'll be left with just a yellow-gray glow, at least until we drive away. I wonder when he'll decide it's safe enough to start walking. The others are already leaving him behind.

22

We arrive in Monterey a little after nightfall. After checking into our room, we wander around for an hour, taking in the shops, restaurants, fish markets, and Cannery Row, avoiding the overcrowded wharf. I like the old-fashioned streets and quaint buildings, the smell of fish, the low-hanging burgundy archway that reads MONTEREY CANNING CO. But most of all, I love and fear this coastline, so different from our own. Rocks, boulders, cliffs. A chorus of seals not the least bit intimidated by the dramatic waves crashing over and around them. There isn't a sand beach in sight.

Choosing a small Italian restaurant for dinner, we sink into a dimly lit booth and look at the menus with glazed-over eyes. Ayla has been sober for three years because she says alcohol turns her into a crazy person. I haven't drunk around her because of this, but tonight I have a glass of wine with my spaghetti, feeling a little guilty as I do. She doesn't seem to mind. The fatigue from driving heightens the effects of the alcohol; I grow self-conscious, aware of my steps and speech patterns as we walk back to the inn in the darkness. I can't remember the last time I got tipsy on one glass.

I am in over my head. I know that.

Things Ayla and I will never be able to do together: (1) go on a road trip where we take turns driving, (2) get drunk, (3) go on roller coasters.

Once in our room, we undress down to our underwear and T-shirts and collapse onto the king-size bed.

"Babe, can you do me a favor?"

"What is it?"

"I need to do something called the Epley maneuver. Helps recalibrate my inner ear. Should clear up the last of my vertigo."

"Okay." With great effort, I sit up and try to ignore my own swimming equilibrium.

We turn down the comforter and toss the small, frilly pillows off to the side. Ayla sits in the center of the bed, facing the scalloped headboard, checking to make sure that when she lies down, her head will completely hang off the edge of the bed.

"Where do you need me?"

Sitting up, she points to the right side of the bed. "Just support my head while I lie back. I have to hold four positions for thirty seconds each."

Standing over her, I cup her temples with both palms and wrap my fingers around the back of her skull, careful not to cover her ears. Then I lower my lips to her forehead and kiss her. Together, we turn her head so that she's looking directly toward her right diagonal. "Lean me back, quick," she says. "Let my head hang off the bed, but not all the way."

As I help her hold the awkward position, Ayla shuts her eyes tight. Her eyelids bounce with a spastic fury. After half a minute of this, she says, "Help me turn the other way but keep the same angle." We move her slowly. "Oh, that's better." I watch as her eyelids smooth over. "That's so much better."

We finish with her sitting up stiffly, staring at the headboard again. After she's held that final position for thirty seconds, she relaxes and begins to move like her normal self. The change is striking. Since our first date, I've tried to picture Ayla in uniform, standing at attention or marching. It's almost impossible. At some point her shoulders started rolling forward, her eyes drifting down. Did she stand and sit and walk that way before going into the army? Or did she begin folding into herself because of her three years in it?

"Where'd you go?" she asks.

My vulnerability feels stretched taut; I shift from one foot to the other, watching her. Ayla reaches up, circles an arm around my waist. We lie back, legs entwined.

"One of these days you're going to let me in there," she says, her eyes on my forehead. "It'll be your turn to go to confession." I feel myself blush.

She rubs her thumb across my forehead, down the sides of my cheek and jaw. She kisses my temple, my ear, the side of my neck. Maybe I should say something but then I realize she's not expecting me to. She reaches to the nightstand and turns out the light.

Ayla lies on her side, back toward me, and I spoon her from behind, my arm wrapped tightly around her waist. The darkness of this room is more than what I'm used to, the mattress softer, and there's no noise other than the occasional conversation of people walking on the street below us. She makes it look so easy. Earlier she said I was steady, but what if she knew the truth?

My arm, wrapped around her waist, starts to tremble.

"I've always been kind of quiet," I say, the words rushing out. "When I was a kid, the only person I ever really talked to was my mom. At night, when she tucked me in, she always asked what I was thinking about. Or at least that's how I remember it. And I'd go on and on."

Silence. Ayla's breathing is too deep, too even. I prop myself up to get a look at her and, sure enough, she's asleep, a wistful, almost childlike expression on her face.

Peering around the room, I can just make out the shapes of the Dutch furniture, where one thing stops and another begins, the ball-and-claw feet intersecting with rose-colored carpet, the shadows blending in with the wallpaper. I remember Ayla's ex-girlfriend, who used to yell her name in the middle of the night, how Ayla would only sometimes wake up, and I continue, my voice barely audible. "I've spent my whole life trying to figure out how not to think about her. Trying to will her out of existence. And when something does remind me of her, it's like everything shuts down."

I look at the bare shoulder next to me, rising and falling with each breath. "I'm scared to tell you that I'm bi. Not that being bi is bad, but you'd be surprised. The last woman I dated, Diane, was so horrified. Like

I was *ruined* because I'd been with men, like my skin had been tainted with something foul. Why are people so weird? When Diane found out, she broke it off but pretended that wasn't why. I'm bad at math. I'm jealous of everyone you've ever been with, especially your first. I don't mean crazy jealous, I just mean—some people really enjoy this part but I find it so hard. Walking around with my insides quaking all the time, wondering if you feel the same way."

What else?, my mother used to ask me every night at bedtime. *What else?* And I would answer.

I close my eyes. Picture the road as a river of tarantulas. Think about the guy I worked a day car with the other day, whose name was Mike or Steve or Tim, how every time he laughed he said, "Ha ha ha," which made it sound like he wasn't actually laughing. And eventually I fall asleep.

23

The trailhead for the hike looks treacherous even to me. "What's the name of it again?"

She looks at the map the inn gave us. "Soberanes Point. The trail should take us right down to the ocean after we go through some kind of canyon."

We set off, Ayla leading. I'm cranky. I didn't get enough sleep; I'm hungry and we didn't bring any food with us. Now Ayla is insisting we go on a hike. But the sight of her legs is distracting—I've never seen her in shorts—and as I watch her shapely calves flex in front of me I think maybe it's not a bad idea.

It's beautiful already. Two shades of blue hang in front of us, where the sky meets the ocean. The first drop into the tree-filled canyon is almost vertical, and when I slip a little, a cascade of small rocks tumbles past Ayla. She pauses, re-centers herself, and keeps moving.

"Why'd you pick Monterey?" Ayla asks. "Have you been here before?"

"Once." She's clearly waiting for me to say more so I add, "When I was little."

"With your whole family?"

"Yes." I don't feel like talking about myself. I woke up in a panic that Ayla had heard everything. If she did, she's really good at pretending otherwise. "We stayed at some hotel that had a pier. You could walk right out to the ocean. And I saw a family of otters, and all of them had wrapped themselves up in the kelp forest."

"They'd done what now?"

"It's so they don't float away while they're sleeping."

The trail levels off somewhat, and we pause to admire the view before taking the next descent into the canyon. The rolling, wildflower-covered hills look as soft as plush toys against the severe coastline.

It was the last family trip we ever took. Dad drove up the 1 freeway in our old Volvo, loaded with games and books and clothes, and when Mom wasn't breaking up fights between Ryan and me, she was pointing out the hawks overhead, or telling us about the aquarium, leaning her head out the window, her hair so long it lifted in the wind and brushed against the back window.

In the canyon, light pokes through the evergreen and redwood trees and lands in a pied pattern on the trail. I find myself thinking about depth perception and balance, the difference between Ayla's brain before she got hurt and Ayla's brain after, all the while admiring the muscle definition in her arms as they swing in front of me and the obvious strength in her back. Her head tips forward as she makes her way down the side of the canyon, looking up now and then to be sure of where she's going, her bangs uncharacteristically swept out of her face.

"Ayla, when you drink, what is it you end up thinking about?"

She points out a tall pine that was struck by lightning, one blackened half falling away, the other half alive. "Well, I had a bit of an adrenaline problem when I came home. It was hard to settle. Alcohol made it worse, but it's also—do you remember what I told you about intrusive images?" In her tone there's a touch of pride. Somewhere in Ayla's planner are notes on what we talked about that day at Venice Beach. "I had those real bad for a while. Not that I ever did anything too drastic—a buddy of mine had it much worse. When he first got back, he drank too much one night and pulled a gun on his girlfriend. Thought he was in a firefight back in Taji."

In front of us the trail forks, the left path taking the higher road and the right one dropping at a more severe angle. Ayla hooks left without pausing.

"Shouldn't we look at the map?"

"Nah, we want this one. It'll curve around and then drop down to the beach."

I look behind us, trying to memorize where we've come from, and see a smaller trail up the hill to my far right. Five hikers lean their weight into the incline; all of them have walking sticks that look like ski poles. When I turn my head, Ayla has almost disappeared. When I catch up to her, she continues.

"The way it worked, for me at least, was that some memories would sort of layer themselves over reality. So I never thought I was back there or anything—I never got confused about what was real—but I couldn't stop the images from coming."

We talk about my becoming an EMT and I struggle a little bit from trying to keep up with her and talk at the same time; meanwhile, she's charging ahead, both hands hooked lightly on the straps of her backpack. I tell her I might go into nursing, that I've always found medicine interesting. Probably because she can hear the breathlessness in my voice, Ayla stops walking and retrieves the water bottle from her backpack. Passing it to me, she asks, "What's the real reason?"

"How do you mean?"

"Saying you might want to go into nursing is not a reason to become an EMT."

"Oh. I got tired of feeling helpless, I guess. I went through a rough patch, had a bad breakup, that kind of thing, and I just wanted to feel like I was doing something."

Along the steep wall of the canyon, one tree is growing sideways, its trunk curving up toward the sunlight. Ayla takes the water bottle I hand her without looking at me; she seems preoccupied.

"Bad breakup how?"

"I got lied to a lot."

"How long were you and she together?"

"Four years," I say, not bothering to correct her.

"Well, she sounds like a little whore."

I laugh. She crouches down to put the water bottle back in the bag. "How does it feel to save a life?"

"Exactly as good as you'd think it would." I dig the toe of my hiking boot into the ground, bringing the smell of pine and saltwater earth. "Ayla?" I stomp on the raised dirt, flatten it. "What did you see?"

She stays balanced in a low squatted position, hovering. "Well, when a body's been blown up there's not really any blood left. Just… I don't know, burned stumps of *parts* of humans. Sometimes all you see is a femur or two in a pile of ashes. And then the flies, everywhere, tons of them—for years I'd shut my eyes and see flies covering everything. Explosives in the carcass of a goat, the face of my buddy right before he got killed. He was there one minute, and then he was gone. There and gone. There and gone. You know. The usual shit."

She stands up but still won't look at me; her eyes have an unfocused look. Slinging the backpack over her shoulders, she says, "A friend of mine got raped by a guy in her unit, and when she tried to report it to her commanding officer, he didn't believe her. One day she walked into the mess hall, walked right up to him, and pointed a gun at his head."

"The commanding officer?"

"No, the rapist."

"Why didn't the commanding officer believe her?"

"He probably did, but if the rapist was a good soldier…"

"Did she kill him?"

"No, me and a few others took her down before she could fire. Later she told me—she said for weeks after the rape, she just kept trying to get through it. That's how she put it. She'd wake up every day, go out on assignments, try to avoid the guy, try to do her job, day after day she kept pushing through, and then one day she woke up more clear-headed than she'd been in months. That was the day she walked into the mess hall with every intention of killing him."

She looks at me with an air of resignation. "When I got back I kept trying to be normal. I'd drink with my friends, with my family. I'd have one beer and be thinking about that stuff, and then I'd *keep* drinking to try to stop thinking about that stuff. And meanwhile, no one wants to hear it. People ask the dumbest—just the dumbest questions. You're sitting there, watching a football game." She draws a circle in the air in front of her forehead. "*Trying* not to think about all the horrible shit in your fucked-up little head, and they're saying things like 'So how hot is it in Iraq? I hear it's pretty hot?' Or 'Did you kill any bad guys?' And you want to—you just want to strangle them." She pauses. "I mean, not really."

"But kind of."

"Yeah."

The air gets cooler as we descend. I listen for the sound of the ocean. Occasionally there's a bird call, but other than that it's quiet. My stomach whines for food. The trail looks less and less like a trail; it gets increasingly cluttered with shrubs, branches block the way, and sometimes I lose the thread in a pile of rocks before finding it again. I scramble over a fallen baby redwood that even sideways is taller than I am, and once I'm on the other side, I struggle to find anything resembling a path leading away from it. "Maybe we should check—" I start to say, but Ayla's gone.

People like to think that if you get hurt or lost, an EMT is the perfect person to be with. If Ayla were hurt somewhere, if she broke a bone or passed out or got attacked by a mountain lion, and assuming I was even able to find her, I'd be useless. I don't have anything on my person, no phone or flashlight, much less a jump bag or any meds. I guess I could make a tourniquet out of my shirt and a thick branch if I had to.

After some futile searching, after calling Ayla's name a few times, I go back to the fallen tree and lie down. My back against the striations of the trunk, I look up at the redwood canopy. All the trees seem to lean in toward the radius of my vision. I remember hearing once that you're supposed to stay in one place when you get lost, so you're easier to find.

She should have let me look at the map. She should have listened when I told her the hike seemed dangerous. At some point I will have to tell her that I have also dated guys, and it's entirely possible she will do what Diane did: assume I am actually a closeted lesbian, or a straight girl experimenting, and dump my ass immediately.

Behold the praying mantis, bright green head balanced on her body like a teacup on a pin, leaf-wings like coattails, devouring her mate after sex and starting with his head. Falling in love is so dumb. I'd rather be home in my bed eating a ham sandwich. She's lost. We're lost. What does it matter? I was sunk before our first date. Why can't I be like Marla and find someone who's safe and practical? I remember Tom standing in our kitchen and the answer comes to me immediately: because Marla's dating someone who probably looks apologetic when he orgasms.

I wanted to come to Monterey because coming here is the last happy family memory I have, but now Ayla and I are separated, and lost, and the sun is going to set soon, and I'm starving and cranky and cold and tired, and even if I found mushrooms or something to eat they would probably be poisonous, and for all I know Ayla fell to the bottom of a ravine.

"Piper?"

I sit up so fast my ass slides against the grooved bark. "Damn it."

"Having fun?"

"Where did you get off to?"

She looks sheepish. "Took a minute to realize I'd lost you and then when I tried to backtrack—"

"There was no trail."

"Right." The map the inn gave us is in her hand. She shoves it into her pocket, climbs over the tree I'm sitting on, and walks back in the direction we came from, moving so fast I practically have to run to catch up with her.

"Hey, I think I should lead the way back to the car."

"Not finished yet, more hiking to do."

"What? That's ridiculous! We've already gotten lost once."

"Don't be a quitter. You call that getting lost? The ocean is just this way." When she finds the fork in the trail again she veers down the steep slope.

"Fuck that!" I yell after her.

She turns around, startled, her arms stretching out to the sides to catch her balance. "Excuse me?"

"You haven't let me see the map even *once*, it's going to get dark soon, and I was *worried* about you, Ayla, I thought you were sick or in trouble somewhere, and all you've been thinking about is this stupid hike?"

She stares at me. Her expression is thoughtful. "Do you really want to do this?"

My hands are throbbing. My head hurts. "Do what?"

Ayla makes a looping gesture with her finger that ends pointing at the sky. "This." Climbing back up to where I'm standing, she digs the map out of her pocket. "Here you go." The folded paper in her offering hand is a creased, once-glossy brochure.

I take it from her, mumbling thanks.

She's very close, her face scrutinizing mine. "What's going on?" Wrapping her hands around my wrists, she shakes my arms, causing my elbows to flop in their joints. "What do you need right now? Hungry? I've got something in my bag, I think. Here." She fishes out a bag of trail mix, obviously old, the raisins a pale version of themselves, the inside of the bag plastered with the dust of peanut skins. "Well, I'm sorry, that's not too appealing—" But I take a handful and shove it into my mouth and it's delicious, crunchy and stale and sticking in my throat. I can't look at her. The inside of the brochure reveals a green oval with crisscrossing trail lines but no landmarks. The back is an advertisement for perfume.

"It says there are spectacular views," Ayla says. "I thought it would be nice to see something spectacular."

"You don't care about the views," I say slowly.

"Not really. What I want is to finish this hike, because now the whole thing is pissing me off, but if you don't want to we don't have to."

"There's something I should tell you. Should've told you. I'm actually bi."

She considers this. "Meaning you've fooled around with guys or meaning you've been serious with a guy before?"

"Both. I mean, I've known pretty much my whole life. Had a crush on Billy Mendel in first grade, Sara Janssen in fourth."

"What's your stance on monogamy? If you're dating a girl, do you feel like you also need—"

"Very. Very monogamous."

"Good." She shifts the backpack on her shoulder. "This relationship you've been talking about—"

"It was actually with a guy."

"—did you and he talk much?"

It takes me a minute to register the question. I nibble on peanuts. "I don't know. We did a lot together. Threw parties, went out a lot, saw different bands. He taught me how to— No. We barely ever talked."

"And he cheated on you?"

"Yes."

"When was this?"

"We broke up two years ago. I haven't really dated anyone since." I'm surprised when she looks at me with a friendly expression.

"Want to hear something funny?"

"What's that?"

"I didn't used to be into girls at all."

"What?"

"Yeah. Before I hit my head, I liked guys. In that first year after the TBI, when I'd made most of my recovery, I started looking at women completely differently. At some point I realized I'd turned gay."

My shock is impossible to mask. "But that's *incredible*."

Ayla nods. "I know."

A breeze comes through the trees carrying the smell of seaweed. Ayla gestures up the hill, toward where my car is parked. "No," I say. "Let's finish it."

Still stunned, I follow behind her down the trail. At some point I notice her shoulders are shaking. The backpack bounces more than it should with each step.

"You asshole!" I scream, catching up to her and almost knocking her down. "I can't believe I be*lieved* you."

She's almost convulsive from laughter, her eyes are tearing up, and she's radiating pure joy. "You should have seen your face," she says.

* * *

It takes another thirty minutes to reach the ocean, and when we do, we trudge toward it, exhausted, holding hands. We find a seat in the flattest part of the landscape, on a pile of smoothed-over blue stones, and stare out at the half-moon shape of the shoreline, the craggy rocks, the swirling breakwater. Feeling calmer than I have in weeks, I ask Ayla the question I've long been wanting to. She's quiet at first. She finds a thin branch among the stones and breaks it in half repeatedly. When there's nothing left to halve, she sprinkles the fragments. "The day I got hurt," she says, "we were running security on a supply convoy. Going down a road that always had IEDs."

Her face looks hollowed, her dark green eyes almost blue. I watch her hands, the restlessness in them.

"By my second tour it was truly hell. I was there for the fall of Baghdad, but it didn't take long for things to get really messy. Kids, ex-soldiers—hell, it seemed like everyone but us—knew the location of hidden ammunition dumps buried throughout Iraq. After a while it was impossible to tell who hated Americans and who didn't mind them, so you just expected everyone wanted to kill you. Hajis used rocket-propelled grenades, mortar attacks, IEDs, land mines. They packed vehicles with explosives and detonated them next to a target. And of course there's the suicide bombers."

She finds a new branch amid the rocks and inspects it, begins plucking at it, removing small pieces from one end. "Everyone's nerves were shot. I mean, it felt like a matter of time. You'd hear things—people getting blown up every day, losing limbs, eyesight, hearing, whatever. You'd listen to the stories and feel in your gut that you were next. I'd been hit by a few already, but nothing serious."

"Hit by what?"

"IEDs. Improvised explosive devices."

"How many times?"

"I don't know—probably two or three times? But we just kept going. No one was badly hurt."

Ayla tells me that on the day she got hurt, the IED that detonated was much stronger than any her unit had encountered before. Probably the device had been assembled from several projectile explosives, and linked together by a daisy chain of single charges. She found out later that the bomb had completely destroyed the vehicle in front of her, killing everyone in it, as well as flipping over several other vehicles in the convoy, including hers.

She doesn't remember any of this. When the vehicle in front of her blew up, and blast waves, sand, and shrapnel hit her Humvee, lifting the two-ton vehicle off the ground and throwing it onto its side, what she remembers are overlapping cries of "IED!" "*IED!,*" the air filling with a frantic "*aiee.*"

Later she would wake up in Germany and then at Walter Reed; she would meet the new version of herself over and over again: the shuffling steps, the coaxing memory games, the lessons on how to multitask, how to follow a conversation even when music was playing. She would meet her anger over and over again, too. She would endure the torment of watching people recognize her as someone other than who she had been.

In the actual moment of the explosion, Ayla shut her eyes tight. She heard the sand raining against metal, the piercing cries layered over the echo of the blast; she pictured a woman floating. A woman with a sad, fierce face, her long dress and hair whipping in the wind. Somewhere between losing gravity and slamming against foreign earth, Ayla was back home in Wisconsin, being tucked into her childhood bed, listening to her mother tell their favorite ghost story.

24

All the cells in your body replace themselves many times over the course of your lifetime, with the exception of neurons. What sprung to life remains until death: neurons of varying size, width, length, and complexity, neurons shaped like shooting stars, like trees, like insects—as familiar in appearance as they are startling and indescribable—with names like "spiny stellate" and "star pyramidal." This alien machinery is part of you, as biological as your bones and eyes and teeth.

When you think about neurons, you think about your brain, about spidery cell bodies stretching out in all directions within the confines of your supercomputer's gelatinous folds. But what about sensory neurons, the layers and layers of them, living just under the surface of your skin? If you want to talk about emotions, if you want to talk about what's visceral, you start here.

Every memory ever formed starts with sensory input. All experience begins with the subtlest of subconscious observations: the location of your hands in space, the textures of all the surfaces intersecting with your body, the weight of your clothing, the temperature of the air. Your experiences start with your posture, how relaxed or tense your shoulders are, if you're hungry, if you need to pee.

Picture your skin, the body's largest organ, stain-resistant and waterproof. Picture the peripheral nervous system like the tentacles of a jellyfish, nerves shooting out from the cracks of your spine, white-hot and responsive, winding around bones, snaking across neck and clavicle, twisting through the muscles of hands and feet. These nerves culminate in neurons, embedded in your skin, raw ends clawing for the surface, as if trying to break the seal where water meets sky.

Some sensory neurons specialize in pressure changes, others in temperature, and still others in the spatial arrangement of your limbs. They work together to create a composite picture. Your emotions aren't based on singular input—after all, when your face grows hot, that flash of crimson could be a sign of shame, or of blushing happiness, or of visible fury. What distinguishes your emotions is how all the various feedback integrates. Say your sensory neurons collect the following observations: your clothes feel tight, your seat uncomfortable, your voice too loud. As you sit, fidgeting—eyes retreating into their sockets, the skin of your forehead constricting, your jaw clamped tight—your amygdala stiches together these incoming sensations and singularly labels them *anger*.

Expansive breathing + bursting sensation = *joy*.

Rising pulse + trembling hands = *fear*.

Keep in mind, what science has yet to quantify or comprehend is the mechanism by which your past gets triggered. Old emotions spike abruptly, with piercing, visceral conviction. You smell the stink of the long brown cigarettes your grandmother used to smoke, and you can see and sense and hear her, the way her hip bones jutted out from flower-patterned dresses, the yellowed fingernails gripping your shoulder, the dry-as-a-leaf laugh. All this visceral sensitivity, stored in your antennae-studded nervous system; your skin all that separates you from constant daily stimuli. And you, a living conduit.

25

During our last night in Monterey, Ayla's body startles mine awake, her muscles twitching in her sleep, and at first I'm in a panic, tumbling toward reality from a dream, my hair plastered to my neck with sweat. I listen hard and hear nothing. My eyes adjust in the darkness; I realize it is actually very early morning, that today is Sunday, our last day here. Her muscles twitch again, a small spasm in her lower back that travels to the hand curled underneath my shoulders. Impulses course through reflexive limbs; I think of sparks of electricity like frenzied fireflies—glowing, darting, bursting, extinguishing—all without ever having had a particular destination. Just before falling back asleep I am seized with the conviction that I must remember this, tomorrow, when I am on an ambulance, but what exactly I must remember is not clear.

26

I arrive at Station 710 before 7 a.m. and finish a full rig checkout and restock. I'm grateful to be back after my time at headquarters; it's easy enough to settle into my old routine from training. At 0659 my new partner arrives and dives for the phone, calling Dispatch to clock in before he'll be considered late. After he hangs up, he comes out to the lot and lights a cigarette. He takes note of the finished checkout form, balanced on the bumper, while I squat by the large tires, checking their tread and air pressure.

"You don't have to do that," he says. "I looked at them just last week."

I don't believe him but don't say that. Our introduction is clumsy—we don't shake hands—and I'm distracted by the way the sour suck of his cigarette creates two freckle-covered ravines between his cheekbones and jawline.

William Leone is about twenty-five years old, very tall and pale, with thin auburn hair that sticks straight up. Wide brown freckles cover his entire face, so much that it's hard to see what his features look like underneath. With the narrow-framed look of someone who should be lean, whose body should create the shape of a long thin reed, he isn't and it doesn't. A bit of a paunch fills out his uniform, just above where the belt cinches up his pants, and his arms look soft and unused.

"They always stick me with new hires," William says. "I bet you're pretty green."

Proceeding to lecture me in what is meant to be a voice of exhaustion, he insists on being the driver rather than the attendant, emphasizing that he doesn't like being in the back with patients. He doesn't like talking to them, assessing them, or doing paperwork on them, and—because I'm new—I should pay my dues, in blood, vomit, and paperwork. I look behind him at the parked Silverado truck, plastered with fire department stickers.

I note the LAFD undershirt and belt buckle. It's so obvious he wants to be FD someday, so I remind him that the majority of fire department calls are medical runs.

"Or did you not want to be a firefighter?"

He doesn't like this, either.

Our first call comes in at 0948 for a difficulty breather, and William warns against acting as navigator. "Do *not* try to map me!" he yells over the sirens.

"All right, it's just how I was trained."

"I know some tricks and shortcuts it's gonna take you years to figure out. Put your goddamn Thomas Guide away."

William likes to tell me what I do wrong. The way I fill out a rig checkout form is too detailed (don't bother to put the mileage), and I use incorrect radio speech (say "en route," not "in route," and say "copy," not "copy that"). His refusal to let me drive the ambulance makes me feel like a little kid denied rides at Disneyland.

We park in front of a peach-colored residence, drag the gurney up the driveway and down the little walkway that leads to the back house. Near the open screen door of what looks like a shack, a circle of firefighters and police officers stand, looking down. Our patient lies facedown on the cement, his arms bent awkwardly underneath him, his slightly bloody face covered with ants.

I don't want William to know this is my first dead body. I listen as one of the firefighters confirms absent lung sounds, absent pulse, fixed and dilated pupils. I observe rigor mortis and dependent lividity for the first time, having learned in EMT school that these are "definitive signs of death," along with putrefaction and decapitation. Ruth used to warn me that calls come in incorrectly sometimes, and I find myself wondering about the caller, how close that person got before deciding to disappear.

"Is that blood?" A cop points to a small red blotch underneath the man's right knee.

I squat down along with one of the firefighters. We grab the man's shoulder and waist—his skin is so cold even through my gloves, probably from lying on concrete overnight—and dislodge him. When we roll him onto his side, his arms come with him. I watch my hands to make sure the ants don't transition from crawling on his face to crawling on me.

"A body you can turn by the ankles," the firefighter jokes. We all look to where his right knee had been.

It's a push pop. The man has been lying on top of an unfinished push pop, one of those frozen sherbet treats with cartoons on the side. After noting this, and that there are no signs of trauma, we roll him back to where we found him, which doesn't feel like the right thing to do, but no one wants to look at his face.

William gets permission from Dispatch to post at Vermont and Vernon.

"Why?" I ask him.

"I need a couple things," he says.

He parks at a 99-cent store, and as resentful as I am that he didn't ask for my permission, I go in.

The store's aisles are stacked with gaudy trinkets. There's one just like it in Hollywood where I used to live; when I was practicing to be a bartender, I would throw parties and go to the 99-cent store for supplies, neon tiki shot glasses and tiny foldout paper umbrellas, cheap limes and generic mixers. I'm trying to remember the names of all the stupid drinks some of the customers at Mad Dog Bar & Grill liked to order, names like Naked Girl Scout and Red Death and Painkiller, when I almost collide with Jared. He's coming around the corner of the hardware aisle, holding a tube of toothpaste.

"Piper?"

"Jared."

His hair is cut too short, exposing pronged and angry-looking temples. He's lost weight but he was always a little skinny. It's Aim toothpaste he's holding, a brand I've never heard of; he's chosen the kind made especially for sensitive teeth.

I'm surprised by his beaming smile; he looks like he wants to hug me. After a small lean forward, his arms lifting, reconsidering, Jared settles back onto his heels. "You look—it's great to see you." He takes in the uniform, the badge, even looks at the boots and nods, as if he can see the steel plates hidden underneath the skin.

"Firefighter?"

"EMT."

He looks appropriately impressed. "That's so great."

He tells me he's teaching at Hydrian Art Center, over by USC.

"Still living at—"

"Yup, you wouldn't recognize it anymore. Just redecorated, made a new lamp for the living room, turned out pretty good."

We talk about our old neighborhood. My favorite hole-in-the-wall noodle restaurant has closed; he reminds me how the place inspired me to put *togarashi* chili powder on absolutely everything for a little while. His technique classes are always filling up; he's trying to sell a collection of hand-blown plates at some fancy boutique. I still love him; I still hate him; this stuff never goes away. He tries so hard to appear effortless; there's always something awkward about him, a little off, which is maybe why I labeled him as some kind of kindred spirit in the first place.

"Is the EMT thing full-time or you still doing gigs as an extra?"

"Hell no. The same week I turned in my last round of dues, that assistant director was such a prick I couldn't take it anymore."

"He was a piece of work."

"A strange one. Definitely."

"He had a thing for you."

"What? No. He was into blond wannabe starlets and his poor wife had—"

"Blond starlets and you. He wanted to give you that speaking role in— what was that movie?"

"No, the first AD thought I should get that line. I'm telling you, Ben despised me."

"Same difference. He wanted to rip your clothes off."

It's still there, some kernel of attraction, a nudge at my center, the distant memory of how good the sex was, all mixed up with the feeling of having been duped, of wishing for triumph in a stupid situation when there's none to be had. As if he can sense a weakness in me, Jared leans forward and says, "I've missed you, you know? It's really good to see you."

He used to leave small sculptures around the apartment for me, bits of tangled glass with specks of opaque green and curving turquoise, and other creations, too, like the time he welded two five-by-seven steel plates to a hinge to make a kind of book, small and heavy in your lap, and even though the pages inside were empty, waiting to be written on, you could close the book and secure it with a giant padlock as if it held secrets. Somewhere in my unpacked box of belongings is that book, the key to the padlock taped to buffed steel, the pages inside still blank.

"Jared," I tell him, "I don't ever want to be friends with you."

"I know," he says.

We smile at each other then, even break into laughter. As we walk out to the parking lot I mention Ayla, and, for the first time since she and I started dating, I settle into the news. I am not hung up on him anymore. I finally crawled out from hiding, and, anyway, look at him. Jared tells me he is dating someone named Christy, who he talks about in an offhand way, like it's new still, like he hasn't made up his mind how he feels about her, but then he mentions they've been together for over a year.

"You're as big a dick as ever, you know that?"

"What's that supposed to mean?"

"How many people did you cheat on me with, anyway?" He doesn't answer. He draws himself up and leans his head to one side, the way he always did when he was pissed. Four years we were together. It's so easy to imagine him talking about me in some offhand way. For all I know, Christy could be living with him, wearing his engagement ring, and Jared would still make sure to leave himself a way out.

William comes out of the store carrying a bag filled with candy and energy drinks. "We got to go," he says.

"Do we have a call?"

"Nah, they just need us back. Two-car got a move-up."

I don't look back or say goodbye. Jared stands there, next to the same broad-nosed orange Chevy pickup truck he owned the day we met, and watches me walk away.

Of all the days to be slow. By 1200 we've run only a couple of calls; I met the two-car crew briefly before they left to post in Malibu all morning. William and I have already taken to avoiding each other. I sit at the dining room table with my laptop while William watches television. I look up EMT-related blogs, rants, chats, journals. I start a list of medical slang, the acronyms and nicknames these kinds of websites like to throw around. PFO. Pissed and fell over. CATS. Cut all to shit.

TF Bundy. Totally fucked but unfortunately not dead yet.

"Good weather today," William says. He's slumped so far down in the recliner I can just see spikes of his hair and the tops of his ears. He waves the remote control at the screen, where a woman with a white-blond bob, black eyebrows, and a V-neck sweater points at animated cloud clusters. "It's always going to be good weather when Sherri's showing lots of cleavage."

AGMI. Ain't gonna make it.

Code Brown. Patient has defecated. Code Yellow. Patient has urinated.

"Yes!" William says, when he finds a rerun of *Rob & Big*. "Do work, son." He throws the remote control onto the seat of the nearest recliner and coughs without covering his mouth.

AMF-yoyo: Adios, motherfucker, you're on your own.

A black sedan glides through an obstacle course, its windows too tinted to see any sign of the driver. A man's resonant voice layers over a symphonic swell; he promises a better life because of new mattress technology. A woman with teeth so bleached they look removable discusses wings on maxi pads and pours tinted liquid from a glass beaker. William has grown still; it's possible he's fallen asleep. I search websites and find a few more acronyms to add to my list. CC. Cancel Christmas. DILF. Doctor I'd like to fuck.

What bothers me the most is that I should know, better than anyone, what untrustworthy people look and act like. That's my inheritance.

At 1302 we get a call for a "man down" outside a shopping mall. This kind of description is as vague as it gets. It can mean anything from a medical cause (syncopal episode, seizure, low- or high-blood-sugar diabetic, stroke, heart attack, drunk or drug overdose) to a traumatic one (assault, stabbing, gunshot wound). The man could be sleeping or he could be dead.

William and I arrive at the Slauson Super Mall, more of an indoor swap meet than an actual mall, where you can buy anything from stripper shoes to speakers to fittings for the bling on your teeth. The fire department arrived before us and located our patient, standing in the parking lot near the awning-covered entrance. He's dressed in loose clothing, khakis and a half-unbuttoned shirt, and he looks meek, a little uncomfortable, a little sad. When asked what hurts the most, where his pain is, what his reason was for calling 911, he says the same thing over and over.

"I can't function."

We walk him to the rig, sit him on the gurney inside, and the lead medic and I climb into the back. The barrage of questions begins. Pain in your head, chest, abdomen? Difficulty breathing? Is there ringing in your ears, is it difficult to see, can you squeeze my fingers and wiggle your toes, do you have heart problems or diabetes, do you feel confused, weak, dizzy? Have you fallen, been hit or bruised, can you describe how you're feeling, do you have any pain anywhere, has this happened to you before? What have you had to eat or drink, what medications are you taking, what kind of medical problems do you have? Drugs, alcohol? Anxiety, stress, panic attacks?

"I can't function."

He's alert and oriented but to every other question says the same thing: he can't function. He's not taking meds, he ate lunch not that long ago, he feels "warm" from standing in the sun, he doesn't want to hurt himself or anyone else, and one more thing: he can't function.

At first it's kind of funny, then it's annoying, then it's sad. The lead medic sits there, asking, asking—going through his store of medical information, the mental checklist. Interrupting, I report the guy's vitals one by one. His breathing, pulse, and blood pressure are fine; his lungs are clear bilaterally. His blood is fully oxygenated and traveling to the farthest reaches of his body. His pupils are equal, round, and reactive to light, his skin signs are normal, he's not altered in any way, and his blood sugar is perfect.

There is a moment of silence and we all sit there. "All right," the lead medic says. He thinks for a moment. "Was there any hospital in particular you wanted to go to?" The man shakes his head. William mumbles something about our tax dollars as he shuts the back doors.

The two-car on B shift, 7102, consists of the puffed-up Steve Chang, who makes impressive use of the equipment in the exercise room, grunting, and the docile pre-med student, Phil Hall. When we arrive back at station, we find them yelling at each other from the recliners as they play a video game. Even sitting down, Steve's physique is noticeable, his lats and triceps inflated, like the orange floaties kids wear in pools. Phil's curly brown hair frames his pleasant face with springs, and a mustache crouches on his upper lip. A & O Ambulance's policy on facial hair allows mustaches but not beards; most of the guys appear too young to grow either. William sinks into one of the recliners with a bored expression.

"How was it?" Steve asks without looking up, the controller twisting violently in his hands.

"We totally saved a life," William says.

Phil's use of the controller is less frantic, more precise. "I'm sorry to do this to you, man—"

"You dick!" Steve says. He tosses the remote to William. "Here. Whatever you want." But William turns the television off. For a moment it's silent.

"You had any good calls?" I ask, spooning peanut butter onto a plate filled with carrots and celery.

"You mean like our move-up to Malibu?" Steve replies. He turns to look at me, holding his index finger to his temple like it's a gun. "Or taking in a frequent flyer?"

Phil stands up to stretch, throwing his chest forward and raising his arms overhead. "Don't forget about our hypoglycemic this morning. She was practically convulsing, and when we asked how long she'd been like that—"

"Her husband said, 'About two hours,'" Steve finishes.

"We had a guy in perfect health call 911," William offers.

"That's this neighborhood for you." Phil drops his arms back to his side. "Too early and too late. Nobody calls for anything in between."

"My worst BS last year was a dumbass who 'overdosed.' Two hits of Motrin on an empty belly and he was sure we'd have to pump his stomach."

"I responded to a paper cut once. I shit you not. A paper cut on a grown woman's pinky finger, and before you ask, yes. We transported her."

"I showed up to a residence once where an old man wanted help finding his remote control."

"What was wrong with your guy?"

"He didn't even know," says William.

I sit at the table with my plate and a glass of water and open up my laptop. They continue to joke around but I find myself unable to join in. Our patient walked out of a shopping mall on a Wednesday afternoon. He didn't make a purchase. He walked toward his parked car, or the bus stop, and then stopped dead in his tracks, not knowing if he wanted to go home, stay put, or go back and buy something. Not knowing if he was hungry, thirsty, tired, lonely, restless, anxious, sick, or crazy. Only knowing he didn't know. It's not a medical complaint, and there isn't a thing we or the hospital can do, but all the same. What do you do when you can't function? You call 911.

The day my mother left she dropped me off at school as usual in the morning. I was in fourth grade. Mom was forever forgetting things, so the entire way to Crestway Elementary I kept reminding her not only to come to my soccer practice that afternoon but to bring food. It was her turn to bring a snack for all of us to eat; I kept whining at her not to bring orange slices like she always did. I hated the stickiness the juice left on my fingers.

When we took our break someone else's mother went to the store and brought back Popsicles. I was angry Mom forgot to come, forgot to bring us anything; even orange slices would've been better than a mother who simply hadn't showed. But when I got dropped off at home, Aunt Judy was there, and Dad couldn't get a handle on anything, and Ryan told me there was a note from Mom we weren't allowed to read. It didn't take long before I was convinced she'd left because of me. I drafted a hundred apologies that night and many nights after, silently bargaining with her, swearing not to complain about anything ever again if she would just come back. And my shame deepened and warped and spread; it flared up when I had to withdraw from soccer, when I got special treatment from the homeroom teacher, when I would come home to a lopsided household, and Dad would steal sips of Scotch, thinking Ryan and I didn't notice. All through fifth grade I got into fistfights with a crew of bullies; three times I got sent home, once with a black eye. They knew, the way kids just know, that something was wrong with me. And when I graduated from high school, Ryan and I went just once to visit Mom and Sergio in Colorado, and the two of them acted more like teenagers than my teenage friends did; they did LSD together and offered Ryan and me each a white paper tab so we could trip "as a family."

I look up from the computer to find William watching me. I don't know how long I've been staring at the picture of the pale pink jellyfish that serves as my desktop image. He grabs his lighter off the counter and heads outside to smoke. Steve makes his way to the exercise room.

"What're you working on, Piper?" Phil plops down across from me with a massive textbook and an assortment of highlighters. When I realize he's referring to the list I started this morning, I slide it over to him.

Phil reads the whole thing and laughs once, a high-pitched *hee-haw* sound, which is all it takes to endear him to me. "That's hilarious," he says. "You should add 'WNL.'"

"Within normal limits?"

"We never looked."

He cracks open the giant book and flips pages until he gets to a drawing of a skinless man flexing his bicep. An inset reveals the layers of muscles found in the upper arm. "So what are you in for?" he asks.

I look at him blankly.

"You going police, medicine, or fire?"

"Oh, probably nursing. You're pre-med?"

"Yeah. I used to want to go fire but I went on a call a while back that changed all that." He tells me about a stroke patient who had symptoms for five days before his wife finally called 911. What would have been reversible by thrombolytics became permanent paralysis of the entire left side of his body.

"Too late," I say despite myself.

"It was so depressing. Made me want to go into medicine. With an emphasis on education."

Even more endeared by him, I have a moment of relief when I realize I'm exactly where I need to be. Everyone around me is in a state of career limbo, trying to figure out their next steps.

"Did you know William's last partner?"

"William hasn't had a steady partner in a long time. People get on this shift and then they bounce—maybe it's the high volume of calls, or maybe it's him. He seems all right to me, but I've never run calls with him."

Phil tells me Steve used to be skinny, but he's made a steady transformation into meathead over the last year. He highlights every single line as he reads. I watch him use the yellow highlighter for a couple of lines, then pink for a paragraph, then green for a whole page.

"Hey, Piper, there's something you should know about William."

"What's that?"

"Don't ever ask him what his worst call was."

"I wouldn't."

"No, you seem like you know better."

From the workout room, I can just make out the sound of a Britney Spears song, coming from a very tiny speaker or a very loud pair of headphones. "Is that—"

"He thinks we can't hear it," Phil says, grinning.

27

When Marla gets home from work she climbs the stairs without putting her bag down or taking her shoes off. Poking her head into my room, she says, "We're going out." She hooks her thumb in the direction of the street as if I've never been outside before. "Unless you need to get it over with here?"

We've been texting all day, so she already knows about running into Jared, the DOA covered in ants, and the series of naps I've taken to make up for getting three calls after midnight.

"Get what over with?" I ask from my position under the covers.

"Didn't you run into your asshole ex-boyfriend?" She grabs a box of tissues from my dresser and pitches it at me.

I swat the box onto the floor. "Screw you if you think I'm still crying over him."

"Good girl. Now get dressed."

We go to our usual place, Bumper's, on Santa Monica Boulevard. Every time we come here I make the same observation: Bumper's doesn't know what it wants to be when it grows up. The furnishings look like garage-sale ware, beat-up barstools and mismatched crushed-velvet armchairs, yet the floor is an expensive wood parquet. Tiffany lamps hang overhead, tiny colored panes of glass making careful awnings over subdued light, but arcade games with flashes and bells take up one corner. Besides the fact that this bar is walking distance from where we live, the Skee-Ball keeps us coming back.

Marla orders some horrible thing with peppermint schnapps in it, and I get a Jameson on the rocks. We perch on barstools at a small round table close to the arcade area, and wait for the Skee-Ball station to open up. The woman rolling the wooden ball up the ramp is wearing bright pink leggings and a striped shirt that fits tightly across her chest. Her manicure looks too elaborate to endure indoor sports. She plays Skee-Ball the same way I do, always aiming for the ring that says 50, launching the ball so hard against the ramp it either sinks right into the top ring or bounces off and falls into the gutter.

Digging through her giant purse, Marla says, "Can I show you something?" She slides toward me a thin stack of paper that's been folded in half. I open it to discover a three-page Excel worksheet, the most complicated one I've ever seen, with a tiny font and colored headers.

"What is this?"

She pulls back her sleeve to show me the eczema that's taken over her left arm, small patches of white and gray dotting her usually smooth skin. It's easy to forget Marla has allergies. She reacts so rarely—an itching in the throat here, a mild bout of eczema there—and when she went to see a doctor a year ago, she was told it would be next to impossible to figure out which food was causing it.

"Tom made it for me," she explains.

He must have spent hours. The first two pages list food allergies, their corresponding symptoms, and the kinds of dishes that contain trace amounts, and the last page outlines a plan for stripping away foods one at a time in order to narrow down the culprit. The ever-practical Marla has met her match.

"Wow."

"I know." She puts it back in her purse carefully, as if it might explode. "He's so sweet, but sometimes the way he's sweet makes me miss Alexander even more."

"You mean like where are the puppies?"

She laughs. "Yes, actually. Didn't matter what Alexander and I did, we had a good time. With Tom, like when he gave me this, he worked so hard on it, it's amazing he did this for me, but—it feels like we're doing our taxes. Where are the puppies?"

I imagine Tom at his desk, limp ponytail trailing down his back, surfing the internet for hours, fashioning an Excel sheet with all the fervor of true love. When Marla and Alexander were together, they were always talking about the future, about how much better things would eventually be. Even when Marla found out about his heroin use she insisted he was better than that, insisted he loved her despite how he'd taken to treating her. For a while, it was enough to be right.

"I'm going to try to be friends with him," she says.

"With Tom?"

"No, Alexander. He's trying to get clean now. He checked himself into rehab about a month ago."

"You didn't tell me you were talking to him again."

"Just some texting here and there. I haven't seen him. Plus, he's not allowed to have his phone while he's in rehab." She sees the look on my face and adds, "You worry too much."

I tell her not to get too close and remind her that we're talking about someone who stole her money and lied to her all the time. Marla makes a gesture as if that's all old, unimportant history. Behind her, the woman with pink leggings walks off. Marla pulls a roll of quarters out of her purse and warns me of her impending ass-kicking. When a column of wooden Skee-Balls cascades into the slot, Marla picks one up, weighs it in her hand, and looks at me with the crazed expression of someone to whom winning means everything.

"It's just Skee-Ball," I say.

She sends the ball up the ramp, scores forty points, and picks up the next one. I find myself talking about Jared, how our break-up turned me into a lunatic or a snap turtle or both. She sets a ball down and turns to me.

"It's not like it was just the breakup."

"You mean I'm always a snap turtle?"

"Piper, don't you remember? You called me from Colorado. From your mom's funeral. It took me the longest time to understand what you were saying."

"I have no memory of going to her funeral."

"The service had already started and you were bawling your eyes out, and besides the full-blown panic attack you were having about having to sit there while strangers sermonized about your mom, you kept talking about Jared, how you couldn't believe you had to be there without him. You kept saying—"

"I mean it, I really don't remember going to her funeral."

"You kept saying, 'First her and now him.'"

Bumper's has been filling in steadily, so we're surrounded by people who posture and cackle. The Skee-Ball station dings and chimes as it racks up points, and yet Marla's voice is low and clear through the roar around us. "He's also the reason you lost your job, Piper, the reason you kind of lost your mind. Why can't *I* run into him? I'd have a couple things to say to him." She sends the last ball up the ramp and wipes her hands on her jeans. "You really don't remember this?"

I think before answering. "No, I do. I thought I remembered everything—getting on the plane with Ryan and Dad, how we sat in the same aisle and didn't talk. The silver matchboxes in a glass bowl at the hotel. I carried the urn filled with her ashes in my lap, all the way to the canyon. But I don't remember her funeral. And I definitely don't remember calling you."

Marla's looking at me in what I imagine is a motherly way, as if at any minute she's going to pat my hand, or bring me into her bosom for a good cry. I'm used to this, to her treating me like I'm some kind of fragile, explosive creature. I'd be lying if I said I didn't like it.

"Piper—"

My phone vibrates in my pocket and I dig it out. "It's Ayla." Marla waves for me to answer.

Outside the air feels cool and clean; I take in big lungfuls and resist the urge to flail my arms around in space, to air out my armpits and the sides of my body.

"Why aren't you in my bed?" Ayla asks in a groggy version of her voice.

"Are you sleep-dialing me?"

"Why aren't you?"

"Maybe I don't want you to get sick of me."

"No. Come over."

"You'll be asleep by the time I get there."

"Tomorrow?"

"The day after. I work tomorrow."

"Lame."

"Make sure to miss me."

"If you're not over in five minutes—"

When she was the mystery girl at Sustainable Living I coveted all the little moments I couldn't witness, the particular way she brushed her teeth, what position she read books in, how she looked when she fell asleep. Now she's lovelier than ever and all the things that are mine—my problems, my fears, my past—are slamming into each other, making me feel grotesque, almost dangerous. I want to believe there was some kind of turning point between then and now, something to keep me from feeling so flawed and needy, but standing here, holding the phone to my ear, one arm paddling the air like a broken seabird, I know it isn't true. These are not the gifts I'd wish for her.

"Good night, Ayla."

28

William and I arrive at 8963 Budlong Street and walk inside. Our patient is a large woman with a puffed-up barrel chest who wheezes loud enough to be heard without a stethoscope. She sits in a La-Z-Boy wearing a drenched purple tank and green sweats. To get her into the dining room, William and I have to maneuver the gurney through the kitchen, and as we do, I notice the Styrofoam, plastic, and paper containers of every fast-food restaurant in the area spread out on the table and counter, spilling out of the aluminum trash can.

In the dining room I question her tentatively, writing her name and age on my glove, mentally trying to hold my nose shut against the muggy smell of sun-cooked wrappers. As usual, seven firefighters aren't far behind, and soon the lead medic, whose jet-black hair frames her face with a pixie cut, takes over the initial assessment.

Kneeling between the La-Z-Boy and the medbox, I listen to her run through the pecking order of questions as I assemble the components of an albuterol treatment kit. It's a little like putting Ikea furniture together without any instructions, but I finally figure out which way is up, screw the threaded plastic together, and pour the medication into the reservoir. William collects most of the woman's vitals, scrutinizing my blundering work. When I hand the finished product to our patient, she puffs on it gratefully, and the medication begins to vaporize. Droplets suspend in white clouds around her red face.

"How long have you been short of breath?" the lead medic asks.

"About three... *pant, pant,* days," she manages. Two-word dyspnea. I make a note to write that on my paperwork later.

The medic shakes her head. "You can't wait this long next time. Call us sooner."

I marvel at the simplicity of her blunt words. "Call us sooner." How many patients have I already seen that needed to be told that? I notice the woman's cool, sweaty skin and wide yellow toenails, and look around for something to keep her feet warm on the way to the hospital. I find only extra-large men's slippers that probably belong to her husband, but when

I hold them up, asking, "Will these do?" our patient nods desperately, nostrils flaring.

We load her up, careful not to entangle her in the tubing or the sheets. I sit the back of the gurney fully upright to help her breathe and then run to get the heavy side, since William assumes I am too much of a girl to do the heavy lifting and I am anxious to prove him wrong.

Leaning against the corridor of the CRH hallway, I impale myself with the flat edge of my already-dented metal clipboard, keeping it balanced as I write, pressing my pen through three layers of carbon copies. William meticulously cleans the gurney. It seems this is the only task he enjoys doing; he complains about everything else.

On their way to the parking lot, the two paramedics from our call stop to introduce themselves. They work out of Station 2860 on B shift, Magdalene "Dag" Ramirez and Noah Tyson. I like the look of him, the absence of flirtation, the friendly smile. Tyson's rugged face has seen too much sun but appears only wiser for the wear.

"You're new, Piper?" Tyson asks, shaking my hand with his callused one. I try not to groan—why does everyone know this about me? Although I fumbled on scene I thought I had a pretty decent hustle and sense of what to do next. Tyson sees my disappointment and chuckles. "Easy," he says. "Just a guess. I hadn't seen you around and the guys said Ruth was training a newbie."

As soon as they exit the double doors, William says in a thick voice, "Dag. So hot. Married to a Redondo Beach firefighter, but I bet you her husband's got nothing on me."

In full disagreement, I attempt diplomacy by saying, "I didn't see a wedding ring."

"Why would you?" William snorts. "Think she wants her hand degloved when she's fighting fires and pulling people out of cars?" He hangs his thumb off the edge of the gurney. "I didn't realize Ruth was your FTO. Talk about balls in your face—not only is she lame, she prides herself on being a hammer. But Carl is cool."

I don't stick up for Ruth. If William knows it will bother me to speak ill of her, he will speak of nothing else. As we head out to the parking lot, he boasts about the fire academy he completed two years ago. I am not heartless enough to hint he might not get hired (considering the kind of shape he's in now), but when he berates me I am cruel enough to hug these observations like old friends.

The nine-year-old boy stands alone next to the loading dock of the abandoned warehouse on 112th Street, blinking in the sunlight, an open fracture in his left arm, the broken bone exposed. He doesn't cry or complain. His fingers are coated with spray paint, his jeans covered in blood. On the way to Crossroads, I look at the silent little man on the gurney, his arm in a splint and sling and swathe, his open wound held tight with a pressure dressing. His gaze is on the view out the back window, the brightly lit, shabby storefronts, the perpendicular shadows of the lampposts. I think about Ayla telling me I don't know shit about Iraq, and I look at my patient, at the boy's narrow face, set chin, and slumped shoulders. He's nine years old and the large eyes on him are all that still belong to a child. I can sense that any kind word would be like speaking in baby talk to a teenager.

"Want to hear a joke?" I ask him.

"Okay."

"I only know Irish jokes."

He nods.

I tell him the one about three men who walk into a bar: an Irishman, an Italian, and a Frenchman. Three flies swoop into the bar after them, and one lands in each man's beer just after he's ordered. The Italian man plucks the fly from his glass and says, "*È bello*, it's fine," and continues to drink. The Frenchman goes up to the counter and makes a fuss, demanding a new beer from the bartender. And the Irishman grabs the fly by its wings and shakes it over his glass, yelling, "Cough it up, you thievin' bastard!"

The boy's face gives way some.

I tell him about the Irishman who tried to blow up a car, only to burn his mouth on the exhaust pipe, and about the man who invented the Irish jig because he drank too much and got locked out of the bathroom.

At Crossroads he remains impassive despite flirting nurses who offer him juice and graham crackers, and when we get him into a room he hunches down on the bed as if to disappear. As we leave, I hear Shilpa say she's going to have to call his mother, and he yells at her with real fear in his voice and then starts to cry.

Once we're in the ambulance, William says, "Gangbanger-in-training." He waits for a reaction. I don't give him one.

We drive past an auto shop with a wall of rims on display, sparkling like Christmas tinsel—custom rims, spinner rims, chrome rims with spokes shaped like flames, like blades, like spaceships. A busted fire hydrant on Gage Avenue spews a geyser of water that gets encircled by laughing kids. We pass a church you wouldn't know was a church except for the skinny cross that's precariously buttressed on the roof.

I want to fight with William, tell him how wrong he is about everything I know he assumes about that boy, but I keep thinking about what Ayla said. I don't know shit about any of this. So I stare out of the window. I spy lumps of blanket-covered humans, new graffiti on the side of the video store, a Cadillac SUV with its windows blown out, and a pair of child's tennis shoes dangling from a wire.

* * *

I eat dinner with the two-car crew at the Station 710 dining room table, my homemade meal of vegetable stew not as aromatic as their greasy burgers and thrice-cooked fries. We chatter about the latest A & O gossip; we argue over who the worst dispatcher is. Steve tells us about a new product that helps you burn twice as many calories in half the time. He swears it's legal while I make lame juicing jokes and Phil lectures us on the physiological aspects of the human metabolism. My list of medical slang hangs on the fridge door; someone has added "GPO"—good for parts only.

After washing my dishes, I pause at the front window and pop apart the blinds. William always stands in the same place when he smokes, the southeast corner of Station 710's parking lot, probably because it offers the best view of strippers heading in and out of work at the topless club next door. I'm about to ask Phil and Steve if they've ever run a call at Dy-nasty when the phone rings.

Phil waves his hand at me to go even as he jumps to answer it. Before I release the blinds I see William drop his cigarette and start for the rig in a full sprint. Looking at my pager as I close the station door behind me, I move at my usual pace, confused by William's urgency.

As I climb into the passenger seat, I revert back to my first day of training, when nothing made sense, when all the acronyms were meaningless. Somewhere in my brain is the answer, but I turn to William and ask, "What's a GSW?"

29

Adrenaline comes from your adrenal gland, that flap triangle of tissue perched on the crest of each kidney. The chemical was first discovered by a pair of Japanese scientists, who plucked it from a sheep and purified it, paving the way for the eventual mass-production in laboratories, where it could be bottled in clear glass and dubbed "epinephrine."

The primary messenger of your sympathetic nervous system, the star player of the flight-or-fight response in charge of your survival, adrenaline creates similar effects in animals and humans alike. Darwin was the first to note the trembling, hyperventilation, and signs of overheating. Yet fight and flight are not unanimous. When terrified, you become pale and weak, your mouth dries out, and you experience difficulty forming thoughts and speech; when you're enraged, your skin flushes, saliva pours from your glands, and your skeletal muscles become erratic and overactive.

In most cases, your brain instantaneously chooses between fight and flight; in extreme situations, the body fires both instincts at once. What happens to you then is similar to a mouse being fed to a caged snake. Neither fight nor flight is possible, and in a last-ditch effort to lessen the impending pain of death, all the muscles in your body seize and remain seized. The endpoint is paralysis, a numbness, an out-of-body experience.

You knew its effects long before you were ever aware of its medical uses. Find something dangerous to do, and adrenaline is right there with you, tugging on your nerves and your heart rate, quickening your breath, raising your blood sugar. When it works the way it should, adrenaline is better than most recreational drugs, and perhaps more addictive. Similar effects, of course: the vasoconstriction and euphoria of cocaine, the dissociative numbness of PCP, the sudden jolt of household stimulants. Boxers use epinephrine during fights to stanch bleeding; housewives take it to lose weight.

Of course, the real miracle of this chemical is the way it slows down time. Ten seconds become three minutes, three minutes become twenty. You feel like you're moving slowly even while frenetic, and meanwhile you're stronger than you've ever been, and feel no pain. Piece by crystallized piece, moment by suspended moment, everything becomes fluid. You are floating. You are a superhuman. You are a god.

30

We find him lying facedown on Western Avenue with a river of blood coming out of his head. There's no crowd. There is only the feeling that people are watching. Our patient, the cops tell us, is about eighteen years old. Our patient is a heavily tattooed John Doe; our patient is presumably a gang member.

Police were on scene long before us and didn't bother to call it in. They assumed he was dead. They staged out the area, put caution tape around two of the residencies, and started hunting for clues, witnesses, the killer, and the weapon. At some point somebody noticed blood bubbles popping out of his mouth. He was still breathing.

The firefighters, William, and I descend on him eagerly—already I know a case of true trauma is a coveted event—and the officers watch with bemused interest. One of them gets a notebook ready in case our patient regains enough consciousness to reveal his assailant's name. I am very much a rookie still, but even I could tell that cop to put his notebook away.

The bullet went through our patient's occipital lobe, in the back of his skull, and the larger exit wound shows that it shot out of his left temporal lobe. It must have skirted his medulla oblongata because his ability to breathe remains, amazingly, intact. Slow to form and slow to pop, blood and spit continue to balloon out of his mouth below his swollen eyelids.

I pour sterile saline over his face and wrap his wounds. All his clothes get cut off; he has no injuries below his neck, and we cover him with a sheet and strap him to the backboard.

Once we begin our transport to the Santa Monica Trauma Center, there is nothing to do but monitor his breathing. I'm in the back with Noah Tyson, who watches as I match our patient's respirations with a bag valve mask. Occasionally, he says, "Good. You're doing good." I'm not sure if he's talking to me or to the patient.

His vitals are fine but we know they aren't stable. We know we're looking at a dying person, or at most a comatose one, but his body has yet to admit the obvious. When William hits a bump in the road, the trauma dressing slips from our patient's forehead and a large geyser of blood gushes out of the exit wound. I yank my arms out of the way and slide my foot out from the new pool of blood. I have brain on my pant leg.

"Can you grab another dressing?" Tyson asks.

I watch as my right hand reaches for a new multi-trauma dressing from the top cabinet. My left continues to hold the mouthpiece in place. My body moves as though it belongs to someone else.

Tyson helps tape up the dressing and I resume the simple task of pushing oxygen into our patient's lungs. I try to slow my own breathing even while I control his. It's so strange to watch him. His body is warm and strong; he's lying there oozing with life, impossibly alive. Somebody loves him. His mother, his girlfriend, his brother, his friend. Somebody thought he was invincible. He had thought he was invincible, clearly. The muscle memory in his body reeks of it.

The trauma team at Santa Monica meets us in the parking lot and we quickly rush him into a room. They draw a curtain around him, shouting to each other through their light blue masks as they work. They intubate him, pound on his chest, administer blood, fluids, drugs. He dies among the machinery. His vital signs don't circle downward so much as plummet. Looking at him one last time, I see his body jostle limply on the bed from the team's halfhearted resuscitation. All that yelling across his body; nothing anybody does seems related to him. Where is he in the midst of it? A John Doe dead. A policeman's empty notebook page.

William doesn't think he was worth saving. He tells me this in the parking lot while rolling a cigarette up and down two long, plump fingers. I see he hasn't cleaned up the rig yet. A narrow waterfall of blood drips slowly through the perforated aluminum bumper and onto the asphalt.

Parked next to the rig, the gurney resembles a portable murder scene.

"It's good," William says, nodding. "He'll be the perfect organ donor."

Gangbangers are a cancer, he tells me. They should be rounded up in close quarters so as to more easily kill each other. As he talks I feel sick, but it's not because of the slow drips of blood or the brain matter glued to my uniform. It's because in this moment I hate my partner more than I've ever hated anybody, and we still have twelve hours together on this shift alone.

Dispatch gives us an hour at station to clean up and not take any calls. I take a shower and put on my clean extra uniform while William hoses down the rig. The two-car crew is gone, and the station feels cavernous as I listen to the sounds of running water out front. I use gloves to put my dirty uniform in a biohazard bag, not entirely sure how I will ever wear it again. Maybe I should help William scrub down the back, but instead I wander into the sleeping quarters. Muted sunlight diffuses through the blinds as I collapse onto one of the unmade twin beds. I start dreaming almost immediately.

My dream takes place in a clean white room: white walls, tile floor. John Doe lies on the floor, naked but all cleaned up—no sign of blood or brain or even the wound for that matter—and his skin and tattoos gleam in the light. His eyes closed, he's not yet dead but not alive either, and whatever life exists in him is in the form of coiled-up, angry tension. Some part of him refuses to let go.

I get underneath him. Curled up in a ball, my head lowered, my breathing labored, I inch his torso into a sitting position by leaning my body weight into his back and pushing the ground away. It's slow, meticulous work and he is unnaturally heavy. His arms hang loosely at his sides and his head tilts back, resting on my spine. His mouth is ajar and through the open channel of his throat comes a kind of smoke or light. Every time

I nudge him, his body relaxes a little more, and a little more of that strange substance slides out and escapes, curling up into the air around him.

That smoke, that light, is grateful to be going. It's grateful to be going, and the more it leaves his body the lighter and more relaxed his body becomes. No tension, no ugliness, no holding on. Just a body on a tile floor, with smoke and light in the air around it, and me crouched underneath.

31

Maybe I'm too tired to be driving. But I seem to be doing fine. I watch myself from somewhere else, and the girl who resembles me drives my car without any apparent problems.

No sleep last night for Station 710. Phil and Steve had five calls after midnight; William and I had four. Each call took a little over an hour—if you do the math, that equals no sleep. Every time I closed my eyes, desperate to taste REM, the phone rang with another call. Two abdominal pains, one chest pain, and a legitimate car accident with three patients for us—the paperwork alone took over an hour—and meanwhile the two-car got a GSW at around 0300 that everyone assumes was the retaliation for our John Doe. Their victim was sixteen years old, shot once in the kneecap, twice in the chest. He didn't make it either.

I pass Sustainable Living on my way home. There are barely any supermarkets in South Central. Only fast-food restaurants and roach coaches, as far as the eye can see. Ayla and I got back from Monterey just two days ago, but the trip feels like it happened to someone else.

"What's wrong with you?" Ryan asks. He sounds like he's eating something. I shift under the sheets to get a look at the clock on my bedside table; my body feels at least a hundred pounds heavier than usual. It's 1432.

"What's wrong with *you*?" I say into my phone.

"No, seriously. You sound weird. What's your deal?"

I groan out loud, because at Ryan's words what sleep had solved returns with a fresh ache: I remember drips of blood and the boy's swollen face; I recall the plastic bag, sitting in my trunk, holding a spattered uniform. "Nothing," I tell him. "I saw a kid die yesterday. What are you eating?"

"What kid?"

"On the ambulance. Some gangbanger got shot in the head."

There's silence, more than I can handle, so again I ask him.

"A chicken shawarma gyro," he answers absentmindedly. "Too much paprika, and the currants weren't soaked long enough."

More than anything in the world, what I want right now is to put my head in Ayla's lap.

"When can I see you?"

"I'm fine, Ry."

"Of course you are, you're always fine. Do you want to come over here? Or we could go get a drink. Just don't hole up and disappear."

"I wouldn't."

"Right, of course not. What's the name of that call again?"

"GSW," I say reluctantly.

"Is that supposed to be shorthand? 'G-S-W.' That's two more syllables than just saying 'gunshot wound.'"

"Ryan." I say it quiet and fierce, like I'm going to release a stinging rebuttal. But I can't think of one. He won't let me get off the phone until I agree to see him tonight. Despite my frustration, it is with some reluctance that I hang up.

After lying there for several more minutes, I climb out of bed and pull my EMT textbook off the bookshelf. Toward the beginning, there's a section about coping mechanisms. The EMT must make sure to get adequate sleep, exercise, and have a proper diet. Signs that someone is not dealing well with the stress of the job include, but are not limited to, loss of sleep or appetite, nightmares, abrupt mood changes, irritability, guilt, and isolation. How comforting. I already had all the signs and symptoms of not dealing adequately with stress before I ever started the job.

When my phone rings again it's Ayla. I decide I will listen to the voicemail later.

I look at the section again and start counting. There are four hundred words. In a textbook that's 1,210 pages, less than two of those pages are spent describing how to cope with stressful incidents. Things like treating victims of rape, domestic abuse, amputations, burns, suicide attempts, stillborn births, mass-casualty incidents, and dying or dead children or infants. I slam the book shut, put it back on the shelf, and shuffle around my room, hoping the friction of my socks against the carpet will create a spark of static electricity. Perhaps static electricity is a sign of stress.

32

Ryan picks me up in his restored Volkswagen bug, which has been painted an iridescent green, still has a tape deck, and needs new upholstery. On the way to Culver City it backfires in protest as he yanks us in and out of a traffic-filled carpool lane. I ignore his grumbling and search for the right radio station. My music interests have changed. Gone are the days of indie rock; none of my bands make sense anymore. Lately I listen to what the birthplace of gangster rap booms and hums on a daily basis: Ghostface Killa, Immortal Technique, Lloyd Banks. Much to Ryan's chagrin, I've even started to memorize the lyrics. I know almost all the words to J Dilla's "Reality Check."

"There can't be anything worse than a white girl trying to rap," Ryan says after I manage to utter a few streams of compressed lyrics.

At his house I make his favorite drink, a mix of Kahlúa, Coke, Galliano liqueur, and club soda—which tastes like sugary shit but when I'm with him I drink it anyway—and he makes us sourdough toast. This is what we do when we drink together: we eat thick slices of buttered toast, we drink sugary cocktails, and at the end of the evening he always tells me to take two Advil with a glass of water to prevent tomorrow's hangover and I say, "What are you, my mother?" Then we hug goodbye even though we don't usually, because the buzz of alcohol has loosened us up.

He serves the toast on one large burgundy plate and we eat standing, bent over the counter, melting butter sliding on my tongue, the cracking sound of crust being bitten into.

I borrow a soft hooded sweatshirt from his closet and disappear into it, into the smell of my brother, into the shape that his shoulders have transferred to the threadbare cotton. We take our drinks to the backyard, a plot of grass with a couple of trees and a weatherproof table set. With his usual grace Ryan manages to sit and then lie down in the hammock without spilling at all, and I slouch into a chair that's planted next to a barbecue so clean-looking you would think it was unused. For a while there's just the sound of ice clinking against glass. Even though it's not cold I pull the hood up over my head. Even though it isn't dark Ryan waves his arm so the motion detector porch light will stay on. He tells me that Malcolm is working late again. Malcolm is on a new case. A Beverly Hills homeowner has discovered a beehive in her walls, the bees are trafficking all over her house, but she isn't allowed to kill them or remove the hive because honeybees are protected under California law.

"So what's she supposed to do?"

"Wait until they swarm, and then a beekeeper will come remove them. But she doesn't want to wait. Her entire house reeks of honey. Malcolm said the furniture smells like it's been dipped in it."

Ryan asks about the GSW. I keep it brief. Just the act of telling him what happened makes me feel as though I am losing something, like the sound and rhythm of my speech pattern will codify the experience, will turn it into a story you can tell in your brother's backyard as though it is just a story. My mom left. My ex was fucking my friend behind my back. A teenager got shot in the head.

Ryan sways in the hammock. He's looking up at the sky, where not a single star is showing. He says, "What if you knew for certain he was a gang-banger, would that make a difference? If you knew he'd killed other kids?"

"You sound like William."

"I'm not saying he deserved to die. I'm trying to figure out where you're at with all this."

"I don't know. It's their lives, it's real. It doesn't help that no one gives a shit about them—his death wasn't even reported on the news. The kid who died a few hours later wasn't either. Of course what they're doing is stupid and horrible, but lots of wars are stupid."

"I heard there's something like four hundred gangs in LA now, even though undercover cops brought down a bunch. Now there's a scary job— stay away from that one."

"Not to worry."

We nurse our drinks to their last watery traces and I make another round. Ryan reaches up to take the glass I hand him. "For a while I had this thing," he says, "where I wanted to be the loud drunk girl at the party. You know the one? She's fearless. She's always having fun."

I sit down and stretch my legs out in front of me, trying to position the seat cushion of the metal chair so it pads my tailbone. After a few minutes the porch light goes out. I can still make out my brother's shape on the swaying hammock.

"The loud drunk girl isn't ever the least bit apologetic for being loud and obnoxious," Ryan says, "or maybe she isn't even aware she's loud and obnoxious. The point is, she's impossible *not* to pay attention to, and the next day, out of everyone you met at the party, she's the one you're talking about. In college I always ended up dating or being friends with someone like that." He takes a sip. "Malcolm and I have been seeing this therapist. Terry thinks I hide behind other people. Like I'm afraid to bring attention to myself even though it's what I really want, and I've probably been like that since I was a kid."

"Not everything has to do with—"

"No, I know. I just thought it was interesting." He lifts a hand high and waves it until the porch light comes back on. There's no breeze; the grass blades are as still as sculptures. I remember the nine-year-old boy and his broken arm and realize William might have been right. That little boy probably already knew the violence that would happen later, which was why he played hooky and went tagging. I press the cold glass against my ear.

"Pipes, are you getting enough to eat?"

"Are you going to come cook for me if I say no?"

"Are you sleeping enough?"

It sounds like Ryan did his research. Like he found a website that's just like my textbook. *Signs of stress include...* I realize I'm exhausted. I tell him I've been sleeping just fine.

Ryan swings his legs over the edge of the hammock. He takes my glass from my hand and says, "It's time you learned to poach an egg."

We work in a dim kitchen, guided only by the square yellow light over the stove. He pulls out the carton of eggs from the fridge and on the counter lines up a medium pot, a silver teaspoon, a bottle of rice vinegar, and a slotted rubber spoon. I make another round of drinks and complain. "Cooking will kill my buzz," I whine.

"Hush," he says. "This will be good for you." He tells me to fill the pot with a shallow bed of water and set the burner on medium-high heat. "Keep an eye on it. You put the egg in just before the water boils."

He explains how I mustn't break the yolk and mimes the correct way to crack and split an egg one-handed. The tap is sharp, deliberate. Flip the halves apart right over the water to release the contents. I open the carton and discover I have three chances to get it right.

"It's almost boiling, Ry."

"Add the vinegar. Two teaspoons."

I stir in the vinegar. He tells me to keep stirring until it looks like a whirlpool; I will drop the egg into the center pocket of the swirling water and lower the heat immediately. The egg slides out raw and viscous, a transparent slime except for the yolk and the large fragment of eggshell I get in there by accident.

"It's all right," he says.

The quickly coagulating egg white splays out like the tentacles of a twirling jellyfish, but the motion of the circling water wraps the egg back around on itself, holding it together.

When we were kids and had a lot of time to ourselves, Ryan and I got into a kind of ritual, especially on the mornings when Dad had already left for work. We'd push the alarm time later and later and then race to get ready, sliding on the banister down the stairs, using a variety of dismounts, including a kind of belly-slide-to-handstand flip that I rarely succeeded at, and when we reached the kitchen Ryan would wait at the threshold while I made a big show of climbing up on a stool, the kitchen timer in my hand, forcing him to wait for my signal. It took Ryan a little over a minute to make breakfast smoothies, and only about three minutes to pack our lunches. He'd yell and run around the kitchen, trying to beat his time from the day before, and I would stand on the stool chanting, *go go go go*.

"Did you know Mom was going to leave us?" I dip the silver spoon back into the water, trying to reattach a bit of egg white that has wandered off. "I mean, I know we've talked about this before, but I just… well, you were older," I finish lamely. "Could you tell what was going to happen?"

"Leave it, no poking. Let it cook and we'll do another one." He sets a timer for four minutes and places it on the counter. He asks me to repeat the question. I tell him to forget it.

The water slows its swirl; the egg wobbles and grows brighter colored, more substantial. I've lost track of the eggshell fragment. Ryan wishes he could be loud and drunk and not care who sees; what he knows is how to make the perfect poached egg.

"No," he says. "I couldn't tell. After she left, I thought about those weeks leading up to it, thought about them over and over. She used to have those long conversations on the phone—"

"In the walk-in closet."

"Yeah. And I remember her hugging us a lot. I used to push her away, wipe off her kisses. She seemed choked up, more emotional than usual, but… happy, too. Like anything you or I did could set her off and she'd start crying or laughing. But no. I didn't see it coming."

Ryan gets a bowl out of the cabinet and I pick up the slotted spoon, poised for an egg lift. "Do we add vinegar again?"

"No more. Pipes, things are good between you and Ayla, right?"

"She's amazing. She really is."

"Good. Then don't let her go."

33

Before Sigmund Freud and psychoanalysis there were alienists, acupuncturists, healers, massage therapists, medicine men, shamans, and witches. Some Chinese historians think the first medicinal tools originated as far back as 4000 BCE. During the Stone Age, a Paleolithic caveman (who has since been named "Bian") was the first to sharpen a stone with the intent to cure. He was the first to think of pressing on the source of someone's physical pain, cutting at it, and draining what was underneath. One wonders how long he survived his newfound line of work.

These days you can use a certain amount of historical hindsight to consider types of treatment. No one really ponders Franz Mesmer's "animal magnetism" technique anymore, even though it was wildly appreciated in the late 1700s. Mesmer's patients would tie themselves, eight at a time, to a specially designed wooden bathtub and watch in terrible suspense as he glided around in gold slippers and lilac robes. By waving a magnetic wand over the willingly trapped, Mesmer induced trances, convulsions, vomiting, seizures, and hysterical laughter.

On the other hand, those living in the Nordic and Antarctic regions are familiar with light therapy boxes to ease depression in the long winter months. The idea of light as a healing power can be traced to all ancient civilizations: Greeks, Romans, Incas, Aztecs, and the designers of Stonehenge in 2000 BCE Britain. The Egyptians built temples where sunlight was spectrally diffused, with the help of gems, in order to assign a color to each room; people were placed according to what ailed them. Red to stimulate circulation. Blue to soothe pain. Green to heal systemic problems. And so on.

Besides today's use of light, acupuncture, music, and massage, there are also the ever-blossoming forms of what must surely be an ancient idea: nature therapy, wilderness therapy, adventure therapy.

In sum, if you wish to heal what ails you, the best possible thing would be for you to receive a massage with the aid of aromatherapy and essential oils while soft tunes played in the background, surrounded on all sides by a beatific wild landscape, feeling the sunlight on your skin, the acupuncture needles in your hands and feet, the colored gems arranged on your body's meridian channels, and, of course, while incorporating the psychiatric analysis of the childhood roots of all your stress and anxiety.

Maybe there's an easier way.

After all, the very definition of any type of ritual calls for a separation from everyday routine. A solemn attention to the present moment. Which means that perhaps the most definitive healing power lies in the very suggestion of the intent to heal. Perhaps just knowing that someone is focusing his or her eyes, energy, hands, tools, medicines, ointments, and cures on you is the essential medicine.

Of course, that would also mean that the most effective and ancient form of therapy is what's known today as the placebo effect.

34

"Why didn't you call sooner?" Ayla asks. I lie on the carpet of my living room, my legs sprawled out in a Y, my hands clasped over my abdomen. She sits cross-legged, just above my head, looking down at me.

I don't know how to tell her that some part of me didn't want to call at all. That between feeling hideous all over again after running into Jared and completely shaken by the kid on the GSW call, I also hadn't wanted to give up my role from our road trip as the person who listened, who comforted, who held things steady. I wasn't ready for those roles to switch. I don't know how to tell her that I thought she might hear the story of a boy killed by a bullet and be reminded of Iraq, of her own brain injury, of friends of hers who died, and this would set her off, or at least I would seem insensitive. Or worse—the worst thing I can think of, really—maybe she would hear all about the patient I couldn't save, shrug her shoulders, and say, "What's the big deal? Why'd you let it get to you?"

So I shut my eyes. Ayla tucks a stray piece of hair behind my ear before cupping her hands at the base of my skull. She's barely said a word.

When Malcolm arrived and offered to drive me home, I called Ayla, overwrought and slightly drunk, and asked if she would meet me at my apartment. As soon as she walked through the door, the story of my GSW patient spilled out of me. Ayla listened with a look of concern. She didn't interrupt. Or offer advice, or ask questions.

"Say something."

"Like what?"

"Anything."

She's silent for a while, her hands motionless, still cupped behind my ears. "The first time someone I know died, I was in high school. There was this junior, Robbie Blakeney, who jumped off a cliff. He left his jacket and a note under a rock at the top. I didn't know him that well, but it was—everyone was so quiet the day after it happened, the teachers, the students, and I remember there was this thing some of us did where we met on the field after school and had this long moment of silence for him. After that I started avoiding my parents, especially my dad. He'd had a sister who committed suicide. I knew he knew about Robbie, everyone did, but I thought it would be better to pretend nothing had happened. One day he sat me down and said, 'Two things. This isn't going to go away, and you shouldn't expect it to. Second, don't ever be afraid to talk to me.'"

I turn onto my side and scoot toward her until my cheek rests on one of her thighs. She rubs my back in long sweeping motions, down to my tailbone and back up again.

I tell her about my dream. My eyes shut tight, I ask her, "Do you think I'm crazy?"

Soft lips make contact with my shoulder. "Not at all."

* * *

Ayla and I approach the pool. She's still dressed in her normal clothes, but I've changed into a swimsuit and towel. When she said, "I want to watch you swim," she hadn't meant right away, but although it's nearly midnight on a Tuesday evening, going for a swim suddenly seemed like the best possible idea.

She sits on the edge of a wooden lounge chair, sinking into the faded yellow cushion, her elbows resting on her knees, her hands clasped in front of her. The wrong position for lounging. She appears tense, brooding. The rippled light, cast up on the underside of her chin, makes her look like a hologram. She gestures for my towel and I shyly hand it to her. Her face breaks into a radiant smile as she looks at me standing there.

The clear body of water is too lit up from within to reflect the bright moon sagging in the sky above us. At the shallow end, I place both feet on the first step, feeling my face twist from the cold, the goose bumps climbing up my legs, the jump-start shock in my lungs. I peer down at my ankles. Under the water my feet look swollen, a different color than the rest of me. I take a deep breath and plunge the rest of the way in.

When my mother had her accident, she'd been skiing with Sergio. Somehow they'd gotten separated. The rescue team found her a few hours later, half-buried in the snow.

When we got the news, Dad, Ryan, and I took our first family vacation in over a decade. I hated Colorado, but it had never really stood a chance. When we arrived, every temperature felt wrong—it was too cold outside and too warm inside—and I couldn't get comfortable. I grumbled constantly, willing to talk about everything except my mother, everything except what little I knew or could remember about her. But the worst part of the whole thing was watching my father meet the person my mother had run off to be with. I wanted so badly for Dad to treat Sergio coldly or with bravado or with superiority, to do something besides shake his hand and start crying. I wanted to remind him of the line he'd left on my voice mail a thousand times, the one that goes, *ignore everything you can't drink or punch.*

I can feel Ayla watching me. I propel myself forward despite my sluggishness. My body struggles to shed its extra weight, to savor the feeling of water against skin, of surfacing at the right moment to drag air into my lungs.

How had the rescue team located her? How quickly had they known she was dead beyond resuscitation? What had her expression been like— surprised, terrified? Or did she not even see the tree until it was too late? Perhaps she'd been like the teenager who got shot from behind: her body giving off an assumption of pure invincibility.

When Ayla woke up in Germany, about twelve hours after getting hit with the IED, she found out she would be going home. She didn't understand too well the other stuff the doctors said, about frontal lobes and executive functioning, but she understood the words "going home" just fine.

Her first stop back in the States was the Walter Reed VA hospital, where they put her in a low-stimulation ward for about a week. A place with low light, bare rooms, hushed voices—a place that lacked the overhead paging of hospitals, where balloons, cards, and television weren't allowed. Even the smell of flowers could be overwhelming for some after that type of injury. They taught her to think of her brain as a computer that could be reprogrammed through purposeful repetition. They taught her to treat it as a muscle that required exercise, food, oxygen, and rest.

I try to show off for Ayla, changing from one stroke to another, even doing the butterfly, which I haven't done in years. But then I settle on the backstroke, my arms barely making a sound in the water. You don't have to think about your breathing when you do the backstroke, and this way it's easy to look at the sky, the giant moon looking flimsy and in need of washing, a flattened and dirty white paper globe.

My mother was cremated. When it came time to spread the ashes Sergio was too squeamish to hold the urn, my father too heartbroken, and no one asked Ryan. If I felt resistance in grieving for her, I felt none at all in holding what was left of her body the last few moments before it scattered. A body is bones and muscle, skin and organs, the lattice of cells upon cells upon cells. People use the word *organic* all the time; people use it to mean healthy, intuitive, natural, environmental, sustainably farmed. But the original definition meant none of these things: the word *organic* first meant carbon-based. As in, all life forms on this planet are built from a fundamental carbon chain or ring to which other atoms are attached. My mother's remains were organic.

We sprinkled what was left of her off Westwater Canyon at the border of Colorado and Utah, the light gray granular ash drifting down toward the river, mirroring the clumps of ice embedded in the canyon walls, and the sun shone fierce against the red earth at our feet; it lit up the orange-streaked chasm in front of us, and the glowing brightness of the earth and sky and ice glinted off the river's surface miles below.

Months later I grew perversely curious about the process of cremation. I already knew the basic principle—extreme heat and flame reduce the body to bone fragments—but it bothered me to find out that what was left after cremation was then sent through a processor, one with steel blades and a sifting system, one that turned all the residual skeletal matter into a uniform powder blend, to make what little was left even less recognizable.

It always felt like the actual moment in which my mother was cremated was when the yawning and fiery bright, orange-red canyon walls swallowed her up, the moment when I held my breath and turned the heavy urn over, hoping nothing would go up my nose, and the light gray ash shook out with a thump and dissipated in the wind.

Ayla talks about recovering from her injury as an ongoing daily decision. But since starting this job—maybe since my mother left us—I've been wishing there was a cure. A better answer on how to cope, how to comprehend things that aren't comprehensible. A proven and approved way of life, a pill, an answer, an algorithm...

Unlike six years ago, these days Ayla passes. She passes as an uninjured, non-disabled person 95 percent of the time. Only the subtle things remain—the difficulty she has remembering things, the frequent writing in her planner, the way she closes her eyes when she gets dizzy, the stirrings in her sleep.

Opening my eyes in the water, I picture Ayla in her hyperbaric chamber. Once a month she spends an hour in a cylinder full of pure pressurized oxygen, the idea being that the saturated cerebral blood will prompt regeneration in damaged neurons. Built to fit people one at a time as they lie flat on their backs, the chambers either have a submarine's small round windows or are made of a thick, transparent acrylic. Ayla prefers the submarine style. She'll even ask them to cover the windows so she can't see anything but the curved steel around her. Rather than becoming claustrophobic, she breathes easy. Having spent most of my childhood in a swimming pool, I can understand.

Touching my feet down in the shallow end, I push myself to a standing position against the suction of the water. Ayla, sitting there, watching me, with her wide, flat hands and long fingers, her strong shoulders and loud heartbeat.

Gesturing to the rippling water, she says, "You're very good at that, you know. Do you feel any better?"

"Much," I say, tilting my head, wiggling a pinky finger in my ear, suddenly unable to look at her or make my way toward the steps. She reaches for the towel. "One more thing, and then I'll get out."

I fill my lungs with air and swim to the bottom of the deep end. I stay there, cross-legged, hands circling to keep myself submerged, as if I'm about to have an underwater tea party. My hair swirls against my neck, drifts back and forth in front of my face; my cheeks balloon out; pressure builds up behind my eyes, behind the inner recesses of my eardrums. Everything is quiet.

35

"Did you sleep okay?" Ayla asks as I poke at the last of my parsley-studded omelet wedge with a fork. Except for the lone businessman reading the newspaper by the window, we are the only ones at Luna Café.

"Slept fine." That's not true; I slept like shit. And I know if Ayla hadn't sensed my restlessness last night, my constant dozing and waking up, she could at least look at my drooping face this morning and guess the truth.

"Any dreams?"

"No dreams." That's true, anyway.

"How much have you been thinking about him?"

"I'm fine, Ayla."

"No, you're not. And you don't have to be. But we can talk about something else if you want."

She's obviously waiting for me to respond.

"Let's talk about something else," I say.

My headache and lack of sleep aren't the problem. It's Ayla. As if it's not enough that she twitches in her sleep, she also grunts and sighs. Last night every time I was on the brink of losing consciousness, one of her limbs would jerk or she'd make a sound that woke me.

To change the subject, she tells me about calling home yesterday. "My dad told me about this funny thing that happened," she says. "My mom and I used to take care of this vegetable garden. I mean, it was huge. We had an area for the stuff that you had to replant annually and an area for some stock stuff that could kind of keep itself going. Anyway, after I got back from Iraq I suddenly had this black thumb, so I couldn't—"

"You told me about that already."

It's an almost imperceptible shift, what happens in her face then, but she resets quickly. Her voice comes out a little flatter. "I'm sure I did. Do you want to hear the story or not?"

"Okay." I feel crappy to have reminded her of her memory snags, but I'm still annoyed with her for reasons I can't quite understand. All she has to do to look fantastic is run her hand through her hair. She always wants to go to Luna Café, even though it's where we always go. We're already getting boring.

Ayla tells me one of the last things she tried to plant before giving up on gardening was an apple tree. She cleared a spot where the seeds could get full sunlight, only nothing ever grew. Earlier this week her mother was in the tool shed and noticed one of the walls was caving inward. When she looked at it from the outside, she discovered a three-year-old apple tree growing in the middle of some old shovels.

"Wait, what?"

Ayla grins at me. "I got it mixed up. Who knows, maybe I buried a glove where the seeds were supposed to go."

I smile back at her. "Did you tell your mom you've got a greener thumb now?"

"I told her I lost my job. She thinks it's a good thing. I've been wanting to go back to school anyway."

When I nudge her, she admits interest in becoming an occupational or speech therapist.

"I figure I can work with people worse than me," she says. She talks about Sasha, an occupational therapist at the VA center, who's been helping Ayla ever since she moved to California two years ago. Sasha's been coaxing Ayla to finish her general ed classes at West LA College and apply to grad school next fall. I wonder if that's where Ayla got the idea in the first place. "So she's older?"

"Maybe in her thirties. Why?"

"Oh, nothing. Just wondering how long these things take, you know, to go through school and get a good job." What kind of name is Sasha anyway? An erotic dancer name? I can't help but wonder if she is the reason for the vibrancy in Ayla's voice. In my head Sasha is sultry and coy, with glossy blond hair that flows straight down to her waist. But she sounds like the intellectual type, so I modify the image. Sasha coils her hair into a thick braid that wraps around one shoulder. She wears stylish black-rimmed glasses and bright red lipstick.

"Piper?" Ayla is tapping the side of a beige ceramic coffee cup. I turn my attention back to her from the window. "Where'd you go this time?"

I suggest a trip to West LA College and Ayla begs off. It's such a new idea, she says, and she's not sure she's ready.

"It's only twenty minutes from here." I signal for the check, determined to be more helpful than the brainy, sensual Sasha. "I'll drive you."

Except for a few squat clusters of offices, classrooms, and trailers, the sloping grounds of West LA College are dominated by parking lots and athletic fields. We hike up the hill in the middle of campus, looking for the Admissions and Student Services office, steering around clumps of chattering students.

"Do you see any letters?" I ask Ayla. "We're looking for C-something." She runs a hand over her forehead. "I don't know. I don't see anything." I glance at her. "You okay?"

"Just hot. I feel kind of hot."

"Are you dizzy? Do you want to stop for a second?"

"No, no, I'm not dizzy. I'm—it's fine."

A self-important crowd passes by us, talking loudly and cackling. A backpack bumps my shoulder. No one turns around to apologize. I glare at the group, trying to spot a guilty backside. Everyone carries the same thin pamphlet. "You know, I think it's some kind of orientation day," I say, turning back to Ayla.

Ayla's breaths are too shallow, too quick. Her eyes bulge; her neck and ears have sprouted crimson.

"Ayla? Are you okay?"

She slumps over a little. "Damn it."

More students approach from the top of the hill. I look around for an escape route. To the right of us there's a patch of grass with an anorexic palm tree and an empty park bench. I drag her over to it and we sit, facing a panoramic view of downtown Culver City. She puts her head between her knees and says something, but her words are muffled.

"I can't hear you. Talk to me?"

She lifts her head, revealing a stricken expression. "My heart. It's going fucking crazy, beating way too fast. I can feel it in my throat like a frog is in there. Like it's going to pop. Make it stop, Piper, please—what's it doing?"

A hundred apologies brim inside of me. I flip her left hand so it rests, palm up, on her knee. I place two fingers lightly on the thumb-side of her wrist and find her pulse. Her thumping, steady, urgent pulse.

"How is it? Is it fast? It feels really fast." She taps her collarbone. "My chest is exploding in a million directions. And I'm really hot."

"Hold on," I say. "Just a second." I have the urge to shush her, which of course is the wrong tactic.

Clicking the timer on my watch, I find her pulse again, and wait for the second hand to get to fifteen seconds before beginning the count. When the timer reaches forty-five seconds, I press the button again and do the math: 32 beats in thirty seconds. "Your pulse is 64 beats a minute," I tell Ayla, relieved. "That's a perfect pulse."

"So I'm just being a crazy person right now? Fuck you."

"Ayla." I know that just because this is an anxiety attack and not a medical emergency doesn't abate her symptoms in the slightest. "Ayla, honey, I need you to try to slow your breathing down."

"I bet you think I'm a real idiot, always telling you the same stories over and over again."

"Ayla, no, please. Try to take some deep breaths."

"I used to want to be an architect." Her words are coming out in gasps.

"I used to be really good with my hands. My fucking heart is—it's not like I'm doing this on purpose, you know."

"No, no, I know, just—please. Try to take a few deep breaths. Close your eyes. That's it. Now breathe." Ayla's shoulders rise and fall as she forces deep respirations; I'm reassured when her color starts climbing back to normal. "That's it, babe." I wrap an arm around her shoulders and kiss her cheek.

Her eyes pop open; she jumps up, pushing me away so hard my spine slams against the bench. Her shoulders are thrown back as she stands there glaring at me. For the first time I can see, really see, the physical strength of the veteran in front of me.

"What the hell do you think you're doing?"

"What?"

"Someone could see us."

"But that's—what does that matter?"

"They can't find out."

"Ayla, please, what are you talking about?"

"They'll never let me go here if they know."

I feel a chill at her words. "Ayla, honey, there's no—you're not in the army anymore. Or Wisconsin. No one cares if you're a lesbian."

She looks around, remembers where she is. Her embarrassment is obvious. She walks toward the palm tree at the crest of the hill. When I catch up to her, she's staring at the crisscrossing bark of the palm tree's base, the hairs sprouting out of it. She keeps her voice low.

"What am I to you, anyway? Between the memory shit and the vertigo and the fact that we're both broke, you want to act like it's all just dandy? Let me tell you something. I was doing just fine before I met you. I can handle my own shit, so if this is some kind of pity—"

"It's not like that."

She has the look of someone who wants very badly to destroy something. There's only me and the palm tree.

"I knew it was too soon to come here."

My eyes fill with tears. "I'm sorry."

"I'm going home."

"Ayla—"

"I'll take the *bus*."

"Ayla, wait, please..."

I try to follow, not knowing how to stop her, scared to try to touch her again. She pays no attention to my jumbled pleadings. Throwing herself down the hill, walking swiftly along the sidewalk, she disappears around the corner of Overland Avenue and Stocker Street and I'm left there, looking at an empty intersection.

36

The blond nurse glares at William. "You have plenty of saline," she tells him. "Now go away."

"I need a *banana bag*," he insists. "All those vitamins and nutrients do a body good."

We are a pretty pair, William and me, him with ashy skin from partying all night, and me with hollowed half-moons under my eyes. And yet it's oddly invigorating to be back at work. When I arrived this morning everything looked a little different—just the sight of the ambulance parked in front of station reminded me of the GSW's swollen eyelids and defiant expression—but it also felt good to have survived that shift and then returned. Seeing Phil's friendly face and hearing Steve's corny music while he worked out was like coming home.

The blond nurse is pretending to restock the crash cart but at this point she's just rearranging it. After a glance down the hallway, she turns to him. "I suppose you want me to start the line on you, too?"

He's trying to be charming; it's like watching a hyena flirt. "I'll let you put it in my femoral," he offers.

I wince as I picture the vein snaking along William's groin, but the nurse laughs. "Follow me." They disappear into the stockroom.

An ER tech I've never talked to before nods at me. News of how I handled the GSW call seems to have traveled in roughly this format: Piper did everything she could, got blood and brains on her, didn't have a breakdown afterward. The increased eye contact and nods of recognition aren't helpful; these gestures only remind me of him. People might see grief in me and change their minds.

J-Rock and Pep emerge out of Room 3, Pep pushing a stripped gurney on which fresh linen has been piled.

"Piper!" Pep says. "I hear you owe the station ice cream."

"I swear you two only ever work with each other. Why all the overtime?"

"Our anniversary is coming up." Pep raises his eyebrows meaningfully at J-Rock, who scowls. "How's William? As big a dick as everyone says?"

I know that William is the one who spread the word that I'm a good partner, a decent rookie, and that I kept my head when it mattered, but I gossip about him anyway. They tell me about how Carl almost got written up for mouthing off to a firefighter. As it turns out, the firefighter was trying to ship a legitimate shortness of breath patient without so much as a lung-sounds check or an oxygen saturation reading.

"Ruth vouched for him," J-Rock says. "So the supervisor went easy."

"Yeah, having a partner who's employee of the year comes in handy."

"I bought you a doughnut this morning."

"You're a real sweetheart."

When William emerges from the stockroom, they take that as a good time to leave.

"Happy anniversary," I call after them.

William's arms are crossed to hide and hold in place the banana bag tucked underneath his uniform shirt.

"Nice baby bump."

"Laugh all you want," he replies, uncurling his left arm to show me the line already secured on the inside of his elbow. The narrow tubing zigzags away from the embedded needle and disappears between two buttonholes. "There is no better cure for a hangover."

Our first call this morning is a man on a bicycle who got doored by an eccentric older woman. He's not wearing a helmet, just a T-shirt and ratty jeans; she's wearing a trim little hat with a large purple flower, gaudy earrings, and crooked makeup. She keeps looking at him, lying on the concrete in front of her, at the blood rushing out of his broken nose and the wrist bent at a cockeyed angle. She keeps saying, over and over, "But I checked my rearview mirror three times before I got out of the car." And she holds up three fingers as if to prove it. He responds, his speech slurred by a trauma-thickened tongue, "Then that's *three* times you would've seen me, lady, because I was *there*." And he holds up one finger before passing out.

When William and I go to load our patient, I look into the yawn of the back of the ambulance and feel my eyes burn. Turning to him, I say very slowly and deliberately, "I'm driving," and hold my hand up for the keys. To my surprise, he places them in my palm without a single snide word.

As the day moves on, William and I say very little to each other, but find a rhythm just the same. We get a call for a GSW, and en route to the residence I become anxious, my skin prickling. But upon arriving at 8421 Gramercy, we find a man who shot a hole through his own left foot by accident. He'd been cleaning his rifle and forgot to empty the chamber.

We get put on standby for a bomb threat for about two hours, twenty-five pounds of TNT. Later we find out Dispatch made a mistake—instead of posting us a safe distance away, they put us right on top of the supposed explosives.

We pick up a woman outside the Inglewood courthouse who claims a penis has been stuck inside of her vagina for the last six years, and the firefighters ask me to do the assessment since I'm the only one who isn't doubled over with laughter. I comply, scribbling down notes on their run sheet. Onset: sex with her ex-husband, six years ago. Palliation: gets worse (and grows larger) with thoughts of sex. Quality/Radiation/Severity: 9 out of 10 severe throbbing pain that's intermittent. We drop her off at CRH with a pillow under her knees, and shake our heads when Shilpa asks if we visualized the chief complaint.

I'm grateful to drive; I can understand why William never wants to be the attendant. The driving is relaxing somehow. Organized, methodical. William's brief and confident mapping instructions are impressive—he could probably navigate the entire Los Angeles area strung out and blindfolded. After getting on scene, it's just a matter of loading the patient, driving to CRH, and, afterward, disinfecting everything. If it's a Code 2 transport, drive nice and slow and even. If it's a Code 3, anticipate at least three intersections ahead, try to brake slowly so things don't shift too much in the back, and assume every driver on the road is a half-blind moron listening to music so loud it could drown out a nuclear explosion. I get a delicious shiver every time I jump into the opposing lane.

By our seventh call I'm used to the way the wail of the sirens emulates the singsong repetition in my head. *Will she call will she call will she call...* There is nothing else to do but wonder. I've left messages and sent texts. Stubborn in my mind is the thought that she won't and can't give up, that what has begun between us is simply too good for either of us to let go of, but this thought is coupled with doubt. Maybe I really don't know her. Maybe everything I thought I knew about her is a projection, hers or mine. Maybe she was just waiting to walk away. Maybe I'll be better off if she does.

"8421 Gramercy, at 84th," William says. "Just head down Manchester."

"Again?" I ask. He shrugs.

Will she call will she call will she call...

It's dark when we pull up to the little gray house. The man who lives here was having a few drinks with his neighbor when he decided to tell her the story of earlier, even reenact it for her by propping the rifle in his lap and waving his hands at the freshly bandaged foot. When we prepare to take him to the hospital for shooting himself in the same foot a second time, the man refuses to answer any questions. "I don't want to talk about it," he says, and his neighbor hides behind the sofa in order to cover her laugh. William is not so considerate.

At the hospital, my partner's mood shifts. "We need to clean it again," he says of the back of the rig. "It's starting to smell. I think blood must have soaked down into the floor plates from that kid."

During a break at station, I press my cell phone to my ear with the top of my shoulder so that I can use both hands to rattle the chain-link fence that borders Station 710's parking lot. I can't believe what Marla's saying. "You did *what*?"

"Piper, it was a one-time thing, please don't—"

"Jesus, Marla. Are you going to tell Tom?"

Marla slept with Alexander. The whole world is going to shit. Letting go of the mesh, I look down and start counting William's stubbed cigarettes. About thirty. There are others, too, but I'm counting only Marlboros.

"Please don't overreact about this, okay? Not everything is like your life. This is different."

"So you're not going to tell him. He's an addict, Marla. What were you thinking?"

"It's not like that. Does Alexander look like a drug addict to you?"

"Is that what you're basing this on? Can you even hear yourself?" Marla doesn't respond. Next door the sound of heavy bass booms through the walls of the club amid hooting and laughter. "Well, how was it?"

"It was good. Not anything like what I remembered." She hesitates. "He's lost a lot of weight. And it was… more *urgent* somehow. I don't know, there's something about spending time with him—it's like it makes me stronger."

Back in the days of my post-Jared misery, I remember Marla coming over to Ryan's place to comfort me. I barely let her talk. I was too busy spouting all the useless sayings, the kind of shit you're supposed to say, about things having a purpose, and what doesn't kill you makes you stronger. It was almost as if I was trying to cheer her up. Marla finally cut me off. "Don't do that," she said. "You're strong enough."

"Marla—"

"Forget it. We'll talk about this later. How are you? How is Ayla?"

I know that if I talk about what happened, the thin string that has been holding me up will break. Instead I tell her about earlier, how William and I had been eating lunch with the two-car crew at a fried-chicken joint when we looked out the window and saw an SUV veer into a telephone pole, so decisively the rear of the vehicle lifted up. How the driver popped out like an angry puff of smoke, tore a large stuffed baggie from where it was taped to his chest and threw it as hard as he could into oncoming traffic before turning and running down the street. How by that point the four of us were already on the sidewalk, patting our pockets for gloves, but when we heard the police sirens we said, "Guess they got this one," and went back inside to finish our meals.

I expect Marla to laugh, but she's hushed, waiting for the punch line. We end the conversation awkwardly. I slip my phone into my pocket and swivel around to head inside.

Ayla leans against my car not fifteen feet from me. She pushes up one of her thin sleeves, then tugs it back down. I mentally play back the last ten minutes, starting with when I walked outside to take Marla's phone call. Ayla must have been in the parking lot the whole time. How could I have missed her?

"What are you doing here?"

Her face is puffy, her eyes bloodshot. "I love you," she says. "You probably already know that, but I just thought, in case you didn't…"

I feel a sharp spike of terror at her words and try not to show it. Ayla rubs one shoe over the gravel, back and forth, a scrape-swish sound. "I acted like a real asshole yesterday. I came here to tell you that." She raises her eyebrows. "I guess you know that, too?"

"No," I say, shaking my head. "I shouldn't have—"

"Wait. Listen. I don't even remember half of what I said to you yesterday, but that still doesn't—what I mean is, you don't have to forgive me or anything. That's not why I came here."

It's so hard to move—my legs are stiff, my hands can't seem to do anything but hang limply at my sides—but I manage to walk toward her.

"I'm going to figure it out," she says. "The school thing, getting my degree, all that. I'm not going to let yesterday—"

"Of course you are," I say. We stare at each other. Her hair is unusually flat. "Wait, how did you get here?"

"Took the bus from Silver Lake to South Central. I must really like you."

37

I'm not sure at what point I become aware of William standing there. For a while all I'm aware of is Ayla's generous mouth, but maybe it's a noise—the sound of someone gaping—or maybe it's just his unmistakable tall and freckled presence announcing itself. When I open my eyes William's mouth is hanging open, an unlit cigarette precariously glued to his bottom lip.

"William!" It's all I can do not to laugh. "William, this is my"—I give her a quick look for confirmation; she squeezes my hand—"girlfriend, Ayla. Ayla, this is my partner, William."

"Nice to meet you," Ayla offers.

He reaches up and plucks the cigarette off his face, but even after this slight recovery, all he can manage is a nod. He heads toward his usual spot in the parking lot and lights up.

"Which one is he?" Ayla asks. "I know you… Is he the one who's always joking around?"

"No, that's Carl. William is—" In the back of Ayla's planner, she'll sometimes draw diagrams as a way to remember people and how they know each other. I told her about Carl and Ruth, J-Rock and Pep, Steve and Phil, not to mention some of the firefighters. How could she possibly keep track?

"William's all right. I used to hate him, but he's growing on me."

Around midnight at station I brush my teeth, strip down to my shorts, and sit at the edge of a creaking twin bed, arranging my pants around my boots so that with only two steps and a yank I will be in full uniform again. Ayla loves me. I have a girlfriend. I'm in love. Falling back into bed and pulling the sheets over me, I think about a story I heard long ago, about a king who learned to sleep with his eyes open in order to spook any would-be assassins. Anything is possible, I tell myself, and then proceed to sleep soundly, with both eyes shut.

William and I get woken only once, and it's obvious from the moment we step inside that our call will get canceled. The daughter had called from another state because her mom wasn't returning her phone calls; we discover the woman dead in her small, unkempt apartment, surrounded by fashion magazines and newspapers. The firefighters unstick the body from the floor and roll it onto its side to note the dark blotches caused by collected stagnant blood, as well as the unnatural stiffness of the limbs.

Someone uses a sheet to cover the body, tools and equipment are gathered, and single-file and silent we tromp out the door, down the cobbled steps, past the pool, and out the gate.

I stand in the middle of the street talking to Dag and Tyson while William returns the empty gurney to the ambulance and the police call the coroner. The fire engine has already left, but the gleaming medic squad is parked behind us, its engine still running, its lights still flashing. The rotating glare casts all our faces in horror-movie red.

"I've noticed you're pretty strong for your size," Tyson is saying. "Have you ever thought about becoming a firefighter? We could certainly use more women in the department."

"Do a ride-along with us sometime," Dag adds. "Just let us know and we'll talk to Captain Greger."

Focusing on the weight of the jump bag in my hand, I give it a subtle, unnecessary bounce to reestablish my grip. I feel so distracted by the woman in the apartment. I wonder if this is similar to what happened to Ayla, how even after coming home she would remember the corpses she saw in Iraq, the dead goat whose body hid a bomb. I had been nervous to look at the woman's face because I knew the image would imprint—I can still see the ants, the blood bubbles; I can still remember it was the left side of the dog-owner's face that got eaten off—but in the end, what choice did I have? The image I can add to the growing pile: a woman's glaring eyes, swollen, protruding tongue, the look of absolute reproach.

The last postcard my mother ever sent me shows her smiling face as small as a fingernail, and yet that tiny image is always how I picture her now. It's as if all the memories I had from being a kid got replaced by that grainy photograph.

"I've definitely been thinking about becoming a firefighter," I tell them. Tyson starts to explain the hiring process of different departments, the types of physical training; I nod to show I'm listening.

38

In photos of Ayla in Iraq, she wears tan T-shirts tucked into belted camouflage pants. Dog tags dangle between her small, round breasts, and
well-kept beige boots jut out below the perfectly cinched and tied cuffs
of her pant legs. She wears this outfit when she's at ease, smiling from
inside the tents or resting on the cots. When on duty as a Military Police
mechanic, either prepping a convoy or headed for the arms room, the
camera peers at her through dust clouds, and reveals her in a camouflage
jacket and body armor, a helmet strapped tightly to her pointed chin, an
M249 held with both hands.

These days, the slicked-back ponytail is gone. She wears jeans with
faded sneakers, soft, loose T-shirts that can't hide her strong shoulders,
and, even when it's warm outside: thin zip-up hooded sweatshirts in shades
of gray, blue, and green. Ayla didn't keep any of her uniforms or army
paraphernalia after getting discharged; she returned the entire contents of
her TA-50 back to her unit—her uniform and Gortex, the rain gear and
rucksack, but while there's more variety in color and style, even now, in the
drawers of Ayla's dresser, crisply folded stacks of shirts and socks are stored,
as if at any moment the staff sergeant will be coming by the barracks to
inspect her cleanliness.

Tonight Ayla will meet my father. In preparation, she changed her shirt
three times; when I went to pick her up, shoes were spread all over the floor
of her apartment. Now, outside the restaurant, she wears a green button-up
and skinny jeans. She looks a little panicked.

"Are you sure I look all right?"

Absolutely, I tell her.

Introducing Dad to my new girlfriend was Ryan's idea, and he was vis-
ibly shocked when I didn't resist too much. Having told myself many times
it doesn't actually matter if Dad approves, I feel relatively calm.

"Does he know about me?"

"That you're gay?"

"No, the brain thing."

"I didn't tell him."

Dad picked the restaurant, an Italian family place, Costa Mesa–style—an overpriced menu and huge portions, plenty of garish distractions on the walls to keep the kids cross-eyed, plenty of strong cocktails for the adults. Through the window I watch a small child get "Happy Birthday" sung to her by a group of twentysomethings. They're wearing fake mustaches and crowing boisterously, and, like her, I find myself charmed by the bartender for knowing how to play the accordion.

Dad walks hurriedly to the entrance, almost passing us. It's obvious he came straight from the office—he looks dressed up and slightly out of place in his suit and tie.

"Am I late? Sorry about that."

"You're fine, Dad."

I kiss him on the cheek and introduce Ayla.

"Michael," he says, pumping her hand. "So good to meet you."

When we walk inside, the hostess greets us warmly. Dad requests an outside table, where the noise level is manageable and strings of light bulbs hang over the tables.

"The doc says I got to eat healthier," he says as we look at the giant menus. "I'm thinking about going vegetarian." He peers at Ayla. "You look like you're in shape—are you vegetarian?"

She smiles shyly. "No. I just work out a lot."

He makes a humming noise. "That settles it. I'm going back to the gym."

Eventually a frazzled waiter comes to take our order, putting a basket of bread and some olive oil on the table. Dad orders a Coke and I get a lemonade; Ayla sticks to water. I raise my eyebrows when Dad asks for fried zucchini sticks as a side dish to his entree. "What? That's vegetarian."

As the waiter walks away, Dad says to Ayla, "When Piper's mother was pregnant with her, no junk food was allowed in the house. Very healthy, had to have vegetable shakes every morning. She never wanted to be around cigarette smoke, and this was back when everyone smoked. Those shakes—they smelled like I don't know what. To this day, I have no idea how she drank them."

"I heard about your ex-wife. I'm very sorry."

Dad leans across the table, one bulky forearm flattening the white cloth napkin that's arranged in the shape of a triangle. "Actually, she's not my ex-wife. We never divorced—neither of us ever filed."

I stiffen at this new piece of information. Ayla's foot finds and traps my right ankle under the table, as if to keep me from running away. She returns his smile.

"What was her name?"

"Cecelia. Cecelia Morgan. When I met her she had hair down to her butt and—"

"She always had hair down to her butt, Dad." More than fifteen years they were separated. Why didn't they get a divorce?

"No, they took almost two feet off for a wig once when you were about four. Paid handsomely for it."

Dad asks Ayla what she does for a living and she skirts it a little. She mentions her time in the Army, her plans to go back to school. When she asks him what he does, he tells her he's a software engineer. As he explains that a friend of his helped build a video game for post-traumatic stress, her eyes flicker in that way they do when she wants to change the subject.

"He said the work was very particular. Had to be extremely realistic, with options the doctors could add in, like certain kinds of buildings or roads."

"Right," Ayla says. "They even add a vibrating cushion so it feels like you're sitting in a Humvee."

"Wait, what is this?" I ask.

"They say reliving a bad experience helps it go away," Ayla tells me, "if it's in a controlled setting. Of course, with vets, the hard part is getting them to the doctor in the first place."

I try to think back to the last time I asked my father how his work was going, and how he answered that question.

"He told me simulating combat was the hardest part. There's some center in Texas where they test explosives on animals—"

"Oh, that's horrible." I make a face.

Ayla shrugs. She says her father grew up on a dairy farm, and when he was a kid a cow combusted. She talks about the theory behind spontaneous bovine combustion, and she's wearing her storytelling face now, carefully blank so as not to give away the ending. My dad's eyes light up in response.

"See, it's not just all the methane in their intestines—or the flatulence— it can't be, because if that were the case, there'd be eruptions in every cow field. Not a pretty sight."

"Or a pretty smell." Dad's barrel chest starts shaking with barely contained laughter; I can't remember the last time I saw him look so pleased.

She says if a spark lights off the fat just under the skin, the cow turns into a candle on four legs. The spark can come from an electrical field, or maybe a heat-packed haystack. "Add all *that* to a bunch of methane—"

"And you've got yourself a bovine bonfire," Dad finishes. They're both laughing now.

There's something unsettling about watching the two of them together, how easily they get along. Ayla soaks a piece of bread in the saucer of olive oil, then dabs it on the sides. Her free hand finds mine under the table, squeezes it. Dad looks relaxed and happy, his arms crossed over his chest, his tie loosened around his thick neck. What's unfolding is what I've always wanted, only now that it's happening it's still not enough. I reach for the word and find it. Family. And I can sense how much Dad enjoys it, too.

After Mom left, Ryan used to get horribly depressed on his birthdays.

Dad never knew what to do. Sometimes you could hear Ryan crying in his room even though he was trying to be quiet. Dad would ignore it for a while, then tell me to run up and see if Ryan wanted to watch a movie or something, get his mind off things. He'd hand me a slice of store-bought cake to take upstairs but never went himself, never acknowledged Ryan's grief directly. It's obvious to me now that Dad was helpless against what happened, that he had no idea how to move on and still hasn't. A memory is not a life, a shrine is not a home... but I'm no better. It's been so hard to forgive Dad for what he couldn't give us.

A song comes on in the restaurant, Johnny Cash, I think, forlorn and gruff and true, and it's too much, suddenly. I feel a little sick, a little embarrassed at my own sentimentality. Dad and Ayla are talking about UFO sightings and cattle mutilations, Ayla moving in that restless way of hers, picking at her napkin, rotating her water glass. Dad's blond hair is graying at his temples and the weathered lines in his face stop at his jawline—his large ears look soft and young. A single white hair grows wildly out of one of Dad's eyebrows. The stuff you can't see in pictures.

Our food arrives. We peer at each other's plates and at each other; we nod, hesitating before picking up our forks. It feels like we should say something, recognize the moment somehow.

"Just a minute." Dad fishes around in his jacket pocket. "I can't forget to—" He locates his plastic pill holder case, which has the days of the week labeled on each divided well. "It's my ticker," he explains to Ayla. "Not as young anymore."

"Oh, I get you." She knocks knuckles against the side of her head. "My noggin has bad days sometimes. I got knocked out pretty good overseas."

Dad fishes four pills out from a well and chases them with what's left in his water glass. He oozes vitality. You wouldn't know my father's in poor health from looking at him, but he has an ulcer, some prostate polyps, high blood pressure, high cholesterol... My father is one of my patients,

I realize. If I ran a call on him, I would suspect chronic heart failure and immediately look for the pedal edema swelling of his ankles.

I read a story once about a guy who had been a big Wall Street somebody and then he left everything and everyone and went to live off the grid, in the woods somewhere in a little cabin, eating fish and game he'd caught, buying supplies at the nearest town once a month. When a journalist tracked him down and asked how he could leave everything behind like that, his wife and friends and family, not to mention a small fortune, the man responded, "I just don't think about it."

Now Ayla is laughing and Dad is beaming. "There's only one saying I know," Ayla says, "I think it's Irish, anyway—something about arriving in heaven before hell knows you've died?"

"That's a good one," Dad says. He raises his drink. "May your glass be ever full, may the roof over your head be strong." Ayla and I raise our glasses as well, my voice unconsciously joining his, Ayla's lips moving slightly, as if she's trying to memorize the words. "And may you be in heaven half an hour before the devil knows you're dead."

PART THREE

39

By now you know this neighborhood better than your own. You've run calls at every type of establishment and household, every disreputable office and narrow stairwell, every freeway and restaurant, con home and club, all the high schools—sports injuries, fake seizures, assaults—and all but two of the elementary schools.

At the liquor store closest to station, you buy soda and energy drinks, power bars and beef jerky, to squirrel away in the rig console for the especially busy days. There is no Take a Penny, Leave a Penny. The man who owns it is Jerry; he knows everyone's name in this neighborhood but yours. To you and to all the other EMTs, he makes the same joke every time you enter the store: "Don't arrest me, Officer!" And then he laughs, and you think for the thousandth time that your uniform looks nothing like a cop's. You went in there after a shift once wearing street clothes, and an unrecognizing Jerry just stared at you and couldn't think of what to say.

Your blind spot is less pronounced. By now you're so used to the job's daily decisions, you can take the time to take it all in. There's the mansion on Slauson Avenue, your new favorite, not because of the sweet and elderly owner who sometimes drinks too many gin martinis and calls 911, but because the foyer displays a life-size cardboard cutout of Barack Obama.

You've run calls at the county jail and the courthouse, on men and women smart enough to know that claiming chest pain would get them out of their cells for a little while. You've run calls on drug overdoses and assaults where the police officer leans over and shouts, "Do you want to go to jail or to the hospital?" and even in their fucked-up state (you can almost see the cartoon birds circling), they choose the hospital.

You know which streets are dead ends, which alleys too narrow to fit the ambulance, which avenues and boulevards the easiest to oppose traffic, and when to swerve to avoid the large pothole two blocks from Crossroads. You know the patterns of the homeless, where they sleep and who they fight with, what medications they should be on. Sadie, known in three districts for her consumption of Wild Turkey bourbon, calls every day. One minute she'll be drinking alone and the next she'll be surrounded by seven emergency responders. Her joy at the sight of all those people towering over her is evident. But then she'll remember she's not supposed to look happy, so she'll scrunch up her face and moan. "It hurts," she says, in a voice withered from smoke and drink. "It hurts." And someone will make a joke, and Sadie will forget herself, and she will start cackling all over again.

You've learned which chief complaint is the worst chief complaint. When someone has abdominal pain, it doesn't matter if it's mild indigestion or a life-threatening aortic aneurysm, the treatment is the same. *Drive to the hospital.* That's it. They could have an ulcer, blood in their GI tract, kidney stones, a bladder infection, appendicitis; they could have internal bleeding from a bruised solid organ or the swollen infection of a hollow one. They could be throwing up bright red blood or vomiting "coffee grounds"—digested blood. This could have been going on for weeks or hours.

The most you can do on your way to the hospital is get signs, symptoms, and severity. The triage nurse takes it from there, but god forbid you finish your paperwork on the rig and still have even one minute to go on your ride to the ER. That's one minute more of sitting there, listening to someone scream their head off, ask for pain medicine, and tell you they're going to throw up. You can sympathize with their pain, hand them a basin, tell them no medicine is allowed until some tests are performed at the hospital, but what it really feels like you're saying is, I'm useless. I can't help you. Just sit tight in this overrated taxi and we'll get you there.

And by now you've learned the secret: in your job, it's better when there are things to do. The worst kind of patient is the one you can't help.

40

Hail Jesus God our Father please save him, save my baby let him live please…

I glance in the rearview mirror. I only have a blocked view, but I hear banging, pleading, retching, and terrified shouts, not to mention the patient's wife is sitting in the passenger seat praying her head off. I'm still pouring sweat from struggling with the 280-pound man. The one who went from dead to combative as we loaded him onto a backboard and attempted to carry him down a steep flight of stairs to the ambulance waiting below. We'd found him pulseless, his last dying breath leaving his lungs as his eyes went limp.

We did the usual to bring him back. Bagged him with oxygen, jumped on compressions, pushed drugs through an IV, stopped to shock him twice, and all the while his wife yelled at him in an unbelievably commanding voice: "Breathe, big man! *Breathe,* baby!" I thought at the time that we should bring her to every full arrest. Who wouldn't do what she says?

Because he was big, we had to four-point the backboard, and unfortunately the way out was so tight we had to lift his feet up over the banister

and carry him down the stairs headfirst, all of us squeezed together, shuffling our steps. Halfway down the stairs, all that blood in his brain, his
eyes opened and he started yelling and flailing. He probably had no clue
what had happened to him. There he was, a born-again newborn, and his
first view of the world after dying was a strange angle of the night sky, our
sweaty faces, and the beeping EKG monitor we'd balanced on his chest.

Now his huge arms thrash around and William says, "Calm down, sir,
try to relax!"

"So what happened?" I ask the wife.

She starts her story but I interrupt her right away. "What's his history
of drug use?"

Her eyes go wide and she uses her booming voice. "He does crack
cocaine!"

I nod, fighting the inappropriate urge to laugh. So the patient in the
back is a crack overdose who just got loaded up with voltage and pure
adrenaline. No wonder he's frothing at the mouth.

Please God let him go to rehab, he's been clean for two years God don't
let him die for this mistake, please God praise Jesus let him live let him live...

It sounds like a brawl back there. At this point I'm more concerned that
he's going to hurt one of my coworkers than I am about him dying again.
I oppose traffic almost the entire trip. Stupid cars keep stopping in the
middle of the road—does no one ever pull to the right? My habit of cursing under my breath while I drive Code 3 is in full force. I hope she doesn't
notice I'm countering her prayers with a string of cuss words.

We arrive at Crossroads and I fly out of the ambulance to open the
back doors. That's when I see that the walls, ceiling, floor, and doors are
all splattered with a clear fluid that smells faintly of alcohol. The two paramedics pile out; William hops down. As I stand there, stunned, looking
at the mess, he tells me that our patient threw up four times en route to
the hospital. Also, he managed to free himself from the backboard. The

slamming I heard was that of the board swinging into the rig walls.

"Everyone okay?"

Yes. Everyone knows to get out of the way of projectile vomit.

We walk into the ER with our patient very much alive, sitting crazy-eyed on the gurney, a bright green rubber airway assist still dangling out of his nose. The awaiting full arrest team looks bewildered.

"Is this him?"

"Yeah, it's him. He came back."

We move like a confused school of fish to get him into a room, unload him onto a bed, disentangle wires, hang up the IV bag, hook him up to the hospital's pulse ox, and so on. The lead medic's voice calls out over the scuffle of activity. He's looking at his run sheet for reference: "Good evening, everybody, we have a twenty-eight-year-old male overdose found pulseless, v tach with agonal breathing. Epinephrine was administered at…"

He continues. The last I see of our patient as the swarm closes in are the big man's terrified eyes. He looks no closer to understanding what has happened to him tonight.

William joins me in the parking lot and helps with the cleanup, which is unlike him, but he's in a good mood now that we had a good call. We go through a whole roll of paper towels on the walls and floor and ceiling, then use disinfectant spray and a few clean rags, and then move on to round three—a combination of germicide wipes after letting the disinfectant spray soak for three minutes.

I hear shouts from one end of the Crossroads parking lot and turn to look. There's an EMT named Peter Mohan who used to be a gymnast; he's doing his back tucks again. The nurses who smoke always goad him, and Mohan always says the same thing—"I am not a windup monkey"—and then he does a back tuck anyway.

"Where to after this?" William asks.

"I'm sick of everywhere."

He looks at his watch. "One more minute."

We are boycotting Station 710. We hate the new two-car crew. Phil and Steve are gone—Steve Chang is an ER tech at St. Mary's now, Phil Hall is living at home in Connecticut, waiting to hear back from medical schools—and they have been replaced by Andrew Yurt and Danielle Martin. Andrew is obviously in love with his partner, and the giggling way she takes advantage of this, to get out of any work or cleaning or having to lift her patients, is sickening. I tried to convince Pep and J-Rock to switch to our shift, but besides the fact that they are creatures of habit, both of them bellowed about William being a racist, and I couldn't really argue. Carl is no hope either. He and his new partner, an ex-MMA fighter, have been comfortably seated on their shift ever since Ruth got picked up by the Long Beach Fire Department. Apparently, when she finished the academy, half of her fellow graduates couldn't stand her, and the other half couldn't wait for her to become chief.

"I vote for the Manchester strip," he says. "I want to get a nap in."

"Done," I say. "I really don't care."

We clean the inside of the rig again, calling out to each other what needs to be restocked, and then drive to Station 710 to grab supplies. We don't talk about the call, but we don't ever talk about the call. We're not friends, but we do respect each other. If nothing else, when there is work to be done, we do it and save our squabbling for later.

Lately William has seemed burned out. Not just cocky, not just his know-it-all self, but crispy around the edges. I think he thought he'd get hired by a department by now, or maybe it was the call we had about two months back, the old lady with dementia who kept shrieking at her husband and left deep scratch marks along both of his arms. If I remember right, William's grandfather has dementia, too.

He started drawing comics a few weeks ago, dark, twisted comics that make you laugh even as you feel a little uncomfortable. I've been working with him for almost half a year now and never knew he could draw. One shows a withered old woman in a liquor store with skin like an elephant's; she's wearing nasal cannula attached to a personal tank of oxygen and she's purchasing a carton of cigarettes. He captured the fuck-you expression on her face perfectly.

You hear stories in the field about burnout. The consensus is that everyone goes through it at least once, and it lasts a month or so, if not longer. It can be cyclical or it can be career-ending. Some people are easy to spot, like Frankie Fisher from Station 630, whose hands shake slightly but only when he's not running calls. The first time I met him, he was sitting on the aluminum bumper of his rig, taking his own blood pressure, a habit he became so famous for someone managed to get a hold of some Atenolol and slip it into his duffel bag as a joke. Or Bob Pasteur, who tried to resuscitate a kid who got hit and then dragged by a drunk driver's SUV. To hear people tell it, the boy was so covered in abrasions it looked like his skin was gone, and his ear was found several blocks away with an earbud still in it. Bobby turned in his uniform a couple months later.

With William it's different. He's always been surly and a loudmouth. Burnout on him looks more like apathy. It's been difficult to goad him into an argument, and when he does get mad, it's something. I saw him get into it with a nurse because he didn't want to have to take a transfer patient all the way to Burbank. In the middle of his shouting he turned so red you couldn't see his freckles anymore, and the nurse, an athletic Australian man who towered over William by at least six inches, looked so alarmed I can't believe he didn't report it.

We park at the strip mall on Manchester Avenue and William steps out to smoke. I lean the seat back, turn the radio volume down, and place the walkie-talkie on my stomach so it will wake me when Dispatch calls our rig number.

I've had some bad calls. A while back we arrived at a residence to find a man sobbing into a couch and his dry-eyed wife holding a Mason jar, the lid sealed tight, a tiny human fetus curled at the bottom. And there was the woman whose boyfriend threw her out of his car on the freeway. She'd been all dolled up in a new dress, had gotten her nails and hair and makeup done, and that was the worst part, somehow, the shredded and bloody manicure.

I know burnout will come for me someday but I like to think it won't. As far as I can tell, no one escapes it, not even the lifers who have no intention of ever doing anything else. And as much as I keep telling Ayla how much I love my job, keep regaling her with stories, the triumphant and the horrific, I also keep stalling on decisions about whether to be a nurse or a firefighter or something else entirely. Some nagging part of me thinks maybe after burning out I'll know what to do.

41

She grinds her teeth but she denies it. She swears I snore but I deny it.

During the day, she doesn't twitch. But she does bite her nails.

Sometimes when her anxiety kicks in she gets distant and cold. I ask her what's wrong and she gets defensive. So I slip into being wary and introverted, reading a book while she cleans surfaces already wiped down, while she scrubs at bathroom mildew like it's personal. After busying herself for a while, she'll relax enough to allow herself to be soothed, to be seen, to be touched; she'll welcome me back into the room with joking fondness, like I'm a guest who has just arrived. I can see her constant effort to balance herself. How to live in the world, and how to live with me in it.

When we stay at my apartment, I cook for us; mostly we stay at her studio, where she makes scrambled eggs and country potatoes, tuna casserole, vegetable barley soup. We don't try to cook together. For her it is a reminder of a lesson learned anew since her injury, a not-quite-seamless reintegration into normal living. To keep it from being a struggle, she uses recipes that outline every last detail, with handwritten notes from over the years: what pot or pan or knife works best, exactly what setting to put the stove burner on. A list taped to the microwave explains what materials are acceptable to put inside, and a reminder taped eye-level on the freezer door urges her to check expiration dates before eating anything.

Although she stores her leftovers in a complicated Tupperware system she refuses to teach me, she has no objection to my doing the dishes. By this time, she's relaxed. The cooking is over, the meal eaten. We'll put music on and sing together, my hands covered in suds, her husky voice a surprising low soprano, while she waits to dry each item and put it where it belongs.

Ayla hangs out with a cluster of butch women, lesbians who seem to have read the how-to-be-a-lesbian manual, because they drive trucks and wear baseball hats, watch sports and build things, and seem to have been born into long-term monogamous relationships. More often than not, Ayla spends her time with just one of them, Annie, an ex–army sergeant who is now a security guard in Santa Clarita. Annie and Ayla don't talk much when they're together, but seem to exist on the same subdued but attentive energy, a shared vigilance for all that happens around them. At some point I realized Annie was the friend Ayla told me about, the one who almost killed her rapist in the mess hall. There's something in Annie's eyes that tells me she wouldn't still be here if it weren't for Ayla.

I went with them to the gym in downtown Los Angeles once, and watched as they worked out together, spotting each other on weights, stretching stiffly and half-heartedly, the way bodybuilders do, between reps. The men at the gym treated the two women the same as any other guy in the place: many pairs of eyes stared fixedly in the mirror, flicking from their own straining muscles to those of the women working out beside them, back and forth and back again, before seeming more or less satisfied.

Ayla's new job is dog-walking, and her reputation has spread quickly. Her charge now covers a wide spread of breeds, from a Great Dane to a malamute to a Catalan sheepdog, not to mention your basic terriers and Labradors. There's a mixed beagle/German shepherd named Rocky, an Australian cattle dog named Prawn. While the other dogs run for the ball and chase their own tails, Prawn stays by your side.

On my days off, if we stay in, I quiz her on material for the online biology class she's taking, the warm-up course before fall's fully loaded semester. If we go out, we wander through Silver Lake, passing cafés and bars and boutiques, admiring the murals. We'll go to the parks where she takes her canine clients or we'll walk around the reservoir if the pathway isn't too crowded with strollers and joggers. She'll show me a new residence spotted on one of her walks—perhaps a house shaped like an igloo, but with a porch, or a gated, pallid monstrosity surrounded by palm trees.

On nights when she gets the fierce headaches, I'll wake up, too, thinking for a moment that I heard the phone ring at Station 710, thinking I have to put my boots on and respond to a call. When I remember where I am, I throw an arm around her warm, naked waist and drop back to sleep.

Her body's burdens make her shape and density more certain. I know where her center is. I know where her edges are. I feel cocooned in her arms every night we spend together, I know exactly what I'm holding on to, and it has gotten hard to fall asleep without her weight around me.

And she has yet to strangle me in her sleep.

42

People say there are no seasons in LA, but tell that to the torrential rain. I'm sitting on the couch at Ryan's place, listening to him and Malcolm fight. Malcolm thinks Ryan hides his emotions; Ryan doesn't know why everything has to be such a big deal. Malcolm doesn't feel like his needs are getting met; Ryan rolls his eyes when he hears phrases like "I feel like my needs aren't getting met." When Ryan came out he thought he'd never have to have conversations like this one.

They seem to have forgotten I'm here. I listen to the rain crash against their little house, the rat-a-tat on the roof and the splattering on the windows. Their backyard is taking a pounding. I watch the rivulets on the glass of the back door and think about how Marla and Tom will move in together next month and I wonder what they will fight about. Marla never told Tom about sleeping with Alexander; she swears it was a one-time thing, she doesn't even talk to him anymore, but I don't trust her to tell me the truth about him. She thinks I'm "oversensitive" about the subject. In any case, I need to find a new roommate. Ayla and I don't bother discussing the possibility of moving in together; we know it's too soon. While I'm no slob, she's so eagle-eyed in her cleaning habits I would drive her ballistic. And even though I have trouble admitting it, sometimes when she gets distant I take it personally. I get needy and wounded. Sometimes I'm like a little kid who needs attention. It's worse when I'm sleep deprived, when I ran too many calls the night before.

There are other things, too, like three months ago when she wished me a happy birthday two days before my actual birthday, or how I get snarly when I see other women checking her out, which usually just makes her laugh. "I'm not going anywhere," she always says, and I pretend I don't know what she's talking about.

Now Malcolm is complaining about their sex life, which apparently has been waning for the last few months. Ryan says, "You do know Piper's my sister, right?" I've never seen him so exasperated. I take that as my cue to leave.

It's late—"oh-dark-thirty in the morning," as Carl would say—and my little car struggles to warm up as I turn the screeching windshield wipers to full blast. My car's headlights barely illuminate three feet in front of me, so when the last northbound curve of the 10 east appears unexpectedly, I almost fishtail my car. Swearing under my breath, I check my speed, realizing I missed my exit. Somewhere along this rainy late night drive I started thinking about how Ayla told me that she never masturbated as much as when she was in Iraq, how it was something about the heat, the sand, the homesick yearnings, the restless energy, the hurry-up-and-wait, the frustration that followed her losing sight of any real purpose in being there. She found stolen moments in which to touch herself, lose herself. In her almost two years of active duty, the act of self-service kept her sane.

I get to Ayla's studio, let myself in with the extra key found under the heavy wooden planter with the dead, dried-out rosemary, and slip into bed, waking her up. She starts to kiss me, half-awake, half-slumbering. I take her fingertips and guide them. "Show me," I tell her, my voice in her hair. She doesn't seem to understand and I start to move the hand under mine in small circles. "Show me, Ayla, I want to watch."

Her breathing changes. Fingers move instinctually, eyes closed as if still dreaming. When I am so turned on I can't stand it, I slip under the covers, slide down the length of the bed, and move her hand out of the way. I dip my head to take a drink. The taste is—always and impossibly—better than I remember.

I drink from her with my hands cupped under her hips, pulling her toward me. I drink from her like everything depends on it. The beauty in the sprawl of her naked body: the spill of dark hair against the pillow, the spiraling of legs, the grip of her hands on my shoulders, the twisting of the sheets.

I tease her slowly. I don't come up for air. I know she's shifted when her cries change pitch. Suddenly generous and full and savage, her moan travels from the base of her spine, reverberates through her body, and pours out from her open, arching mouth.

Only then do I stop, the last of that beautiful drink sliding down my throat. I travel up the length of her, curious fingers tracing aftershocks, and we kiss, our breathing heavy. She wraps her arms around me and I tuck my face in the crook where her neck meets her shoulder. This is how we fall asleep: the sound of rain against her bungalow, my face nestled next to hers, her arms gently rocking me, our shudders subsiding.

43

You have billions of sensory neurons, transmitting signals throughout your body, and some of the most concentrated hot spots are your lips, face, neck, tongue, toes, hands, and ears.

There are twenty-five thousand nerve endings per square centimeter of the human hand.

You have ten thousand taste buds. And forty million smell receptors.

Depending on your physiology, less stereotypical areas might be more easily aroused: the inside of your elbow, the arch of your foot, the lining of your belly button. When the sensor-rich outermost layer of your skin gets grazed, kissed, licked, traced, suckled, squeezed, pinched, nibbled, or breathed on, neurons translate these signals into electro-physiological impulses, which result in neurotransmitter release.

Ode to dopamine. Seratonin. Nitric oxide and oxytocin. Ode to epinephrine and norepinephrine, to neurotransmitters and neuropeptides.

When you're experiencing arousal, your body's parasympathetic response, the feed-or-breed contingency in charge of smooth muscle contraction, gets activated. Your pulse slows, your face flushes, your groin swells, and you might even experience what experts call "involuntary vocalizations." Meanwhile your bloodstream rushes to accommodate the oxygen needs of frenetic receptor cells and a chain reaction begins, sending clusters of neurotransmitters spinning from one excitable neuron to the next.

There comes a moment when you have to let go. You have to consciously allow your sympathetic response, that fight-or-flight instinct, to take over. Your body might not know whether it's fighting or taking flight, but it does know to quicken the heart rate, dilate the pupils, and deepen the breathing. When you make the decision to lose control, your neurotransmitters trigger a cascade, releasing a flood of pent-up molecules free to dance on your brain for the seven or so seconds it takes to experience an orgasm.

As ecstatic contractions take over all sensation in your body, the primal voice inside you screaming for flight ceases, because it found euphoric release. Your brain also receives the message that you have beaten whatever it was you were fighting.

You won.

44

Waking up two minutes before my phone's 0530 alarm, I turn it off and silently return it to the nightstand. When I roll back to Ayla's shape next to me, I know my efforts were useless. She's awake.

I snuggle into her. "What are you doing up so early?"

She absentmindedly rubs my hip. "I wanted to make sure I got to say goodbye."

"Well, now you've said goodbye. Go back to sleep."

"No, no, I'm up. I'm awake."

"Ayla, your eyes are closed."

"I'm awake," she argues, but her eyes remain closed. I get up and get dressed, smiling in the dark, and then pause at the side of the bed.

She yanks me down on top of her. I win the short-lived wrestling match that follows because she's still only half-awake. Pinning her hips with my knees and trapping her forearms with my hands, I tell her, "I don't want to go to work."

"Call in sick. We'll spend the day together."

"I wish. What are you doing today?"

"I got a date with the submarine. And I might rock climb with Annie."

Like always, when she mentions her hyperbaric oxygen therapy, I feel uneasy. I picture her in the claustrophobic metal chamber, lying perfectly still. I let go of her wrists and rest the side of my head on her chest, listening to her slow heartbeat.

She wraps her arms around me. "It's safe, you know. FDA approved."

I took Ayla to one of her treatments once. The technician invited me into the room, and I watched Ayla climb into the chamber and lie down. The technician lowered the heavy lid, sealing her inside, and adjusted the pressure settings. Ayla looked so alone and removed in there, so distant and alien, even though she'd waved cheerfully from one of the small round windows. I'd had to look away, and my palms hadn't stopped sweating until we'd stepped out into the sunlight an hour later.

Ayla leans her head back to meet my eyes. "Babe, you all right?" she asks.

"I'm fine," I say, forcing a smile. "Just don't feel like going to work."

She looks at me for a moment before replying. "Be safe today."

I move toward the door, my bag weighing down my shoulder. After her session that day, I'd asked her, "What if there's an earthquake?" She had stared at me, uncomprehending. "Who will let you out?" And she replied that hopefully no one would, at least not until the earthquake was over.

45

When the call comes in, William and I are at Jesse Owens Park because a group of men had flagged us down. We thought someone was hurt but it turned out they just wanted their blood pressures taken. William scoffed at the request, but I jumped out before he could drive away and grabbed a cuff for him, a cuff for myself, and two pairs of ears. Seven men in their mid-forties, some who didn't speak English, some who had clearly been drinking—or perhaps had never stopped—and all of them disheveled and friendly, not quite homeless but profoundly poor, who had probably given up looking for work in the Home Depot parking lot and had come here instead to enjoy the sky's last streaks from a cloud-covered sunset.

When the call comes in, one of the drunk men is sticking out his tongue and saying, "Ah," as if I can look at his throat like a doctor and tell him if he is healthy or not, and I am leaning away from the smell, trying to remember the last time I had any kind of checkup myself, had stuck out my tongue and said, "Ah," or if that was even the kind of thing you did at checkups anymore.

When the call comes in, William is enjoying himself but pretending not to; he's giving a man medical advice in broken Spanish, his ego swelling from the pleasure of being listened to so respectfully, even though as soon as we drive away he will probably say terrible things, since talking badly about people is what he does best.

But the call comes in, and the call changes everything in an instant, because the dispatcher's voice is frantic through the slender black box of the walkie-talkie, resting on the bench seat near the sharps container. And a dispatcher's voice is never frantic.

"You guys, get on air *now*. You got an MCI. Looks like a multiple stabbing on a bus. I'm sending it over." There's a pause in the transmission; already our pagers are vibrating, and in these few seconds between his voice initially breaking through the air and this pause, William and I dismiss the gloves, throw the equipment back, and jump into the cab without so much as a glance at the men we're leaving behind.

* * *

William sits silently for a few minutes, and then starts his energetic drumming on the steering wheel again, presumably in time with the song in his head. We've turned the FM radio off while we wait for updates from dispatch. I look out the window, tapping the backs of my fingertips against the glass, in a rhythm of my own. MCI: multi-casualty incident. I've never had one before, unless you count the car accidents where more than one person is hurt. No one counts those. As we post at an intersection three blocks away from the location of the call, waiting for police to clear the scene and declare it safe, I read the page for the umpteenth time, fidgeting in my seat.

At Manchester Boulevard and Van Ness Avenue there is a public bus with several victims of a stabbing, the extent of their injuries unknown. That is all my pager can tell me, but I keep re-reading it as if it will suddenly offer something new. I can't remember the rules of triage. The colors of the priority tags are black, red, yellow, and green, but what are the cutoff criteria for when you treat someone and when you don't? All I can remember is that this is the hardest part, knowing who gets a black tag and who gets a red one. It shouldn't matter in this case—we'll have plenty of resources to treat both types of patients—but still. Is it that if the person has a pulse but isn't breathing, you declare them dead and move on to the next? Or do you adjust the airway, give a breath, and then if nothing changes, place a black tag around their toe and move on?

A knock sounds on the driver's side, and William rolls down his window. Tyson wears full turnouts, complete with a thick reflective jacket and a battered helmet. His usually relaxed face looks worried.

"You guys hear?" he asks. We shake our heads. "There's a big pileup on the freeway. Everyone's over there. And anyone who's not is at the residential fire on the East Side." He thumbs over his shoulder. "Right now we got the engine and the squad, so plus you guys that's only nine of us. We've called for backup from Compton, but their nearest truck is half an hour out. A & O is calling private ambulance companies to get another unit over here, but you know how that can be." He scratches his jaw and takes a deep breath, his voice louder and more authoritative as he continues. "So listen up. Captain Greger is going to call the shots on this one. And I need you guys to really pay attention. We might have to improvise a bit. It is *not* your job to question how Greger decides to handle this call. It's your job to move quickly, think clearly, and follow instructions. We are all going to have to be on our A-game." He swivels his gaze from William to me. "Got it?"

"Yes, sir."

William thrusts his chin in the direction of Van Ness Avenue. "Any idea what's taking so long?"

"One of their own got shot a week ago, so my guess is the PD aren't messing around on this one. They might be taking quick statements from everyone on board to make sure the stabber didn't slip in with the other passengers."

"Do you know which bus it is?" The question escapes before I can stop it. My temples are pounding. I still can't remember who gets a black tag versus a red one—why didn't I ask about that?

Tyson angles his head to get a better look at me, the front of his helmet almost touching the steering wheel. "You mean like which *line* it is?"

William snorts. "I'm sure the police will get right on that."

"Did you want the specs of the bus, too?"

They continue in this manner while I smile at them, blushing, less bothered by their teasing than by a nagging fear I refuse to name.

The Metro bus looks like a beached whale that's been washed up across two lanes of traffic, its glossy white skin reflecting the emergency lights. Captain Greger leads the nine of us past two officers directing traffic at the intersection, past the semicircular perimeter created by cop cars, past the caution tape and the clump of stricken passengers. We've confirmed there are two patients, and as we climb on board, our team rushes to handle the bus driver at the front while Greger, Dag, and three other firefighters clamber to the back. As I climb the steps into the bus, carrying a jump bag that doesn't feel adequate, my eyes meet those of the bus driver.

Every call I run, every patient I treat, every time my eyes meet those of someone who is sick or hurt or bleeding or dying, I have a moment where I can't remember a goddamn thing.

I give the man a nod and unhook the bag from my shoulder.

He's crumpled in the driver's chair, but Tyson and William grab his armpits and lift him to a more accessible seat, and as the bus driver sinks his weight into it with a wince, I notice he's favoring the left side of his body. The white hair bordering his temples bookends terrified eyes, a thin sheen of sweat coats his round face, and the gray flesh of his cheeks quivers with each terse breath. Crouching next to Tyson, I lift my glove and press the back of my hand into the bus driver's forearm. "Cool, pale, diaphoretic," I call out to the firefighter standing behind me, who is documenting everything on a clipboard, and I start to set up the oxygen tank and a mask.

Tyson reaches for the stethoscope around his neck and then thinks better of it. "Do you have pain anywhere?"

The man gestures to his lower right rib cage, where there is a dark stain, difficult to see because of the dark blue, sweat-soaked uniform shirt he's wearing. William cuts through the thick shirt with trauma shears, peels the undershirt off of the wound, and my arms dance around William and Tyson in order to place the oxygen mask around the man's head.

When the wound is exposed we all pause. It's a deepening gash running in a diagonal line between his eighth and ninth rib, but the amazing thing is that I can hear it: I can hear the hissing, sputtering sound the wound makes as he struggles to breathe.

Captain Greger and the others come up from the back of the bus and unsling the ECG monitor onto a nearby seat. "We're calling her," Greger advises the firefighter with the clipboard. "Too much blood loss; she's asystole; we checked in two leads. We're going to focus all our energy on him. What have we—" He turns to Tyson, who is pressing the bell of the stethoscope into several places on the man's chest. "Sucking chest wound. Dag, set up a needle-D; Sammy, go ahead and throw the leads on him; let's get a BVM ready…"

My fingertips hover over the medbox, suspended in their reach for an occlusive dressing. The thought that we still need to check for possible exit wounds (because we don't know how long the knife was) vanishes. For the first time, my eyes register our second patient.

An arm pushes past me, grabs what it needs from the medbox. "What the hell is wrong with your partner?"

William doesn't answer. He has followed my gaze down the length of the bus.

Her short thick hair is matted from blood. The dark strands plaster themselves across her face. Her head tilts downward, resting against the window, and her shoulders are slouched. Even in death she has bad posture.

"Is that…," William's voice—his pretentious, blistering voice—subdued into a child's hushed awe. "Isn't that your girl?"

Everything inside me lights up in agony but I can't move. A red spray coats the back of the gray plastic seat. A dark pool glistens on the floor. She's wearing a tan, long-sleeved shirt. Her eyes are closed, but if they were open they would be green, because Ayla's eyes are green.

I start screaming. William turns pale and jumps back. His freckles stand out so sharply from his face I have the absurd thought that I could reach out and pluck them. I could gather a few with my fingertips and roll them around on my palm.

My scream trails off and everyone is frozen in place, including the bus driver, whose ragged breathing punctures the silence. I push past the group and down the aisle. I want to call for help. Someone should call 911. Her expression would look almost peaceful if it weren't for all the blood.

A hoarse shout from behind me. "Get her out of here," Captain Greger begs. "I want her off the bus *now*."

Even without turning my head I can feel the confusion of the agitated crew, the voices from outside the bus coming nearer.

I get to the end of the aisle. Ayla's cheekbones sit higher on her face than those of the woman in front of me. Ayla doesn't wear tan shirts. Or silver rings. The woman's left ear is nearly severed; what remains of the half-moon chunk of flesh dangles from a deep hole just below her cheekbone. I stare at it, then at the wounded neck still oozing blood. Her arms droop in her lap like helpless offerings. With a trembling hand, I lean over the woman, press a fingertip to her eyelid, and lift up.

Her eye is brown. The pupil fixed and dilated.

Sliding myself into the neighboring seat I wrap my arms around the dead woman. I rock her limp, still-warm body back and forth. The weight of her slick and heavy head swings against my shoulder.

When the police come to remove me from the bus, it takes three officers to peel my arms from their embrace. "It's not her," I tell them over and over. Pulling me to my feet, the officers half-drag, half-carry me off the bus.

46

A cop drives me to Crossroads, lets me out in the ambulance parking lot, and never says a word. When I'm standing on two feet again, I stare up at the three gray box towers of CRH, feeling like I've never seen them, really seen them, much less the bent sky above or anything else around me. The world is a strange and oblong shape.

Inside, in the hallway near the nurses' station, William is stripping down the gurney. He halts mid-motion when he sees me. "What—"

For once, he is speechless.

"It wasn't her," I say.

I can't read his expression very well. His jaw muscles ripple, his face swinging between pity and disgust.

"How's the other patient?" I ask.

William jerks his chin toward one of the trauma rooms. "See for yourself."

In Room 1, Bed A, the bus driver lies unconscious. Curtains create a circular perimeter around the room, and I watch through the gap as the doctor and nurses prep the man's right side for a chest tube. He's covered up to his waist by only a thin sheet, and both of his arms have been raised above his head and folded across the top of the pillow. He would look like he was lounging or taking a nap if it weren't for all the activity around him.

"We'll need bilateral entry," the doctor says through his light blue mask as he coats rust-colored iodine in a broad circle just below the man's right armpit. "A 32-French for his right and a 30-French for the left."

"Prepping both now," a nurse says. "That was a 30-French for his *left* side, correct? And a 32-French for the side of the injury." From somewhere in the room: snickering.

Tyson stands outside of the inner circle, watching them, his face more pale than the patient's.

"You mean the side with the actual stab wound?" another nurse calls out. More snickering.

"Enough," the doctor says. "Janeen, hand me a Kelly clamp." He has created an incision over the man's fourth rib, and he uses the curved instrument to stretch wider the opening of the cut, to separate the layers of skin and muscle from each other, before reaching the entire length of his gloved index finger into the hole. When he removes his finger and picks up the chest tube for insertion, a stream of clear red pleural fluid dribbles down the man's side, escaping from the lining of his injured lung. Inch after inch of a thick plastic tube gets shoved into the man's chest, and then sutured in place. The bus driver's face is empty, close to death, hovering in the balance. But his vitals begin to rise upon the initial drainage of air and blood from his lung cavity.

Tyson is looking at me, his face convoluted by hatred.

I can picture the whole thing. How Tyson was so flustered on scene that when he went to perform a needle-decompression, he plunged the needle into the wrong side, the uninjured side. I can picture the tip of the needle entering the man's healthy lung, just below the clavicle and above his heart, and how it created a second pneumothorax there. I can picture the crew in the back of the ambulance, or perhaps the ER team that received him, realizing the mistake. They would have had to place a second needle and begin the management of not one but two pneumothoraces. One is enough to kill a person.

This isn't me. I haven't made a mistake this big before.

The curtains get pushed back, and members of the ER team shout to each other as they wheel the man out of the room and upstairs to the OR for surgery. Soon the hallway is empty and quiet. Tyson stands directly in front of me. A call everyone will be talking about for months, and he blew it. My fists hang at my sides, someone else's blood smeared on my arms.

"Piper, that woman back there, did you know her?"

My voice is flat, unmoved, unapologetic. "No, sir. I thought I did. But no."

"Well, listen, I don't know what's gotten into you, but you better pull your shit together." His voice shakes a little. "You got that?"

"I got it."

He leaves, pushing the swinging door so hard it creaks in protest before settling back on its hinges. I take a few steps into the blue-white light of the trauma room. Over a confetti of discarded dressings and crumpled tape, the plastic encasements for IV bags and the no-longer-sterile needle wrappers litter the floor like shelled husks. Despite the silence, the stillness, the room is riddled with evidence of what happened in here. There is a void in the center of the room, free of any debris or paraphernalia: a rectangular-shaped vacancy where the bed had been standing.

I stumble to the double doors of the ER, push them open, and step outside. The cool night air hits the sweat on my temples and neck. I try to stiffen my shape into a less flimsy one as I descend the ramp. My hand on the railing, one wobbling, unwilling foot in front of the other, I manage not to fall down.

What does it matter, anyway? Fuck it. What does any of it matter? People die every day.

There is an oak tree near the hospital entrance, healthy and tall despite the fact that no one ever waters it, its broad branches partially covering the sign that reads CROSSROADS HOSPITAL. It is the only tree for about a mile around and the only tree of its kind in this area: a magnificent, lonely, lumbering beauty.

I vomit somewhere near the base of it.

47

When conducting the triage of a multi-casualty incident—

Green, green, red. Black, yellow, red, yellow.

Start by taking charge.

The mechanism behind memory isn't fully understood. How your brain works remains the fundamental scientific question of our time.

Airway, breathing, circulation. Skin signs, vitals, level of consciousness.

An entire skyscraper filled with peer-reviewed scientific textbooks can't explain a child small enough to fit in your palm.

Consider the events. An unknown number of people traveling on a public bus were stabbed by one of the passengers.

Nothing in you is reliable. Your memory disintegrates, your eyes lie, your inner ear lets the horizon slip away.

Ask for permission to treat. Ask: "What seems to be the problem today, sir/ma'am?"

Green to heal, blue to soothe. The oldest form of medicine is the white pill, made of sugar, designed to be nothing.

Height, weight, age, address, zip code, date of birth, telephone number. You are an abacus. A license plate. A chi square.

The "walking wounded" are the people capable of exiting the bus.

Your only thought is: *Here we go.*

Walk around; take no more than thirty seconds to determine the status of each victim; decide who is dead; decide who isn't.

The most you can do is describe how much it's been hurting and for how long. Perhaps it's a leftover piece of your evolution, a souvenir still lodged within your head, an inner voice screaming for flight.

If there is no spontaneous breathing, put a black tag around the necks or toes so other rescuers will know not to treat them.

If they are breathing at a rate of over thirty breaths a minute, or have a weak pulse and can't follow commands, they are immediate.

Do your best to stick to protocol. Do not treat; only label.

Triage is simple.

Assign colors.

48

Our shift supervisor is waiting for me at the station when we arrive. He gives me just a few minutes to get ready—enough time to remove my uniform shirt, wash the blood off my arms, throat, and face, and pull on an A & O sweatshirt. His name is Jonathon, but everyone calls him Johnny Be Good.

I've seen him only a couple times, dropping off fresh supplies at Station 710. He resembles a weasel with a crew cut, zipped up into an overly starched uniform. His boots have an unholy shine to them.

We sit in a greasy spoon diner, the only late-night diner in the area, whose name is actually Greasy Spoon. We have ten minutes before the place closes. Ten minutes for him to fire me, or scold me, or tell me the meaning of life, or whatever it is he is going to tell me. All I want is a shower.

Johnny Be Good orders us coffees to go, and soon a white paper cup sits in front of me, looking entirely too expectant with its wafts of steam, patiently awaiting the company of cream and sugar. As the supervisor talks, I watch the spiky patch of skin to the right of his Adam's apple, the patch that escaped this morning's shave and has a crew cut of its own. The thick dark hairs reverberate with each syllable.

"Piper? *Piper.*"

I meet his eyes for the first time.

"Is there anything you want to talk about?"

"No."

"Okay. Well, listen, you're not alone in this." He reaches into his jacket pocket, pulls out a pamphlet, and slides it across the table to me. "Feel free to call the numbers in here anytime."

The cover of the pamphlet shows a laughing couple captured with a soft-focus lens, the young woman riding piggyback, her arms wrapped loosely around the shoulders of a cheerful man. Underneath, a caption: "Learn to celebrate life in every moment." Inside, there is a phone number for some kind of support group, and a number for a suicide hotline, and more pictures. Smiles all around. I close the pamphlet and place it next to the untouched coffee cup.

"Death is hard," he is saying. "And we see it all the time on this job."

The inside of my left elbow itches. I wonder, again, if I got all the blood off, or if the itch is simply paranoia. I picture all the ways I could direct violence at the glossy folded paper in front of me. Drive over it with the ambulance, turn it into a shish kebab on a syringe, burn cigarette holes into it, heat it in the microwave until it catches fire, drown it in saline. I want to ask him for more than one copy so that I can prolong the pleasure of destroying it.

He looks at his watch. "Because of, er, the intensity of the call you just had, I want you to know that we're advising you to take some time off. You're a good employee, and we'd hate to lose you, but… this is your chance to take a break. Really think about whether you want to be here, and if this is the job for you.

"We can give you a thirty-day leave before we have to let you go, so ideally you'll be able to come to a conclusion in the next month. And then just let us know. All right?" He smiles. It looks a little like the pamphlet, this smile.

In the parking lot of Station 710, I pour out the coffee that was bought for me because I couldn't pull my shit together. I watch the brown waterfall splatter against the dark asphalt, drenching the weeds poking through the cracks. Going inside, I stop at the office first to shove the pamphlet—damp from my clammy hand, crumpled from the way I've been clutching it—into the shredder, before making my way to the locker room to pack up my bag and leave.

49

She answers the door and I stare into her face, half-believing. It's her but she looks different. As if she's been flattened and reinflated. For the last twenty-four hours, since seeing her crumpled and lifeless shape on that bus, everything has been like that. The same but not the same.

Ayla raises her eyebrows. "You coming in, babe? Or you just going to stand there?"

The smell of the garlic-and-herb chicken dinner she's cooking travels through an open window. Nausea bubbles in my throat. Using the view as an excuse, I convince her to sit with me on the concrete steps leading up to her bungalow. The sky in front of us is unimpressive, a thin brown layer squatting over the city.

I hear myself telling Ayla that I've picked up the night half of a shift in order to help out a friend. She inspects the side of my face as I lie to her. I hadn't intended to do this before coming over here. As soon as she answered the door, looking like some kind of impostor, I knew I wouldn't be able to step inside.

I can't, I keep thinking. I can't do this.

"Sorry to cancel last minute on you."

She nods, raises a fingernail to her mouth to chew on it, thinks better of it, and drops her hand back down. "Is something wrong?"

I shake my head, eyes fixed on that miserable view. "No, not at all."

She follows my gaze, dropping her chin onto crossed arms, and says carefully, "Are you sure you don't want to talk about it? Maybe something happened at work?"

Everywhere. I am going to vomit everywhere.

"Nothing happened at work."

I force myself to look at the Ayla sitting next to me, trying to keep my eyes casual, my face neutral. Perhaps a smile would be appropriate in this moment? I can't remember how I used to act. My eyes find her left ear, trace the shape of it, see it dangling like a bizarre earring from a hole on the side of her head, bloody ribbons coursing down her shirt. The vision disappears as quickly as it arrived, but I'm glued to the concrete, still staring. Look at her, she's alive, she's right here in front of you, it's wonderful. It's all a big lie. Ayla shifts her arms and tilts her head, returning my gaze. I realize that at any moment she might try to hug me or put her hands on me, and with a sudden panic I yank myself to my feet. The last person I touched was dead.

"I'm kind of tired. Not myself. I have to go to work but I'll see you soon? Enjoy your dinner?" I give her a quick kiss on the top of her head and throw myself down the stairs. She calls something out but I don't look back.

In the car, driving, driving, driving—Ayla lives only a few miles from me but I take the longest route I can think of back to my apartment, the 2 to the 134 to the 101 to the 405 to the 10 to the 110, a big horseshoe loop around Los Angeles, gripping the steering wheel, occasionally punching my thighs or tugging at the hair above my ears as if to distract the headache that's sprung up in both temples. Everything is fine, nothing is wrong, everything is.

When a Volvo neatly cuts me off on the 101 freeway, I follow it for miles. I bring my car as close as I can to the license plate that reads FMLY MAN, to the sticker that says MY OTHER CAR IS A YACHT. Honking continuously, shrieking a string of profanities, tears leaking down my face. I enjoy the man's terrified expression in the rearview mirror.

50

About two weeks go by. I fall into a kind of routine. I pretend to work; I pretend to work shift after shift after shift; I avoid people; I use Marla as an excuse not to see Ayla and Ayla as an excuse not to see Marla and work as an excuse not to see anyone. Ryan calls and calls; I never answer, but when I finally call him back, it goes to voice mail. My brother has changed his message to the crooning of Leonard Cohen's "Hallelujah," which means he and Malcolm must be fighting. I hang up.

I can't be around anyone anymore, but when I'm alone, I long not to be. I crave Ayla especially. I picture scouring her face and hands and neck, making undeniable her living presence, fortifying reality somehow. But when I see her everything in me retreats. I shrink and hollow. She's no longer the Ayla I knew.

Every day it happens all over again, the pause before the scream, the recognition before the inventory. If I manage to sleep, my dreams are nightmares—a vibrant bloodstained wash; I wake up shaking—but my dreams are gentle compared to my sour-sick blossoming consciousness. My dreams are a lulling whisper compared to that terrible moment, right after I realize I am no longer dreaming, right before I open my eyes and consider what is true and what isn't, because the moment of my awakening always consists of me standing on a bus, looking down the aisle, and Ayla is dead.

I start to avoid public places. My room is dark and quiet, with very little sound from the street, and this feels best. While Marla is at work or at Tom's, I'll venture out to the living room and watch my old swim meet videos, or footage from the Olympics. I watch Michael Phelps beat his own world record and become the most decorated medal winner in history. I rewind a ten-second close-up of his butterfly stroke and play it over and over again; his long torso arcing through the water like the spine of a porpoise, his legs and feet undulating below the surface; now you see him, now you don't. I watch it on mute so I don't have to listen to the yelling of the announcers.

I can no longer watch regular television. Violent crime shows fill me with a numbing terror; commercials enrage and horrify me.

Most of the time I drive around, pretending to be at work. Sometimes I park, lean the seat back, and try to sleep.

Around me, always, a blur. Deafened sounds. Motion suspended. Motion sped up. A timeless quality, a buffer, a craving. The desire for nothing to touch me, for no one to speak, while I pretend to be out saving lives.

I think about the frequent flyers most. The woman who invents a new name every time we pick her up and asks that we please not take her to the graveyard, the drunk who apologizes profusely when we find him in a pile of his own vomit, the sallow-faced man who always talks in hundreds. There are a hundred lessons to be learned in a lifetime, he'll say, addressing someone we can't see. A hundred ways to say "I love you," a hundred ways to die. When we were kids Ryan tried to explain that despite Mom leaving us, she still loved us; finally I explained to him that for me to move on with my life I had to stop believing that. I want to find the sallow-faced man and tell him: there's just one way to die and that's dying.

One day I'm in the bathroom line at a Starbucks with three women ahead of me, and I can feel it begin. The fear, the loneliness, the unfairness of it all, the anger at having to *wait*, the total shame of knowing I don't deserve even my rage. But it begins anyway; it builds and builds, and when I go inside, I kick the ceramic toilet bowl so hard my shoe flies off, and then I limp out with a vague sense of accomplishment.

I avoid public places. The surges of anger that break across me with a terrifying velocity don't frighten me at the moment they happen, but they frighten me later when I think back on them.

When I saw Ayla two days ago, she asked if there was anything I wanted to talk about. I haven't been myself lately, she told me. I've been distant and withdrawn and it's clear I'm not sleeping well. Am I stressed because Marla is moving out? Do I need to take a few days off work? I wanted to tell Ayla that I can't *feel* anything anymore, not the way I used to. Nothing can touch me. Not Ayla trying to cook for me, or her hand rubbing my back as she says, "Why don't you swim anymore? Maybe swimming would help." I want to be left alone; her hand is a million miles away; swimming won't help.

The visions are always so much worse around Ayla. Whenever I see her, I wait for her hair and face and body to mutate in front of me. There it comes. Here it is.

I am frightened all the time now and I can't tell anyone and I don't know why.

Every day it happens all over again, and this is what I know: there is an ear, and it is almost severed; there is slick dark hair plastered against a familiar face; there are two fleshy palms upturned in a dead woman's lap. These are the things I think about at the supermarket, where Ayla no longer works, walking up and down the aisles of Sustainable Living as if I am looking for something, and also when I drive around in the middle of the night, pretending to be on shift, because I don't want anyone to know I don't have a job to go to anymore, and the other night when Marla said, "Tomorrow? But I thought you worked yesterday," behind her I saw a pool of blood on the kitchen floor, and I blinked and it went away, and Marla said, "Are you all right?" and I caught myself right before answering, "Yes, it's gone." This is what I know, that sometimes in these visions I am holding a corpse in my arms, rocking it back and forth, feeling its heavy head swing against my shoulder, while other times it is Ayla, it is a half-dead Ayla, and I can't remember how I'm supposed to save her, I can't do anything but weep for her, and she keeps asking for my help.

51

I come home and find Ryan waiting for me, sitting in his Volkswagen bug with a clear view of the walkway to my apartment. As soon as I catch sight of him I freeze. We stare at each other through the windshield. He gets out and approaches me as if I am something from the nature channel. I think about inviting him in and decide not to. Perhaps this conversation will be shorter if we have it in public.

"Pipes."

"Ry."

"I've been calling you."

"I've been busy."

He nods warily. His wavy brown hair falls around his ears; he needs a haircut and a shave. In his expression I see the face of my brother when we were teenagers, angry because I borrowed his CDs without asking, annoyed because I took too long a shower when he needed to get ready. I realize I've missed him.

"I talked to Marla again. She's worried about you. We both are." He tells me I can't keep doing this.

"I've just been working," I say. "Marla's moving out so I thought the extra money might help." I'm proud of the lie until I start to panic. Did I tell anyone I was working today? I can't remember. I think I pretended to work yesterday, which means I should have been getting off shift at 0700 this morning. Which is probably what Marla told Ryan, and why he was waiting for me.

Ryan watches me, makes sure he has my full attention before saying, "That's not what I'm talking about." His voice gets louder. Listen, he says. He tells me about all the times I've disappeared, starting with when Mom left. He cites the friendships I've walked out on, and says he can tell I'm avoiding Ayla.

"Just stay out of it, Ryan!" For some reason I start to laugh, maybe at his ignorance, but the sound collects in my throat. "You're being stupid. And it's got nothing to do with her."

"Oh, don't even get me *started*. I mean, Mom was a piece of work. I know that. When you didn't want to talk to her anymore, I couldn't—"

"When *I* didn't want to talk to her anymore? When *I* didn't—"

"But then you had to go and make Dad out to be some kind of Antichrist... It's like you lost all respect for him because he never got over her—how is that his fault? He loves you, Pipes. He's not going to live forever. You act like he's such a pain in your ass, but you're his favorite."

I wave my hand as if to shoo him away. "And you've got it all figured out, is that it? Maybe I should take notes from you on how to be a perfect communicator?"

He catches my right wrist. "What happened to your hand?"

"It's nothing."

This morning I bought a new phone. I'd been trying to send a text to Ayla yesterday explaining that no, I couldn't think of a good day for us to have a date night, and when the damn thing kept trying to autocorrect my words, I beat it against a brick wall until it shattered. The knuckles of my right hand are raw, covered in newly formed scabs. Ryan drops my wrist and looks at me with concern. I liked the anger better. "Pipes, what's going on with you?"

It's all I can do not to flinch. Don't panic. Just act like he's overreacting. Everything is fine. But at some point someone will guess I'm not actually working anymore. Marla will talk to Ayla just like she talked to Ryan. Someone will call the station looking for me.

Ryan searches my face. "Pipes, I mean it. You can't let go of people every time you get too close."

"Oh, for—*enough*, Ryan. Goddamn it. Who are you to lecture me?"

"Who am I?" he says, his face darkening. "Who am I? I'm the one who holds everything together! If it weren't for me, you wouldn't even make time to *see* Dad." Ryan never gets mad but he's really shouting now. "I'm the one who's always making sure everyone is okay, I'm the one who—"

"You and Malcolm broke up."

I should've realized right away. It's not like him to behave like this, to bellow and criticize, even in a well-intentioned way.

Ryan doesn't say anything, he just kind of crumples. I catch his sagging shoulders and hug him tight. We stand in the street for a long time, my brother's body shaking against mine, my arms awkwardly wrapped around him, trying to hold him up.

There was a game Ryan started when we were younger, after Mom left. He would leave me notes with secret missions or assignments scribbled on them. I'd find them folded up inside my shoes, or taped to the back of the cereal box. The notes usually referred to small objects found hidden in my room. First there was a small glass jar and then later a note taped to my bedroom lamp: "Find something to put inside." I chose the intact body of a large beetle. The green sheen of its hard shell faded quickly, but I lost the jar before I ever got to see it decompose. A week after finding a cloth purse with gold coins in my closet, I found a note tied to my toothbrush that said, "Figure out which coins are fake." But my favorite was a foil-covered owl pellet I was instructed to dissect, because inside the mixture of bones and hair and feathers, nestled in with the rodent's tiny skull, was a flat red button Ryan had taken the time to place, as if to suggest that the mouse had been wearing it when the owl ate him. Nothing says love like a small red button in your owl pellet.

But the fact that Ryan deserves a better sister has never been more obvious than right now. I hold his shaking body even while I resent his presence—I try to comfort him because I know I'm supposed to—and meanwhile I can't feel my arms at all, or the weight of his body leaning into mine. It's as if I'm watching the girl who looks like me hug the boy who looks like Ryan.

52

"Can I help you?" the woman with the hairnet asks.

She sounds as exhausted as I feel. I admire her gold front tooth, how there's just one, how this bull's eye of a first impression is the only decoration she wears. I scan the objects under the heat lamp, of which there are many. This place serves fried chicken, pizza, hamburgers, and fish tacos. Somewhere behind that dirty counter there is even ice cream, as advertised on the overburdened sign outside.

I stare at the personal cheese pizza. Its grizzled face and mozzarella cheeks take up a circle no bigger than my palm, flaring out concentrically: the puffy dough rim with its burnt-orange shrapnel of Parmesan.

"How much?"

"Three dollars."

I don't cook anymore. I used to bring meals for each shift, fresh fruit and vegetables, or Ayla would pack me leftovers using her complicated Tupperware system that I found so baffling and endearing. For the last three weeks, everything I put into my body is white or orange or an overly processed shade somewhere in between. I will drive all night, all over Los Angeles, and at 2 a.m. decide that I need an Oreo milkshake from Jack-in-the-Box, and at 4 a.m. decide it is a good idea to fall asleep in my car, still holding the cup with its coagulated remains.

"Ain't got all day," the woman says. "What's it going to be?"

Death is a grizzled personal cheese pizza. It's being revived under an unsentimental heat lamp.

"I'll take it."

I drive to Manchester Boulevard and Van Ness Avenue and park in front of the auto repair shop. Sitting cross-legged on the roof of my car, I look out over the intersection.

It is, of course, like nothing ever happened. Four lanes wide open for traffic. The steady rhythm of cars coming and going, going and coming, the swollen pause of a red light followed by the sound of bass-heavy beats streaming by and fading away. The yells and waves to people ambling on the sidewalk, or waiting at the bus stop, and no one is any wiser, least of all me.

Tonight Ayla is coming over. I have the vague feeling I need to make a decision of some kind. Maybe I should even try to tell her what happened. But I don't know how to do that. I can't remember the events of that night very well, or the order in which they occurred. Did I look? Did I ever really look at her face, or did I just lose it? I can't remember.

I scan the tarmac, looking for tire track marks or stains, looking for evidence of any kind. Nothing. And yet this is the only thing that's real. When I am really honest with myself, I can admit that I haven't felt the same since that day because it *wasn't* her, and maybe some sick, twisted part of me was kind of relieved when I thought it *was*, because then I could just stop worrying about what I know is inevitable.

From the newspapers I found out that her name was Debbie Heinemann, thirty-three years old, from Hancock Park. The argument between her and the man seated next to her escalated until the man pulled out a knife and began to stab her. Other passengers panicked and the bus driver pulled over and attempted to investigate, at which point he was also stabbed. The prime suspect is Willie Thomas, the woman's boyfriend, who is believed to have escaped the scene on foot. The bus driver remains in critical condition at Crossroads Hospital in South Los Angeles.

If I hold the newspaper about a foot away from my face, close my right eye, and squint my left, the grainy black-and-white picture looks exactly like Ayla.

Hopping down and climbing into my car, I take another look at the seemingly benign intersection before driving away. This is where I lost my mind.

53

Ayla comes over. We don't talk much. It's as if we're both worn out by a conversation that has yet to take place. We sit on the couch watching television, sharing a blanket, our bodies almost touching. Eventually we go to bed.

As we climb under the covers she burrows into me, wrapping my arms tightly around her, but once she's asleep I withdraw, the arm trapped beneath her more difficult to remove, the crook of my elbow a perfect cradle for the side of her neck. Sitting up and looking at her, I take in the glowing, perfect skin, the way her lips shove against the pillow as if kissing it. For the first time in weeks I see Ayla and not the phantom, and with this clarity comes my first selfless thought in a long time: I don't deserve it anymore. I don't deserve to be so close to a person whose skin looks like that; she will be better off without me.

When she comes downstairs in the morning she finds me sitting at the kitchen table, staring out of the small window above the kitchen sink at the thin gray light of dawn. I've been here for hours.

Most of Marla's stuff is already gone. The three-story wooden spice rack, the wide-lipped blue margarita glasses, all the refrigerator magnets. Perhaps the most glaring void is the space over the stove, where the rooster oven mitt had hung like some kind of kitchen mascot.

Ayla sits down across from me. "Did you get any sleep?"

"Not really. It's okay, though."

"Is it?" Her voice has gone flat. She looks briefly at me before dropping her gaze. Her eyes are red-rimmed, her face sunken. "It doesn't feel okay," she says. "I don't know what's going on but I think you do."

I think of the bus driver in critical condition, two puncture wounds in his ribs. Tyson raising his arm, driving the needle in, getting it wrong. Because of me. Because there is never just one consequence.

She leans toward me. "Whatever it is, Piper, you can tell me. Did something happen at work?"

There's no way to shield myself from the images. "Nothing happened at work."

An explosion doesn't just blast an object into the air. Shock waves also travel through the object, causing blunt trauma, imploding trapped pockets of air.

"You haven't been acting right—at all—you haven't been sleeping, or eating—"

And then there's the force of the object hitting the ground afterward.

"Whatever it is you don't want to talk about, you can tell me."

All of this happens in seconds.

"Even if—" Her breath catches and then she goes on. "If there's someone else, you have to tell me. Whatever it is, I need to know."

It doesn't ever stop.

"That's not it," I tell her.

"Then *what*?" When her voice cracks my eyes lock on her face. Ayla never cries. Not when she told me about the IED, or her buddy's head exploding when he got shot in front of her, or how none of her friends knew how to talk to her after she came home with a brain injury. But she's crying now.

"Stop." I push the chair back using the table's edge. "Just stop."

"No. I won't *stop*. Whatever you're going through, you have to tell me. I'm not going anywhere until you do."

Ayla and I could be like that couple on the pamphlet cover, but the queer and fucked-up version—her with her headaches and memory problems, me with my mood swings and visions. *Learn to celebrate life in every moment.* But who would be giving whom a piggyback ride?

I tell her she needs to leave. The words are hard to say but I feel a weight lift off me, just a little, once I've said them. "I'm sorry," I say. "But I can't—"

"Tell me you don't love me anymore."

"What?"

She leans across the table, eyes narrow and lit up. "Piper, I know you love me."

I'm flooded with a sense of wonder. She doesn't want to let me go.

I raise both of my fists above my head and bring them down onto the table as hard as I can, with the single-minded conviction that if I strike hard enough, I will cleave the table in two. It doesn't work. After the cracking sound dies out, the thick wooden surface still stands, barely shaken. Meanwhile my hands reverberate in the air, distress signals blinking crimson, enough pain shooting through my palms and fingertips to offer each digit its own throbbing pulse. She jumps up and takes a step back, her arms thrown up in a defensive gesture.

"Get. *Out.*" The voice is not my own. "Get the fuck out, Ayla."

Her arms float down and hang at her sides; her breathing is heavy and even. I can feel her staring at me and I don't look up. The earthquakes in my fingers travel all the way to my teeth.

She grabs her overnight bag from the bottom of the stairs, hoists it onto her shoulder, and leaves.

54

You're pretty sure the Egyptians had it right. When deciding what to keep and what to throw away, pull the brain out of the nose with a long hook, separate and preserve the digestive system into canopic jars, and let a son of Horus watch over the removed lungs. But leave the heart right where it is.

Modern science tells you the heart isn't responsible for feelings or decisions any more than your intuition resides in your gut. It tells you that despite Hindu gurus naming the heart a primary chakra, and the Roman physician Galen calling it the seat of emotions, and the ancient North African city of Cyrene using its shape as the symbol for romance—despite these things, colloquial terms like open-hearted and brokenhearted, wearing your heart on your sleeve and letting your heart guide you, are wrongly named. Falsely inspired.

No, the real wonder of the heart lies in its physiological properties. Each and every cardiac cell a living and microscopic battery, the SA node acting as a conductor for rapid-fire electrical signals, the valves and chambers opening and closing, emptying and filling, and the left ventricle pushing out blood from its trenches with enough force to fight gravity, with enough power to send that crucial fluid to the farthest reaches of the body and back.

But even so. None of this explains what you know to be true. You house trillions of exquisite living sculptures daily, blooming neurons extending spindly arms, the curve of your ear and the spiral hiding inside it, your lungs like bellowed instruments, swaying in the tides of your breath, the visceral triggers and rhythm-keepers, the molecular messengers and music-makers, and none of these structures can tell you what you most want to know, any more than the grandparents of origin themselves, those mirror-twin circular staircases spiraling up and around each other, could predict not just who you are but all you would become.

Feel the tug of vulnerability—that pure agony of fear and passion—and you will touch your chest in wonder as it swells, glows, expands, consumes. And when people from around the globe and for thousands of years have felt the pain of loss, it is to that hollow, undulating organ beating within the rib cage that they point. "Here," they say. "Fix it. Fix it, please. This is where it hurts."

55

"A & O Ambulance, Jonathon speaking."

"Hi, Jonathon, it's Piper."

"Piper Gallagher. How are you?"

"Good, sir. Thank you."

"Excellent. What can I do for you?"

"I'm ready to come back to work."

"Hey, that's great news! We could really use you. Let's see, I've got a double opening at Station 710. On the A shift, with J-Rock and Pep. How about I put you with a rookie from our last training group? That sound all right?"

"Sounds perfect."

"Excellent, excellent. And Piper?"

"Yes, sir."

"I'm going to need a favor… You ever work a 72?"

Tom and I flip the heavy wooden kitchen table so it lies flat, then lift it by the legs and slide it into the bed of the rented U-Haul pickup truck. Marla has stopped pretending to help with the carrying of heavy furniture, and has now settled into the role of supervisor. And interrogator.

"Piper, for the love of—answer the question already. What do you mean you don't know how she is?"

I shake my hands out, lean against the side of the truck. "We haven't been talking is what I mean. What do we need to grab from inside? If there's any more furniture, we should get it now."

When Marla gets frustrated, her lower jaw thrusts forward like a four-year-old about to have a tantrum, and her heart-shaped lips puff up even more than usual. "Just the tall plant in the upstairs hallway, I think."

"I'll get it," Tom says. I watch him bolt down the walkway that leads back to the apartment and try not to roll my eyes. Traitor. I've already gotten lectured once today: when Marla found out my plan to work a 72-hour shift in South Central, she was almost epileptic. I started to tell her I needed the money, but stopped myself when I realized how much more I would have to explain.

"Ayla and I broke up."

She sputters for a minute, then asks, "When did this happen?"

"Three days ago."

Three glorious days of the visions in my head thinning out, becoming a dull and barely-there presence, like a television that's been left on in a different room. Three days of sleeping soundly. Of not remembering my dreams. Of going for long runs. Three days of looking at my phone every fifteen minutes, reassuring myself that Ayla still hasn't called or texted, and ignoring everyone else who has.

"Move in with us," Marla says. Before I can answer she rushes on. "No, listen, I was going to ask you days ago but I haven't seen you. There's a little room we can fix up, and a garage for your stuff. You barely own anything anyway. Stop looking at me like that."

"I might move in with Ryan, actually."

She starts to say something, hesitates. "I've been really worried about you."

"I know."

"You guys are going to kill each other."

"Probably, yes."

She still looks guilty, like she can't believe she didn't drop everything to take care of me. I wish there was a way to tell her I'm glad she didn't.

"Malcolm threw plates at him. Did Ryan tell you?"

"He threw *plates* at him?" This news sparks jealousy—I feel oddly left out.

"And broke the stereo! Fussy little Malcolm, who would have thought? Poor guy. Don't tell Ryan, but I'm going to miss him." She peers at me closely, as if looking for a mark or scar. "You're really trying to tell me that you broke up with Ayla but you're okay?"

"Yes."

"Aren't you still in love with her?"

"That's not the issue," I say, tired of the question. "It's just the right thing to do."

"Hello? Hello?"

"Dad, it's me."

"Piper?"

"That's the one."

"Hi, honey! To what do I owe the pleasure?"

"No reason. Just, you know, wanted to call and tell you that I love you."

"Hold on, I can barely—" He fumbles with the earpiece, experiments with speakerphone, and finally places the phone next to his ear. "Hello?"

"Still here."

"That's much better. What were you saying?"

"I love you, Dad."

After Marla and Tom have left, and the apartment is barren, and I call my father, and I sit around, realizing how little I own, I decide it's time to do laundry. I throw in all three sets of my A & O uniform. The one that used to have dried brain matter like a gray crust around the left knee and now has a mark on the tags as a way to remember, the one with the late Debbie Heinemann's blood, and the last one as inconspicuous and pliable as a fresh white diaper. Adding enough detergent for several extra-large loads, I lean against the wall of the laundry room, listen to the hum of the washer, and wait for the moment when I add the bleach.

56

"So, Piper," J-Rock says, "I heard you went crazy."

"I did. But now I'm back."

"Well, welcome back."

"That's not all," Pep says, dropping a heavy hand on my shoulder and shaking me. "She's not just back, she's working a 72."

I shrug. "What can I say, I missed the place."

"Man, have you ever worked a 72 before?" J-Rock scowls. "Plus it's a full moon tonight."

Pep makes a sound like a bomb exploding. "You are so in for it." He plops down at the table, unable to look anything but charming no matter what the topic. "Tell us, Piper. Did you forget what your ankles look like?"

"It'll be fine."

"The last time I worked a 72-hour shift," J-Rock says, "I was hallucinating by the end."

The three of us are ignoring the rookie, who's making a fresh pot of coffee to go with the large box of doughnuts he brought. This morning I arrived to find J-Rock in his gym shorts and slippers, lecturing the gangly, fresh-faced boot on how *not* to wake up the sleeping crew who worked the previous shift, and maybe noisy activities like vacuuming could wait a damn minute. It was the first time I'd seen J-Rock without his hat on, his closely cropped hair a slick smiley face from the back because of the permanent indentation in it. I was relieved when the hat found its right place again.

My new partner's name is Shel Lawrence. *Sheldon.* He's already been warned we'll find him a nickname.

"So what's the gossip around here?" I ask. "Besides me, I mean."

Pep and J-Rock mull it over. "Well, William got fired." J-Rock sees my face and adds, "It was because he was late one too many times."

"Right," I say, nodding.

"You remember Toothless Eric? He died."

"Eric was pretty young, wasn't he?"

"Meth ain't exactly the elixir of life."

"Peter from 830's got bit by a crackhead."

"How bad?"

"I still say it's bullshit."

"Nothing crazy, just in the hand."

"Wait, you mean Peter the *germaphobe*, Peter?"

"That's why it's bullshit."

"Piper, who you working with for the rest of your 72?"

"Carl tomorrow and then Sheldon here again for the last 24."

We all look at him, standing a few feet from the table, shifting from one polished boot to the other, clearly waiting to be invited. He looks no older than sixteen but must be at least legal. J-Rock kicks a chair at him and says gruffly, "This isn't the fire department, buddy, and you're not in training anymore. Re-*lax*."

"That's perfect," I say. " Your nickname is 'Buddy.'"

My new partner is what they call a black cloud, and in eight hours' time we run a hemorrhagic stroke, a trip-and-fall, a nausea/vomiting, a crying baby stuck in a high chair, and a lawnmower accident where much of the time was spent studiously searching for the man's missing thumb. It feels so good to be lost in the work: chasing 911 like a drug addict, the sound of sirens and assessments and station banter filling my head. I don't even mind that Buddy is always underfoot and about as useful as an extra gurney, his safety glasses neatly wrapped around the back of his collar, even during meals, because it gives me more to do. Coffee coursing through my veins, watching my hands fly from medbox to patient to steering wheel to paperwork, anticipating the needs of whatever person-of-the-moment is in front of me, I discover that it all goes so quickly, one call after another, the minutes rushing by, the hours soaring.

Buddy and I have barely cleared the Santa Monica Trauma Center when we get our sixth call, for a forty-year-old difficulty breather at 76th Street and Victoria Avenue. I tear back to our district, ignoring Buddy's suggestion to take the 10 east during rush hour.

At the intersection of two small residential streets, our diff breather is easy enough to spot. She alternates between shrieking and hyper-ventilating—wild hair ballooning over an orange bathrobe and pink miniskirt—and she keeps pointing at something in the middle of the street.

We park the gurney on the sidewalk, and I try to calm her down.

"Ma'am, what seems to be the problem?"

"*Do* something, do something!" she bellows, both of her hands gripping my forearm. "Look at my little Figueroa..." Despite her rapid breathing—about forty breaths a minute—she's got great skin color and a healthy tidal volume. The clump of fur in the middle of the street was once a cat. She breaks down into sobs again.

I awkwardly pat her padded orange sleeve. "I'm so sorry, ma'am," I say. "Really I am." Buddy's fingers jab into our entangled limbs, trying to get the woman's pulse as I look around, half-curious to see if I can catch the guilty look of the person who ran it over. The neighbors fidget in silence. I coax the woman to take a seat on the gurney, explaining that we need to take a look at her. If I can get her away from her pet, she might calm down enough for a proper assessment. She refuses. I insist. She places two flat palms on my chest and shoves me.

Finally I get it.

She isn't our patient, and never was. From her gesturing I realize she expects us to do something to save her cat. Buddy pulls his safety glasses from around his collar and puts them on. "Well, maybe we could try—" he begins, and moves toward the smear of mangled fur and muscle.

Hooking him by the elbow I yank Buddy so hard he stumbles backward and almost falls. "Sorry," I say, and pull him out of the woman's earshot. I explain to him that supposing the cat was a viable patient, and not a mutilated carcass, we don't know how to do animal CPR, and we don't have the right equipment for it. Even our pediatric oxygen masks wouldn't fit correctly over a cat's nose.

Buddy's face is like a windup toy coming to a slow halt: his mouth opens and closes, stretching a blank stare. All of a sudden I want to shake this rookie's neck until I see true comprehension streak his eyes. A cat. A fucking cat. We didn't work up a woman who'd been stabbed to death, who'd only just gone cold, because there was no chance of saving her, and he wants to work up a scattered piece of roadkill.

I beg the neighbors to help the howling woman, reiterating that there's nothing we can do. One man, long, lean, with kind gray eyes, takes a few steps toward her, his hands spread wide.

57

She tries to run away but he chases her, dodges traffic, gets cussed out by an irate taxi driver, and, when he finally catches up to her, shakes her violently. She is crying; she beats his chest with tiny fists, tells him to leave her alone even while her eyes tell him to never let her go. It's a love story, and there's no story more violent than love. She is telling him everything now, all the things she wanted to but couldn't. At least I assume that's what she's saying. J-Rock turned the television mute during one of the commercials and never bothered to turn the volume up again.

"You're lucky I don't out you," I say, shifting to find a better position in the unfurled recliner. "You like romantic movies more than any girl I know."

He sits squarely in his upright easy chair, both feet planted, occasionally lifting a plastic cup to his mouth, spitting tobacco juice into it. "I'd deny it," he says. It's almost midnight. Our partners went to bed over an hour ago. I already told J-Rock, in a confidential tone, about how Buddy holds the rig's radio transmitter up to his ear in order to hear Dispatch better, even though the stereo system is behind him. It was almost impossible not to tell him about Buddy's *Ultimate Rookie Move*, starring a cat named Figueroa, but somehow I held back.

"I have a theory," J-Rock says, "about those safety glasses."

"Let me guess—" I remember J-Rock's particular obsession with survival plans.

"He's preparing for the Zombie Apocalypse."

"Of course."

"Think about it. Eyeballs are mucous membranes. Very infection-prone, an easy way to transmit disease. Buddy is more prepared than the rest of us."

"He asked me what my worst call was."

J-Rock winces. "Of course he did."

We'd been driving back from a late-night dinner at the taco stand on Lennox when Buddy asked me, "So what's the worst call you've ever had?" I pulled the rig over so quickly he threw his hand up against the window to brace himself. Turning toward him, I said in a low voice, "Don't ever, ever, ever, ever, *ever* ask an EMT that question. Just don't do it." Buddy had nodded his agreement even though his face sprouted only more questions.

A preview comes on for the next romantic comedy. This one I've seen: it ends with him declaring his love at an airport, right before she's supposed to get on a plane, or maybe he surprises her on the airplane. J-Rock picks up the remote, as if to raise the volume or change the channel, and then puts it down again.

"Hey, Rock?"

"Yeah."

"What did you hear, anyway? About me going crazy, I mean."

He glances sideways at me, his backward hat forcing an extra crease in the skin above his eyebrows. "Heard you ran a call on your girl."

"She wasn't—I mean, it was somebody else."

"No shit. Doubt you'd be back here if it *had* been your girl, am I right?"

I laugh, resting the side of my face against my palm so I can wipe at my eyes without looking obvious. "True."

Staring at the screen, elbows resting on his knees, he says, "We all get it, you know. I definitely get it. If I ran a call on my mom or my grandma, I would bug out."

"So you don't think I'm crazy?"

"We're all a little crazy." He spits brown liquid into his cup. "I don't even like my grandma."

58

Carl has been so easy to work with, while I have been one of the zombies J-Rock is always talking about. I stopped trying to compensate for my monotone hollowness twelve hours ago, when I realized I still had forty hours left on this unending shift. It hasn't helped that we've been on con home duty all day, taking elders to dialysis from their houses, or to the ER from a rest home, wrapping up shunts, removing bed pans, rolling blankly staring bodies on to the gurney like logs. We call the worst ones "Triple D," for dim, disoriented, and drooling. But it's somehow worse when we take a spry, intelligent eighty-year-old man to the hospital for a broken hip, because he looks around at the bodies piled on the gurneys, at the bottle-neck shape of the traffic flowing into the emergency department, and says sadly, "We were never meant to live this long. I think I'm ready to go now."

Carl and I skip dinner. We opt for ice cream instead, and swivel on the stools like children. "I bet you're going to be the cat lady type," Carl says, and I can't really argue. He swears up and down that when he turns sixty he's going to get the words DO NOT RESUSCITATE tattooed on his sternum, or maybe even on his forehead. We discuss the logistics of overdosing on heroin, or opium, as a way to die pleasantly and with some dignity.

At 0217 we get woken to do yet another transfer, this time a middle-aged patient who's a pickup from the Huntington Park Surgical Center. But when we try to drive the woman home, she can't remember her zip code or any cross streets, the hospital face sheet has only a numeric address, and there are so many varieties of "Central Avenue" in the Thomas Guide,

Central Avenues running east, west, north, south, and diagonally. What side of the city does she live on? I have the bright idea to call someone who knows her. I pull over on the big, empty street, a half mile from the hospital, and set the hazards blinking. Once in a while a car zooms by and the rig slowly rocks from side to side. Carl in the back, digging through our patient's purse, exhaustion affecting him now, too, finds the tattered piece of paper with a phone number on it. I dial it on my phone, forgetting it's the middle of the night, not recognizing the New York area code, and wake the woman up. Her voice, brittle and paper thin over the bad connection, grows with warmth and volume as the conversation progresses. She didn't know her sister had been in the hospital. After helping me out with the address, she says with a choke in her voice, "Tell her to call me when she gets home? Please?"

I assure her, hang up, put the paper slip back. I drive again, my hands at a perfect ten and two on the wheel. I know where I'm headed, easy does it, this is a simple transfer, I'm just tired, only twenty-eight more hours to go, no problem. "Ridiculous," I whisper. But then I give myself over to it, to the rolling grief that pummels me from all sides. Something about that concerned voice on the phone, and the empty, dark streets, and the sad, lonely character in the back, the one who doesn't remember where she lives, who didn't tell her sister about her medical problems, who is now a double amputee.

When we get to the house and struggle to fit her through the narrow hallways in her new wheelchair, she tells us to lock the door on our way out. There are seven dead bolts and nothing inside worth stealing. I remind her, with a sense of responsibility: "Call your sister, okay?" She looks at me, nods reluctantly, and, just before we squeeze ourselves out and into the night, gasping for fresh air, I see her pick up the old rotary receiver and stare at it.

59

Jumbled bones, aching teeth, my eyes feel puffy, and where is my other boot? I shuffle around, pants pulled loosely over gym shorts, the belt buckle swinging wildly. Found it. Practically behind the television. Of course. I should take a shower, or at least put on new socks, because these are glued to the bottom of—but I put the boot on just the same. People are watching, eyes on me: straighten up, look normal, everything's fine, nothing to see, and there's Buddy, standing nervous and tall, you remember him.

"Hi, Buddy," I croak. My hands are like the flapping wings of a pigeon, trying to locate the carabiner on my belt loop, forgetting that my belt is lower than my waist because my pants aren't on. "Here you go." I hand him the rig keys. "You're driving today, can't. Dangerous."

He looks at his palm like he's never seen keys before.

She has too many missing teeth to count. She grabs a fourteen-gauge needle out of the medbox and raises it over her head, as if to plunge it into the nearest heart. "You aren't going to put one of these in me, no, sir." I look at her, unable to move or think. Adrenaline like a dull old friend. A firefighter politely asks for the needle back; everyone exhales when his request works. At the hospital she asks me, "What's it like to be beautiful?" Her cackling mouth reveals her few remaining teeth, crooked and stained, and yet I can't figure out why she's asking me that.

Attempt naps. Buddy wakes you for calls. Punch him in the arm and call him by your brother's name. Remember where you are and apologize. Coffee stopped working a long time ago. Drink it anyway.

You no longer eat solid food.

You're close to having a widespread organ mutiny.

The man's throat was squeezed by a cop's hands almost to the point of asphyxiation. His face is a smear of purples and his lips are ghostly. His eyes—the last thing to regain normalcy—are bulbous and blank, but they start to move through emotions as if ticking off a checklist: comprehension, fear, anger, relief, desperation, reproach...

The emaciated curmudgeon says in a clear voice that he has been choking on his iron pill for two days. He demands that you give him CPR.

The kid with the snapped clavicle and sprained wrist, who jumped her bicycle from the roof to the pool on a dare, points at all the objects in the rig compartments with her good hand. "What is that? And that? What does it do? Why?"

At Buddy's urging, I agree to eat something. I struggle to open my last dented can of clam chowder with Station 710's rusted can opener, feeling suddenly that I might start crying. By the time I get the soup into a bowl, I decide to eat it cold.

"Piper? Can I ask you something?" Buddy leans against the counter a few feet away, twisting a pen in his hands. "Did you tell anyone... about the cat?"

I rummage through recollections of endless calls, trying to find the one he's talking about. "Oh! The *cat*." I smile at him. "The one you wanted to—no, I didn't tell anyone."

Buddy's long arms around me, armpits clamping down over my

shoulders, "*Thank you*, Piper, thank you," and the bowl of soup suspends itself between us, pressing against my chest in an increasing diagonal, the plastic rim digging into my sternum. Finally it capsizes, sending chunks of soup down my shirt, and Buddy is flinging paper towels at me and at the floor, promising to lend me his clean extra shirt and buy me dinner. Buddy, who thought he would have to quit his job, maybe move out of the county.

The man who tried to hang himself used wire, several feet of it, around a ceiling fan. The thin cable snapped, dumping him onto the ground, leaving a slit in his neck. He looks at me with his newly spliced Adam's apple, a strange texture in his eyes, and says, "I'm so glad it didn't work."

Halfway through my shift with Buddy, as if surfacing from a long movie, I remember with a jolt that Carl and I had a GSW last night. How we arrived at a parking lot around 0400 to find two firefighter paramedics, one getting a line ready, the other sitting on the ground holding our patient in his lap. The lead medic was new, probably on his first big trauma call, and wore a stunned expression. It would almost have been sort of funny, the way the whole thing brought to mind a badly done TV melodrama—the boy in his lap looked like Jesus after the crucifixion, lolling and ghastly, and the lead medic kept asking, "Can I get some help?" as if he'd forgotten who we were, as if he hadn't already run four calls with us that day—if it weren't for the fact that the boy was so clearly a goner, shot not once but five times. The image of the two of them on the ground like that lasted only a second because soon the four of us were working hard to keep him alive; we dropped him off alive and who knows if he stayed that way. Every serious trauma call I run is somehow that first boy all over again, dying from a bullet to the brain, and even the stunned paramedic appeared similarly, fusing with the boy in his lap and the boy in my memory, bewildered palms turned out, offering and accepting benediction, forgive me, forgive me.

I massage the hinge of my jaw with my index fingers, feeling two persistent nubs kick back against the pads of my fingertips. Eight more hours to go, but I can't remember what happens after that.

Of course I miss her.

60

The morning air has a chill to it; the sun is out but hasn't warmed yet. I drag my stuff to my car, freshly washed hair dripping on the clean sweatshirt and jeans I had the good sense to pack four days ago, and shiver a little. This morning, at 0725, a member of the oncoming B shift crew came into sleeping quarters to wake me up. I was reluctant to hand over the set of station keys and walkie-talkie that for three days had been attached to my belt. These objects: my new appendages. The crew member had to tug a little before I let go, and although I wanted to ask him how it worked, the real world—what kinds of things were supposed to happen, how I was supposed to behave—I didn't know what questions would get me the answers I needed.

Into the open mouth of my trunk I throw a sorry-shaped mountain of uniforms, towels, bedding, boots, and paper bags. Then I stand there, wiggling my toes against the thin rubber of flip-flops.

"What do you think?" I look up to see Carl leaning out of the back window of a Toyota 4Runner, a bright red hoodie pulled over his head. Pep is driving, and J-Rock waves at me from the passenger seat.

"She looks like a walrus on Oxycontin," Pep says. "Not ready to be returned to the wild."

"Piper!" J-Rock yells from the passenger seat. "Can you tell me your name?"

Carl laughs. "Hope you don't do your assessments like that." He waves his hand at me like he's a magician about to do a trick. "Where are you right now? What day is it?"

"Station 710. B shift."

Pep moans and slaps the side of the driver door. "*Mayday*," he says. "We got to take this one in."

"Come on, guys, seriously—"

"Oh, we are serious," Carl says. And J-Rock nods emphatically.

"Get in," Pep says. "You're in no shape to drive."

Breakfast at McDonald's. Carl has to buy it for me, because I left my wallet at station. They've been drinking since the night before, so I have to catch up. Thoughts of Ayla push against me no matter what I say, what I do, how loudly I laugh. As if to declare: you can't run forever. But I can and I will. I have to even if I can't remember why.

Drinking out of paper bags on the Santa Monica boardwalk. Belligerence beset by more belligerence. Carl heckling a bronzed woman in a pink bikini who Rollerblades by us, me running at every clump of seagulls I see so I can watch them fly away, J-Rock repeatedly trying to wrestle with Pep, who keeps fixing his hair. The four of us storming the Mexican restaurant on Ocean Avenue as soon as it opens for brunch, ordering pitchers of margaritas to go with our food. By now I can no longer remember how much money I owe Carl, but I'm promising him the world as if it were mine to give.

"The world," I tell him, dragging out the sound. "The woorrrl."

After that things go dark. We get separated somehow. I'm in Pep's car, my eyelids so thick and heavy it hurts to open them, and everything is swimming. Pep is trying to drive to his house in Baldwin Hills; I have the vague feeling his house is not where I want to go.

Hearing my own voice in a slurred singsong, asking him where J-Rock and Carl are.

"I told you," he says. "They went to pick up ladies on the beach."

Close my eyes. "That's right."

Pep sees a cop and pulls over, not wanting to get a DUI. "Take me home," I tell him. But he doesn't want to drive to Echo Park right now, we can just take a nap at his place and go back later to pick up the boys from Santa Monica.

Everything will be okay, he tells me.

When I wake up the sun has dropped low and slanted, my temples are pounding, and the buzz of alcohol has vanished. It takes a moment to disengage my cheek from the passenger seat of Pep's truck and my tongue from the roof of my mouth. For the first time in a long time, I feel as though I *slept*. I must have slept for hours and hours.

I stir in my seat and look around. We're parked on a small rundown residential street, with tiny box houses spaced evenly from each other. A cherry blossom tree hangs above us, its bare branches casting spindly shadows on the hood of Pep's 4Runner.

Pep's in the driver's seat next to me, one hand tucked into the waist of his pants, his tongue loose in his open mouth, his face collapsed at a severe angle—if he weren't so motionless, he would look like he was trying to lick his right shoulder.

My watch says it's 1716.

I swivel my pounding head, spot a gallon container of water in the backseat and the signs of the intersection directly behind us. We're on Orange Drive at Jefferson Boulevard. Tugging the container of water into my lap with both hands, I drink as if from a bowling ball.

Pressing the back of my skull into the headrest, I massage the jagged imprint in my thigh, created from sleeping on top of my keys. Time for inventory. I have my clothes, my keys, my flip-flops, my phone. I'm missing my wallet. My car is parked at station. I have to take a piss.

Another pull from the water jug. "Pep." I tug hard on his sleeve, my voice cracking the silence. His loud breathing is the only response: sharp sucks of air followed by lengthy exhales. "Pep, I want to go home."

He doesn't stir. I stare at him, realizing that instead of saying "home" I said "hospital."

61

I decide to walk to Ryan's house in Culver City. It's not too far from here. Even if he's not home I know where he keeps the spare key.

I set off, thinking of nothing, my head curiously empty. I stop at the Kenneth Hahn Family Clinic on Jefferson Boulevard and ask to use their bathroom. As I push open the door of the women's restroom, I eye the familiar stick figure, clothed in a white triangle, the dark blue circle behind her creating a reverse silhouette. The light inside comes on automatically, illuminating a rusted and dripping sink, a spotted mirror, and an unassuming toilet.

It's after I flush and wash my hands that I notice the sign taped above the mirror, its slanted font and bright red border:

IN CASE OF EMERGENCY,

PLEASE ASK THE FRONT DESK

FOR SANITARY NAPKINS

I read the sign several times, my lips barely moving.

I remember my father carrying me home after a party one night, how I'd pretended to be asleep in the backseat—despite my mother nudging me and saying, "Piper, sweetie, it's time to wake up," and despite how through barely cracked lids I could see Ryan rolling his eyes—because I had wanted to feel my father's careful hands lift my weight into his arms and carry me up the stairs to my room. When she tucked me in, Mom would always ask if there was anything else I wanted to tell her. She was the only person who listened to even my most ridiculous thoughts without laughing or changing the subject or making me feel bad or getting annoyed, and I can't remember what I would tell her, I only remember how it felt. When she left I ran away. My red-eyed father found me a few blocks from our house with my thumb stuck out, wearing a pink backpack stuffed with cheese sandwiches and Ryan's faded dinosaur pajamas. I remember how brazen it felt, how right. Trying to make it all the way to Colorado.

And I remember Ayla, the real one, the living one, how from the first day I saw her I knew I wouldn't be able to do anything but fall in love with her.

So, yes, Kenneth Hahn Family Clinic on Jefferson Boulevard, pretty please and yes, I would like a tampon. Because if that doesn't solve it, I suppose nothing will.

62

For the first time in weeks I know exactly where I'm going and why. It's a long way, and no one walks in LA—especially not this far—but when it hits me how right this is, nothing else makes sense.

At first I move as if I'm flying, not bothering to pace myself, eyes open, vision unclouded. Reality is intoxicating, every moment a seduction. Greedily I drink in the cozy cracked-asphalt streets of the Crenshaw

District, the beige houses, the rumble of the 10 freeway, the low-slung sun casting a pink glow, blending green yards and gray walkways.

My phone says it will take about two hours. The blinking blue button an eternal *You are here.* My own car is too far to retrieve, and although I consider calling Ryan or Marla, or even my father, and asking someone to drive me, I shake off the desire. There's only one person I want to talk to. She's seven miles away.

It goes like this: take Harcourt Avenue north, because it will take you under the 10 freeway, then turn right on Washington Boulevard, left on Crenshaw, right on Wilshire, left on Vermont, and finally a little zigzag, a little lightning-bolt dance, under the 101 freeway and up the hills into Silver Lake. You will get there, knock on the door, and tell her you're very sorry, because you are sorry; you will tell her you missed her, and of course that's true, and then she will take you back—she'll wrap her strong arms around you, and…

A tiny speck scurries by on the sidewalk. I stoop down to look and it grows still. Smaller than the face of Abe Lincoln on a penny, it pulls its dark red legs close to its bell-shaped body and waits for the shadow leaning over it to lift. It's no use. Hiding is such temporary shelter.

To pass the time, I count parked Honda Civics. Fire hydrants. Streets named after vegetation. I hum snatches of songs, the melody of the verses dissipating; I end on a chorus on repeat. Ferndale, Palm Grove, Vineyard, Hickory. A man climbs out of his still-wheezing vehicle and walks up a driveway. He's wearing a collared peach shirt, stern expression, thick mustache. Two small children in the doorway wait to greet him, yelling-laughing-kicking-each-other, white teeth flashing in their faces.

The world is a gray thing recovering its color.

My left knee itches. I'm hungry I'm thirsty I'm sorry I love you. I will tell her everything if she'll hear it. I travel under six lanes of a groaning, traffic-filled freeway—the suction of sound like a monstrous seashell against your ear—and emerge in a new neighborhood, less cozy, more activity. In the spaces between the houses and the cleaners, the gated apartments and the video store, small groups of people huddle. All the stop signs get ignored by speeding cars. Not even halfway there. A dead bumblebee on the sidewalk, one wing pointing at the sky. Birds fly overhead; I had forgotten there were even birds in Los Angeles.

I think about being an EMT, how it means you get to say to someone, "We're here to help." Even now I crave an algorithm. My life spilling onto a whiteboard, boxes and circles around crucial events, every arrow pointing to—what? It used to be that any memory of my mom caused horror, spasms of shame and disgust. I still don't forgive her, maybe I never will, but something has shifted, unseating my ability to deny the obvious, and I can finally permit what Dad and Ryan have been trying to tell me for years—that she loved us. In her own hurtful, distracted, confused way, Mom loved us. The arrows point to my feet, solidly on the ground, moving toward Ayla. To flip-flops slapping against concrete. The arrows point to conclusions too small and innumerable to name.

And then I'm on Crenshaw Boulevard for a long time, moving slowly against the backdrop of a palm-tree-studded skyline. The streets widen; intersections take longer to cross. Impatient cars swerve by so close I could reach out and touch them, so close I could trail their sides, flat oil from my fingers leaving residue on their gloss. The smell of fried toxins hits my nostrils; I spot a Jack in the Box and ache for even five dollars, mechanically checking my pockets, though they've been checked and rechecked. Yesterday we ran a call on a woman who wanted a ride to work. Her car had broken down, she didn't have bus fare, and I was too exhausted to yell at her for calling 911. Was that really yesterday? Time flies when you've gone crazy.

The sky darkens, the streetlamps come on, and because Los Angeles was never designed for pedestrians, the blocks are long and dark and lonely, each bright intersection a carnival. A billboard's spinning pink and blue lights twirl on the image of a sports car; an eighteen-wheeler, thundering by, sends shudders through me; the silhouette of a pigeon, nesting in the green orb of a streetlamp, serves as the go signal. My skin has split open and been subverted, my nervous system exposed. This is all there is. Each nerve, raw and eager, shrieking its sensitivity, bending toward the sounds of laughter and music, toward the early evening sky. Every time I think of Ayla I want to break into a run. I tried so hard to avoid thinking about her but now I'm looking for her everywhere.

An ambulance goes blaring by, not an A & O rig, but a dark blue beast with yellow stripes and a different siren. I spy strip malls, churches, a sign boasting BEAUTY SUPPLY & WIG, a stand set up in a gas station parking lot that's selling furry car seat covers and animal skin rugs. Maybe Ayla would want a neon-pink leopard-print car seat cover?

My body leans forward, weight transferring from the heel-arch-toes of one foot to the heel-arch-toes of the other, hips shifting slightly to counterbalance, arms swinging. This simple momentum—passing ads, benches, street signs, bus stops, traveling below concrete pillars and telephone poles, seeing your reflection in shopwindows and many-mirrored office buildings—while all the cars, trucks, motorcycles, and the smell of the city race by.

At the corner of Wilshire and Norton, a man in a white shirt halves limes under the rainbow umbrella of his fruit stand. I'm so hungry. I watch him help a customer. Mango, orange, pineapple, watermelon, coconut, and cucumber, loaded into a plastic bag as heavy in your hand as a soiled leather boot. Chile, lime, salt? He looks at me and places a toothpick spearing a trapezoid of mango between my fingers. I force myself to eat slowly. The flavor permeates all the way to my hair follicles. "Thank you, but—" He waves a hand in the air. Using his knife to brush several desiccated limes toward the trash can, he's surprised when I stop him. "*¿Quieres?*" Yes. He laughs as I pucker from the sour pulp; we wave goodbye like old friends.

The air is getting colder. It occurs to me that I will never get there.

I will spend the night shivering in someone's yard, sipping sprinklers for survival, and in the morning forage breakfast from trash cans. My former self would be so disappointed with me; I don't even have a backpack. But then I round the corner from Vermont Avenue. I step onto 1st Street and catch sight of the 101 freeway. My heart begins to race. Almost there. How does it go again? She will—

My right flip-flop breaks away from my foot and I retrieve it by the loose strap, sprung up like a released spring. My feet are disgusting. Two skin-colored lines travel through solid grime and disappear into the crack next to my blackened right big toe. The top edge of the flip-flop has torn open, the side strap is about to come loose, and the back has a suspicious-looking crack, like the heel is about to snap off completely. I'm scared to see how the left is doing. All of a sudden I can't stop laughing. Practically a mile still to go and I'm down to one flip-flop.

At a liquor store on Virgil Avenue I hobble in, trying to use my naked right foot less than my left—as if it matters!—and ask for duct tape. He stares at me. "Duct tape," I say again. "For my shoe?" For the first time in my life someone points at the sign, WE RESERVE THE RIGHT TO REFUSE SERVICE TO ANYBODY. I nod at the man and move on.

I go into a Vons and leave immediately. The glare of too many fluorescents burns spots into my eyelids. Inside a pawn shop, a large, curvy woman with large, curvy hair lays newspaper on the counter and proceeds to put my flip-flop back together with superglue, adding Scotch tape like a garnish. If I survive today these flip-flops will get bronzed and hung on my wall. I leave my watch on the counter as thanks.

My stomach churns; my bowels threaten to eject the lonely piece of mango. I will get there and immediately need to use her bathroom. I will vomit before I ever get there. How much farther? My phone is about to die; the damn blue button hasn't moved for over an hour; I must have been walking in place all this time. Why didn't I call Ryan or Marla? I'm starving.

I'm dying. I'm exhausted. This is stupid. I'm stupid. What happens when I get there and she refuses to talk to me? It will only hurt to look at her. If I went home, and left talk of second chances for another day. This will be so much easier when I'm rested. I'm not thinking straight. It's not too late to change my mind.

The last time I saw Ayla, she tried to tell me there was no way out but through. Now, even while I resist, even while some part of me throws a tantrum—imagining all the ways this could end badly—I know my only choice is to keep moving forward, and I'm so glad.

The steps to Ayla's studio: remember to tell her you don't deserve her. I'm done with counting. I won't count anything ever again. Not hours or minutes or miles or freeways or reasons or steps or stars. I see movement in one of the windows and feel a jerk of fear and relief. She's home. It's time. I'm so very tired of being so afraid.

As I climb the final distance into the hills of Silver Lake, the sky above me dusted with light, I find a hose between two bungalows, take deep gulps of water from it, and spray down my throbbing, filthy feet.

ACKNOWLEDGEMENTS

Especially Damara Ganley, Dave Reid, Katherine Redington, Rachael Lincoln, Noel Plemmons, Charlotte Wheeler, Rachel Nagelberg, and my mother, Tracy Grant: this book wouldn't exist without your love and support. Much thanks to Erin Minnick, for focusing her expert eyes on the details, Liz Curry, for just generally being a badass, Tom Christie, for pushing me past the daydreaming that might have remained the ghostbone of this book, my editor, Andi Winnette, and Stephen Beachy, whose feedback alone was worth the price of graduate school.

To those who granted me interviews—Kurt Schmitz, Susan Voglmaier, Tyler Pew, Linda Noble, Janeen Smith, David Schoppik, Starlyn Lara, Akiva S. Cohen, Tara Fagan, Sarah Kotowski, and others—I'm so, so grateful.

Chris Black, thank you for being you. I feel lucky every damn day.

A moment of reverence for the SF Giants, who won the World Series while I was writing this book. Twice.

And certainly not least: Danny Wolohan, without you, maybe none of this would have happened. Thank you.